this delicious death

PRAISE FOR *MY DEAREST DARKEST*

"A spine-tingling thrill ride that calls on classic prep school dynamics and eerie gothic imagery."

— *Publishers Weekly*

"Cottingham's debut opens with a gut-wrenching first chapter and doesn't let up, juxtaposing vivid and unsettling horror with Sapphic teenage angst."

— *Kirkus Reviews*

"Cottingham succeeds in crafting a truly inventive, gruesome horror story that fans of blood and gore will relish."

— *School Library Journal*

"[A] call back to '90s teen horror movies à la *The Craft* and *The Faculty*."

—*Bulletin of the Center for Children's Books*

"Fans of cult-classic film *Jennifer's Body* and similar scary tropes will revel in Cottingham's atmospheric, spine-tingling horror-romance."

— *Booklist*

"A sweet, queer romance makes this a good option for genre lovers in search of more diverse characters."

— *Youth Services Book Review*

"The tenacity of youth, love, and friendship go to war with the horrors that create nightmares, and it really is uncertain who will end up the winner."

— *Missouri River Regional Library*

ALSO BY KAYLA COTTINGHAM

My Dearest Darkest

this delicious death

KAYLA COTTINGHAM

Copyright © 2023 by Kayla Cottingham
Cover and internal design © 2023 by Sourcebooks
Cover design by Natalie C. Sousa
Cover image © Micha/Shutterstock, Moustache Girl/
Shutterstock, Second Studio/Shutterstock
Internal design by Laura Boren

Sourcebooks and the colophon are registered trademarks of Sourcebooks.

Published by Sourcebooks Fire, an imprint of Sourcebooks
P.O. Box 4410, Naperville, Illinois 60567–4410
(630) 961-3900
sourcebooks.com

Cataloging-in-Publication data is on file with the Library of Congress.

Printed and bound in Canada.
MBP 10 9 8 7 6 5 4 3 2

To Ally, Alex, and Simone—
I don't know if I believe in fate, but if there is something out there
pulling the strings, I'm so grateful it brought us together.
And that it made sure we didn't peak in high school.

CONTENT WARNING

This book contains the following:

Alcohol consumption by
  minors
Anxiety disorders
  (mentioned)
Blood and gore depiction
Body horror
Cannibalism
Captivity & confinement
Dead bodies & body parts
Deadnaming (deadname
  not stated)
Death of a grandparent
Death of a sibling
Drugging (fictional drug)
Drug use (mentioned, not
  explicit)

Fire
Grief & loss depiction
Gun violence
Intrusive thoughts
Murder
Needles & syringes
Nightmares
Parental neglect
Pandemic (fictional disease)
Scars
Sexism
Suicidal ideation (implied)
Transphobia (mentioned,
  not explicit)

one

Am I still a monster
If I run my fingers through your hair
And kiss you to sleep?
Baby, you're in too deep.

—*"Monster" by No Flash Photography*

When my parents asked if I wanted a Mini Cooper for graduation, I didn't think ahead to whether or not it would have enough trunk space to accommodate my cooler full of organs.

Also, the cooler with all the sparkling waters, but that was less of a priority.

"Can you stack the coolers on top of each other?" my best friend, Celeste, suggested, pointing to my trunk with a finger that ended in a sharp pink acrylic nail. "Or put one of the back seats down?"

I shot her a look, one eyebrow raised. Celeste Fairbanks was white, with pink hair, a slim build, and long legs that seemed to go on for miles. She was taller than me by a good half a foot, accentuated by the fact that she was currently wearing white platform heels. They paired nicely with her pink heart-patterned pinafore and pearlescent eyeshadow—both newly purchased using her growing influencer income.

Leave it to Celeste to look cute before 8 a.m., the absolute monster.

"They're too tall to stack," I pointed out, crossing my arms. "And unless you want Valeria to sit in your lap the whole way to the festival, we need all the back seats."

Celeste hummed in agreement, grimacing. We were currently standing in front of the Fairbanks house, packing up the Mini for our first-ever road trip to Desert Bloom, a music festival in the Mojave Desert a few hours' drive away. The house was a modest box-shaped bungalow with a lush garden of desert plants adorning the front. Solar panels glinted on the roof, unlike most homes in Aspen Flats, whose occupants were far too stubborn to consider converting to sustainable energy—despite recent proof of the consequences of not doing so.

"You're gonna have to consolidate," said Wendy, Celeste's mom. She was nearly a foot shorter than her daughter, but she made up for it by wearing tall leopard-print heels. Despite living in California for decades, her thick Jersey accent still clung to every syllable she spoke. "See if you can fit it all in the bigger cooler, and I'll take the other one back in the house."

Celeste sighed. "It feels…kind of wrong to put seltzers in the flesh cooler."

"The *flesh cooler*," I repeated under my breath, biting back a smile.

Celeste's lip twitched for a moment before she cracked and broke into laughter.

Which immediately made me break too, with an inelegant snort that made Celeste laugh even harder. Something about seeing her double over trying to catch her breath only made it worse. Playfully, I shoved her shoulder and she batted my hand away, giggling behind her hand.

"All right, all right." Wendy opened the cooler with the sparkling water and added, "Help me consolidate these. You're burning daylight and I don't want you to have to drive out there in the dark. That's when all the creepers come out."

Celeste and I both groaned—though we were both still smiling—and stooped down to the other cooler to gather an armful of plastic-wrapped organs. We took turns tossing them in the cooler with the drinks. Each one was branded with the required LAB-GROWN SYNTHETIC TISSUE, FOR CONSUMPTION ONLY sticker across the front—I guess to dissuade someone from attempting an at-home organ transplant. They each made a faint crunching sound as they landed atop the ice.

"Sweetie, you sure you don't want a few more livers?" Wendy asked Celeste. "You know I got a whole bunch from Costco during that half-off sale—"

"*Mom*," Celeste said. "We're fine, seriously."

"All right, all right, I get it. My little girl is all grown up now and doesn't need her mom telling her what to do all the time." Wendy leaned over to me, her big blond curls nearly smacking me in the face. "But the offer stands if you want any more, Zoey. You just let me know."

I flashed her a toothy grin. "Thanks, Wendy."

Wendy was one of the few people who could actually make me smile and mean it. She'd been like a second mother to me since

Celeste and I became friends in elementary school. She was always the first to offer me a place to stay or someone to talk to when I needed it. Whenever June rolled around, she drove me and Celeste to LA for the pride parade, and she was always the one yelling the loudest, wearing trans and bi flags in celebration of her daughter. She wasn't the perfect mom, but she was pretty damn close.

It took a few minutes, but the three of us managed to shove all of the SynFlesh into the other cooler and wrangle it into the back without much incident. I closed the trunk and exhaled a breath, sweat already beading on the back of my neck even though the sun had barely risen. I prayed I didn't have pit stains.

"One more thing before you go," Wendy said, taking a few steps back. She pulled her phone out of her pocket and tapped the screen. "I want pictures."

"You're the one who *just* said we're burning daylight," Celeste said.

"That was when you were dawdling! This'll only take a second." When Celeste scowled, she added, "You're going on your first road trip by yourselves! And your first music festival! You're gonna want to look back on this when you're my age, I'm telling you. Now get together and look cute—I'm putting this on Facebook for your Nana."

Celeste sighed and shook her head, but the smile never left her face. The two of us stepped together as I held up a peace sign and did my best not to squint too much when I smiled. Then, Celeste put her arm around me and leaned in next to my face. The heat from her cheek sunk into mine.

My heart puttered and my stomach flipped itself into knots.

"Say *hot girl summer*!"

Celeste grinned and said, "Absolutely not," at the same time I repeated it, voice cracking.

"Beautiful!" Wendy beamed at the screen and then held it out to us. "You look great."

If by *great* she meant tense and sweaty, then yes, I did. My hazel eyes were wide, pale cheeks flushed, my chin-length chestnut hair stuck to my sweaty forehead at a weird angle. I was smiling, kind of, but it was lopsided and forced. Celeste, meanwhile, had a sweet smile on her face while her hair fell in soft waves down the front of her shoulders. I looked like I was her fan and this was a picture from an extremely awkward meet-and-greet.

Celeste withheld a snicker. "Nana will love that."

"You'll be the talk of her nursing home, without a doubt." Wendy tucked her phone into her pocket. "Well, you two should get going. But be safe, okay? You take care of each other no matter what."

"Always have," Celeste said brightly.

Her mother went on her tiptoes and kissed Celeste's cheek, then turned to me and pulled me into a big hug. "I love you girls."

"Love you too," Celeste and I both said.

"All right, get out of here before I cry." She sniffled. "Safe travels."

Celeste and I said our goodbyes before climbing in the car and driving away, Wendy waving behind us as we went.

The mid-June sun beat down on the roof of the Mini as we crossed town to pick up Valeria and Jasmine, the two remaining members of our high school friend group. Before the Hollowing, Valeria and Jasmine had both been infinitely more popular at school than Celeste and I, and our paths only crossed because Aspen Flats was a tiny three-stoplight town where everyone knew each other. Before the Hollowing, Valeria had been a cheerleader for the Aspen Flats Rattlers and Jasmine was already taking college-level courses in addition to playing on the softball team. Meanwhile, Celeste and I were the sort of people who ate lunch in our freshman year English teacher's room through most of high school and spent most of our time sending each other TikToks and fan fiction links under our desks. If it hadn't been for the Hollowing, Jasmine and Valeria probably never would have given us the time of day.

When we got to Valeria's house, I threw the car into park, the cooler rattling in the back seat. Clearly, I hadn't closed the lid all the way when I snatched a SynFlesh heart out to eat on the drive over.

Eighteen months ago, SynFlesh—a substance made by using human stem cells to bioprint large organoids, which were close to, but not quite, the same as real human organs—was dubbed the greatest invention of the twenty-first century by *TIME* magazine. Which made sense, considering the fact that it wound up being humanity's only solution to deal with the Hollowing, dubbed the greatest disaster of the twenty-first century by, well, literally everyone.

The worst part was that the Hollowing was kinda our fault. *Kinda* being the operative word, because the pathogen that made people Hollow came out of melted permafrost, and we'd all learned by now we could mostly blame corporations and the military for electing to sauté the Earth in toxic fumes for profit.

But there was always that thought: *Maybe the last coffee cup that I threw in the trash instead of recycling was the straw that broke the proverbial camel's back and sent us into a borderline zombie apocalypse two years ago.*

The sound of someone tapping on the window snapped me out of my thoughts. Outside, Valeria Vega stood waving in a yellow sundress with a huge smile on her face. Valeria was Latina, with warm tan skin and bouncy brown curls pulled back from her face.

"Good morning!" she sang as she climbed into the back seat. Her smile faltered a bit as she pointed to a spot on her face and said, "Zoey, there's a blood clot on your chin."

"Really? Ah, shit." I rubbed it away with the back of my hand. "My bad."

"She ate a SynFlesh heart with her bare hands while we were driving over," Celeste said from the passenger seat, twisting around to better convey her feelings on the matter to Valeria. "A truck driver saw and nearly drove off the road."

Valeria jerked back. "While you were *driving*, Z?"

"What? I woke up late and needed to eat on the go. Regular people do it all the time." Over Valeria's shoulder, I spotted another figure approaching from the house next door and waved out the window. Once she was close enough to hear me, I added, "You get what I'm saying, right, Jaz? If regular people can get away with eating a McMuffin on the way to work, I can take a few bites of SynFlesh."

"I mean—sure. Until some poor kid in their car seat looks over and sees you unhinge your jaw like an anaconda to swallow a human heart whole," Jasmine Owusu said, crossing her arms. She was Black, with a soft but muscular build and rich dark skin. She'd recently woven her curls into long box braids with light purple streaks laced in. She wore a raglan shirt with the words ASPEN FLATS HIGH SCHOOL SOFTBALL written across the chest, plus ripped denim shorts.

As she climbed into the back seat, she raised an eyebrow at Celeste. "What were you doing while this happened?"

"Sitting in the passenger's seat trying to look normal so the neighbors don't come after us with torches and pitchforks," Celeste groaned, rubbing her temples. "As usual."

Jasmine withheld a snort at that while Valeria sighed and rolled her eyes.

Soon after, everyone buckled in, and the traditional fight for the aux cord began and ended with Valeria sweetly telling us we had terrible taste. She stole the cord and plugged in her phone, blasting some obscure indie pop band that would be playing at the festival.

I rolled down the windows as we hit the open road out of Aspen Flats, the breeze ruffling our hair and sun streaming in. Music throbbed from the speakers, the bassline heavy like a pulse. I pulled my dark sunglasses down while Valeria sang along to the song, Jasmine swaying back and forth while Celeste tapped her foot beside me. A pleasantly effervescent feeling coursed through me like my blood had turned to soda water. My skin was warm and my cheeks flushed.

After what we'd been through the last two years, we deserved to feel good.

Celeste took over driving just outside of Bakersfield, and I started to drift off in the passenger seat.

One moment I was staring at the brush on the side of the road, and the next I was surrounded by redwood trees. I was suddenly fifteen again, with two scraped knees and my dark brown hair— which I'd recently cut myself for the first time—hanging sharply around my jaw. In the silence of the woods, my stomach growled like a starved animal. The trees were massive and silent around me, without even a whisper of a breeze or birdsong to make it feel alive.

"Celeste!" I shouted for what felt like the hundredth time. I pressed a hand to my stomach as hunger pangs shot through me again and my knees threatened to give out. "Where are you?"

A twig snapped beneath my shoe, making me jump. I was nearly a mile away from Camp Everwood, the summer camp Celeste and I had been going to together for the last four years in the northern California woods. It was supposed to be a summer of outdoor activities, staying up late in our cabin, and spending time together.

Instead, half of the kids and counselors had just come down with a weird stomach bug. Some of the kids who smuggled in cell phones shared rumors that people *everywhere* were coming down with a weird stomach bug. But for the most part, they were all back on their feet and normal as ever after three days in bed.

But Celeste and I weren't getting better, and suddenly she'd disappeared into the trees.

The weight of my feet dragging through the underbrush suddenly felt unbearable, like someone had filled my shoes with cement. I stopped, leaning against a tree as I tried to catch my breath, stomach letting out another pained groan. I'd spent days trying and failing to keep down food, only to throw up anything I managed to swallow. What I didn't tell anyone was that the bile that came back up was black and viscous like oil.

As I brushed against a tree, I felt something wet.

Gingerly, I pulled away to discover blood and dirt smeared down my arm. I yelped, immediately assuming I must have cut myself. But as I ran a hand down my skin looking for a wound, I realized it wasn't me.

The blood was already on the tree.

"Celeste!" I screamed ever louder, heart hammering. If she was hurt, I had to find her. "*Celeste!*"

That's when I heard the soft sound of slurping to my left. A chill settled into my skin as I turned. I smelled it before I saw it: the cloying scent of coppery blood staining the air.

Hidden among the ferns was a man's corpse, jaw hanging agape in a frozen scream. A pool of blood soaked into the mossy soil around him and stained his torn khaki cargo shorts and Camp Everwood T-shirt. It leaked from his torso, which was sliced open, revealing the soft pink entrails inside.

I recognized him: Devin Han, one of our camp counselors.

I also recognized the figure slumped over him, licking her fingers.

"Celeste?" I whispered.

When she turned to look at me, it took all my power not to gasp. Her face was smeared with blood, and her teeth were sharp and elongated. Tears cut through the blood, which dripped off her chin and onto her hands where a chunk of...*something* was clutched between her fingers. Her nails, typically short and grubby back then, had curved into lethal-looking talons.

Her lower lip quivered with a sob. "I-I don't know what's happening to me, Zo."

I barely heard her over the sound of blood roaring in my ears as the scent of carnage became stronger and stronger. My stomach snarled, and I felt something poking into my tongue. I began to shake, vision darkening at the edges.

I dove at the body.

Before the dream could progress any more, a hand shook my shoulder. Valeria's voice broke through my sleeping brain.

"Zoey, get up. We made it to the hotel."

I shot up, dazed as my vision came back to me. I was in the Mini Cooper, Celeste, Valeria, and Jasmine all staring at me with furrowed brows. I quickly smoothed my hair and straightened up, shaking my head.

"Sorry," I muttered. "Dozed off."

"Nightmare?" Celeste asked.

I nodded.

"I keep having those too," Val said, a shiver going down her spine. "Like, I keep dreaming that Patricia from EHPA calls me to say that my application to leave Aspen Flats for Desert Bloom was denied and I'm stuck there all summer. It's awful."

"As if Patricia pays enough attention to us to give a shit if we don't get proper sign-offs to leave town," Jasmine snickered. "Who knows, maybe your dream version of the Emergency Hollow Preparedness Association has enough government funding to not watch Netflix on the job and actually monitor us."

"Yeah," I agreed. "That was, ah, pretty much the nightmare. The horrors of our misused tax dollars."

That seemed to placate Jasmine and Val, who offered their

sympathy and slid out of the car to check in at the reception desk. Celeste, though, wrinkled her brow and frowned sympathetically.

"Camp Everwood?" she guessed.

I nodded.

She bit her lip. "Yeah. I get those too. But hey"—she nodded outside toward the hotel—"what better way to get our mind off things than having some vodka I stole from my mom at the pool?"

I cracked a smile. "You're a visionary, Fairbanks. Thanks."

The Hollowing is over, I reminded myself. *And you're okay.*

I opened my door and slid out to follow my friends, doing my best to shove the memory to the back of my mind where it belonged.

two

If you or a family member has been stricken with Hollowness, remember to add your name to the United States National Hollow Registry. Registration will ensure timely delivery of viable nutritional protein to your home from one of our verified distributors. You'll also be sent a link to download the HollowLife app, which allows for local EHPA representatives to remain abreast of your location and for you to log your weekly SynFlesh intake.

Any Hollow person found unregistered is subject to arrest and detention.

Remember: community safety is everyone's business.

—Emergency Hollow Preparedness Association PSA

*C*hecking into the hotel was easy, so it wasn't long before Celeste and I were dragging the flesh cooler to our room. Val strutted beside me humming the lyrics to one of the songs she'd played in the car while Jasmine looked up takeout places nearby that might have SynFlesh options. After a deeply unflattering climb up the stairs, Celeste and I dropped the cooler on the floor of our room, gasping for breath while Val squealed and ran for one of the queen beds.

"This is so cool!" she shouted, flopping down on the pile of pillows near the headboard and splaying out her arms. "I've never had my own hotel room before."

I let my duffel bag slide off my shoulder and onto the floor next to the cooler, surveying the room. The carpet was a dingy shade of mustard yellow, and the beds had floral duvets that may well have been manufactured in the '70s. Still, it smelled like piney cleaning solution and the windows had a nice view of the pool, plus the Joshua tree–speckled desert beyond it, so I couldn't complain.

"You should have been on the softball team," Jasmine said, dropping her hard-shell suitcase, which was covered in BLM, feminist, and lesbian flag stickers, in the corner of the room. "We stayed at hotels all the time. Made for a truly incredible amount of queer drama."

"As fun as sharing a bed with every softball butch in Aspen Flats sounds, I've sworn off activities that require sweating." Val rolled over onto her stomach to look at me and Celeste. "So, you two sharing a bed?"

Celeste and I exchanged a look. At the sight of her faintly quirked eyebrow, something fluttered in the pit of my stomach, which I quickly shoved down.

I said, "I can ask for a rollaway bed at the front desk."

"Why?" Celeste tilted her head to the side and stared at me from under her long, dark eyelashes. "We've been sharing a bed at sleepovers since middle school."

My shitty gay heart did a backflip in my chest.

The thing is, she was right. This wasn't supposed to be weird, because it hadn't been for a long, long time. I'd lost count of the number of times we'd shared beds, either at sleepovers like she said or camping or just hanging out after school and doing homework. It wasn't anything special or noteworthy.

Until a couple weeks ago, when my horrible little lizard brain decided the absolute hottest person on the planet was my best friend.

I opened my mouth to explain myself, but Jasmine cut in, "Maybe this is Zoey's way of finally admitting that she kicks *and* snores."

I started to roll my eyes until it occurred to me that Jaz might be onto something. "Uh—yeah. Sorry, Celeste. I just don't want to keep you awake."

She scoffed. "I'd like to see you try. I sleep through fire alarms."

I forced myself to examine the curtains across the room as my heart sped up. I could feel my face burning, which meant the others could definitely see it. Despite living in SoCal my entire life, I was too pale to hide even the faintest hint of a blush. Sweat beaded on my forehead.

"Um." I tried to swallow, but my throat was dry. "Well. If you're sure—"

Val hopped off her bed and said, "That settles it. Jaz and me here, Zoey and Celeste there. Now, can we *please* get some takeout and go to the pool? We're on vacation; we should act like it!"

"There's a diner a mile from here with SynFlesh options that'll deliver," Jasmine reported.

Celeste's shoulders slumped. "There's a whole cooler of SynFlesh *right there*."

"And you both looked very strong and capable carrying it up the stairs," Val said. "But I hate cold SynFlesh."

Celeste fell onto what was, apparently, *our* bed with a heavy sigh, her eyelashes fluttering and her hair falling in rosy waves around her cheeks.

I gulped.

God, I'm so screwed.

As much as I hated to admit it, Val was right—cold flesh didn't compare to the warm stuff.

I ate a warm SynFlesh steak while sitting cross-legged on the floor, teeth lengthening in sharp fangs as I bit into it. I used my free hand to open the HollowLife app on my phone to log my dinner—I'm sure Patricia, our Emergency Hollow Preparedness Association representative back in Aspen Flats—who was in charge of monitoring us—would appreciate her millionth picture of raw synthetic meat that proved my friends and I weren't out killing innocents. It was kind of a pain to have to log all of my meals, but I understood that it was the government's condition to let Hollow people walk around like everyone else. Sure, it was a little invasive to have to be tracked all the time, and to have to submit applications to leave Aspen Flats, but I much preferred that over the alternative, which was keeping ghouls in prisonlike facilities like at the beginning of the Hollowing.

Meanwhile, Val made an excuse to grab something from the car with her own SynFlesh steak in a Styrofoam box. No one said anything—Val never ate with us. I knew for a fact that it was because she hated people seeing her in her ghoul form, so it didn't exactly warrant much worry so long as she was still eating in general.

When she returned from the car post-dinner, she'd already changed into her swimsuit. The rest of us had to rush to catch up with her as she led the march to the hotel pool. Celeste produced the bottle of vodka that she'd stolen from Wendy, and we poured it into half-full soda bottles we'd bought at the vending machine in the hallway. While we couldn't eat solid human food without getting sick, liquids were the exception to the rule—which was great, because that meant we could still get blasted on vacation.

I took a hearty swig of Fanta and vodka and nearly gagged— *okay, maybe a little too strong.*

The pool was empty when we arrived, much to our cheering delight. The water was pale blue, rippling softly in the low after-noon light. Val took a running start and cannonballed into the deep end while Jasmine readjusted her braids into a bun atop her head before getting into the hot tub. Celeste followed Jasmine, and in an attempt to distract my racing heart, I jogged to the edge of the pool and dove in.

The water was cold enough to bite into my skin, the chlorine burning my eyes as I opened them. Everything underwater was tinged blue, the bubbles rising from my mouth sparkling in the sun. A wicked smile cut across my face as I kicked toward where Val stood in her bright yellow swimsuit. I grabbed her ankle, burst-ing into bubbling laughter as she thrashed and shrieked overhead.

I surfaced with a gasp just as she shouted, "Oh my *god*, you *asshole!*"

She splashed me and I threw my arms up to shield my face, cackling. Val dove at me to try and shove me underwater, and I pushed off from the bottom to glide out of her range. She continued laughing and cursing me out, swimming as fast as she could to catch me.

Before we could get very far, a deep voice from behind us cut in, "Wow. Didn't expect a girl who looks like you to have a mouth like that."

Val and I froze. I flicked away a strand of wet hair and found a boy standing over us at the edge of the pool, a lopsided smile on his face. He was a skinny white guy with black and gray tattoos up and down his arms and on his chest. His hair was dyed black and hung slightly in his eyes. If I had to guess, he was probably in his early twenties.

I tilted my head sideways, frowning. "Can we help you?"

"Sorry, I didn't mean to intrude—I just thought it was funny." His smile grew wider. "I'm Eli, by the way."

"Ignore Zoey—it's nice to meet you. I'm Val." She held eye contact with him, even as I did my best to catch her eye, mentally begging her to tell him to piss off. I spotted the tiniest hint of a blush in the apples of her cheeks, and I nearly groaned out loud.

Val never picked decent guys—it was always assholes like this.

From behind Eli, three other boys came running, diving into the pool with varying amounts of grace. I held up a hand to shield against the spray, scowling. Two of them immediately began trying to dunk each other underwater while another floated on his back.

Of course there's more of them.

"So, what brings you to a nowhere hotel like this?" Eli asked, sitting down at the edge of the pool. His focus was so acutely on Val, it made me feel like I'd turned invisible.

"Going to Desert Bloom with my friends," she said, a small

smile beginning to warm her face. "Sorry, this is kinda weird but you look...familiar almost. Do I know you from somewhere?"

Eli flexed his eyebrows. "You know No Flash Photography?"

Suddenly, Val's face lit up like Eli had just admitted to personally spit-polishing the stars every night. "No *way*! You're *Eli McKinley*?" She clapped her hands together. "Oh my god, *I love you*!"

"Special guy, huh?" Jasmine appeared from the hot tub, dark skin still steaming as she tied a towel around her waist. "Usually, it takes longer for her to say *I love you*. Like, a week or so."

"Jaz, come on! This is *the* Eli McKinley! He's the lead singer for one of my favorite bands that'll be at Desert Bloom! And he writes some of their songs which are, like, *beautiful* lyrically—"

"All right, all right, simmer down." Jasmine held out a hand to Eli. "I'm Jasmine."

"Pleasure." Eli shook her hand and gestured to the pool, where the other boys had stopped trying to drown each other and were laughing about something. "These are my bandmates, Kaiden, Raj, and Cole. I guess you already know we're playing at Desert Bloom."

The boys waved. They had fewer tattoos and looked a little younger, closer to our age. One of them, a redhead with green eyes and freckles—Cole, maybe—held out his hand to me.

"Hey," he said. "Nice to meet you."

I stared at his hand like it was a dead fish floating in the pool.

"This is Zoey," Val supplemented, putting her hands on my shoulders. "Sorry, she's shy."

"No, I'm not," I retorted. "I just don't like being accosted by random guys."

"Not into musicians?" Maybe-Cole asked. Honestly, he was

cute in a scruffy, unkempt sort of way, but that didn't stop me from glaring.

"Not into whatever this is." I pushed off from the bottom of the pool and floated to the pool ladder, pulling myself out. "I'll be in the hot tub."

Cole blinked a few times as his hand slowly sank back into the water. Val didn't so much as flinch as she swam up the edge of the pool to continue chatting with Eli. Jasmine gave me a little shrug of sympathy as I passed.

I found Celeste on her phone in the hot tub. She was in the middle of slapping a filter over a selfie she'd just taken in her cherry-print bikini top and swim skirt before she posted it to Instagram. Despite the heat and steam, her makeup hadn't budged—presumably as a result of an expensive setting spray, or maybe a Faustian bargain. *Jury's out.*

I descended the steps and sat down across from her, folding my arms.

She raised her eyebrows and I explained, "Val met some boys."

"I noticed." She hooked a thumb in their direction. "You don't want to talk to them?"

I wrinkled my nose. "What? Why would I do that?"

Celeste shrugged. "Because you're single and it's summer and they're probably interested? You can be decently cute when you try."

I guffawed at that. "Yeah? You're single too—why don't you talk to them?"

"Please. It takes a lot for me to be interested in a boy these days. And those guys aren't my type at all."

Somehow, that made my pulse quicken—even though Celeste saying she wasn't interested in those boys had absolutely nothing to do with her hypothetical interest in me. Celeste wasn't typically the sort of person to talk about her crushes or dating life—the only people she'd been with in high school were girls, as far as I knew.

I grabbed my vodka-spiked Fanta from where I'd left it on the edge of the hot tub and held it out to Celeste. "Cheers to that."

A small smile crossed her face as she tapped her Sprite bottle against mine. "Cheers. Wanna take bets on how long it is until Val drags those boys over here and forces us to hang out with them?"

"Ten minutes," I said.

"I'll give it twenty. Loser drains her drink?"

"Deal."

Celeste was right, as usual, but it was almost worth it to watch the No Flash Photography boys react as they stepped into the hot tub and I instantly started chugging soda like my life depended on it.

Val sat down in Eli's lap while Jasmine curled up against me, probably to avoid the longing stare of one of the boys, an Indian guy with an impressively tall pompadour and a gold septum piercing. Raj, I assumed. Clearly, he hadn't picked up on the fact that Jasmine was firmly a lesbian.

"This is my friend Celeste," Val told the boys. "She's the one who got us tickets to the festival. She posts makeup tutorials on TikTok and YouTube and gets all the influencer perks."

Celeste blushed a bit. "It's really not that big of a deal."

"Come on—you should own it," Eli said, keeping his eyes on Celeste while he wrapped his arms around Val's waist. It hadn't even been a full hour since they showed up and they were already sitting like they'd been dating for years. "People like us have to earn fame. It doesn't just land in your lap for no reason."

Maybe I was imagining it, but it almost looked like Celeste's eye twitched. "People like us?"

Eli leaned forward conspiratorially. "*Outsiders,* you know? Not those fake-ass Hollywood types. The *real* people with *real* issues."

Celeste bit back a laugh. "Ah, of course. You're right—I bet you and I have had really similar struggles."

Val let out a little sigh while Jasmine snorted into her vodka-spiked ginger ale. Naturally, Eli didn't notice.

"I mean," he continued, unfazed, "just take the last two years, right? Ever since the Hollowing, art's been the last thing on people's minds. It's *ghouls this* and *ghouls that*. Should ghouls be able to go to large public gatherings even with EHPA approval? Was it a good idea to stop mailing ghouls SynFlesh and start selling it in grocery stores next to the regular meat? It's nonstop. How are we supposed to carve out a niche when all that occupies people's minds is whether or not they can go for a walk without their neighbor growing jagged teeth and ripping them apart?"

All of us grew quiet. *Ghoul* was a somewhat pejorative term for Hollow people, and while that's what we usually called ourselves, it definitely didn't have the same vibe coming from Eli's mouth.

Celeste casually said, "Not a fan of Hollow people?"

The other bandmates all averted their gazes at once, not looking at Eli or any one of us. Cole whispered something to his bandmate Kaiden—another white boy with dark hair who'd been vaping more or less nonstop since his arrival—who nodded, while Raj suddenly seemed interested in something on the other side of the pool. If they had any opinions for or against what Eli had said, they didn't show it. Meanwhile, Eli shook his head, slicking back his hair with a slim-fingered hand.

"Nah, look—I get it. It's not like people chose to become ghouls. But listen—the Hollowing *ruined* music for almost a year! Tours got canceled, no one was buying merch—our industry was falling apart. And now people just act like everything is back to normal like ghouls aren't still everywhere. Who knows how long they'll stomach SynFlesh, right? What if one day they decide that isn't enough? Or if the Hollow virus mutates and turns even more people into ghouls? Then we're screwed."

For the first time, Kaiden decided to set his vape pen down on the edge of the hot tub and chime in. "We all remember the Hollowing. You can't honestly look at monsters like that and think they should just be allowed to walk around like the rest of us. We never should have let them out of the cages we kept them in at the beginning of the Hollowing."

Val's skin took on a pale, waxen hue while Jasmine's nostrils flared. Jaz glared at Kaiden out of the corner of her eye while examining her nails. Even Celeste, the most even-tempered of us, was pursing her lips.

But none of that compared to the way that I'd begun to clench my teeth and ball my hands into fists so tight that my nails dug into the skin. *Really* dug in, especially as I thought about how easy it would be to lunge at him and tear out his throat. *God, what a bunch of assholes. I bet they'd taste amazing with Fanta and vodka.*

A trickle of blood dripped down my palm.

Oh—shit.

"Leave it to these guys to always keep the hot tub banter light,"

Raj said in an English accent, his smile doing little to cut the tension. "Ladies, I apologize. Clearly you're just a little kinder about all that stuff than dicks like us. Why don't we open some White Claws and talk about something less…gruesome?"

I stood up, something sharp pressing into my tongue. I struggled to talk around my teeth as I muttered, "No thanks. I'm going back to the room."

Val started to reach out for me, saying, "Zo—"

"Not my scene," I muttered under my breath, stepping out of the hot tub and snagging my room key and towel off a lounge chair.

I kept walking even as my friends called after me, my face heated and pink. As soon as I was out of sight, I ran the rest of the way to the hotel room. I jammed the key card into the slot above the doorknob and shouldered my way inside. Heart racing, I ducked into the bathroom and slammed the door behind me. I gripped the edge of the sink as I tried to catch my breath.

My hazel eyes stared back at me from the mirror, bloodshot and ringed with red around the iris with dark shadows beneath them. All of the veins around my eyes had turned black, standing out starkly against my pale skin. My teeth had sharpened into two rows of long, jagged fangs, my lips around them purple and chapped. My fingernails, now more like wicked talons, clacked against the sink as I steadied myself against it. The bones of my jaw were pliable, prepared to unhinge. Behind my teeth, my tongue was an oxygen-starved shade of blue.

Just as the edges of my vision began to turn red, a knock at the door made me jump.

"Zoey?" Celeste asked. "You okay?"

I quickly closed my mouth, doing my best to banish the image of sinking my teeth into Eli's throat from my mind. I wrapped a fluffy white towel around myself and opened the door.

Celeste stood in the doorway, droplets of water still snaking down her legs from the hot tub. At the sight of me, her mouth rounded into an O.

"No wonder you ran."

Heat filled my cheeks as Celeste gazed at me. She'd seen me like this plenty of times—including when we literally devoured our camp counselor together—but I still couldn't stop myself from turning my gaze to the floor. It had been a long time since I let my control slip.

"Sorry. Kinda lost it back there."

"Hey, it's okay." She gently put a hand on my arm, making my pulse speed up. She gave it a soft squeeze and added, "Don't worry about it. The thought crossed my mind too."

"Really?"

Celeste stuck out her tongue and pointed to a small cut on the edge of it. "Poked myself pretty good. Assholes would have deserved it."

I exhaled a little laugh, my shoulders finally retreating from where they'd tensed up against my throat. As much as I wished that Celeste and I could have avoided becoming Hollow, it was nice to have a best friend who immediately *got it* when stuff like this happened. I never had to worry about being judged around her.

"I just hate guys like that," I said, tucking a lock of dark brown hair behind my ear. "And the fact that Val puts up with them."

"She certainly has a type," Celeste huffed, leaning against the doorframe and crossing her arms. "I'm sure whatever was happening with Eli back there will blow over. Hopefully before the end of the festival."

"It's nice you still have a sense of optimism."

Celeste chuckled. "One of us has to. Oh, totally different topic, but you wanna look through tomorrow's schedule for Desert Bloom and see what we wanna go to? Val's definitely going to be at No Flash Photography, but I had my eye on a couple different options."

"Yeah, definitely." I hiked the towel up over my chest just a bit. "I'm just gonna put clothes on first."

She sputtered a laugh. "Oh, you're not interested in wearing your wet swimsuit in our shared bed?"

Something nearly short-circuited in my brain at the thought of lounging mostly naked together. Which is probably why I responded, too fast, "Of course I'm not interested in that."

I winced as Celeste's smile faltered.

Stupid, stupid, stupid.

Still, she managed to laugh it off. "All right, I was just kidding." She pointed past me into the bathroom. "I'll take a shower while you change. Maybe you can pull up the schedule when you're decent."

With that, she stepped past me into the bathroom and shut the door behind her, leaving me standing there with a beet-red face and a racing heart.

three

When the Hollowing came to Aspen Flats, the town went dark. The streets had emptied as soon as reports started coming in that a strange disease seemed to be ripping through big cities. People locked their doors and boarded up their windows like they were waiting for a hurricane. The town's only grocery store ran out of supplies so fast most people didn't even have a chance to grab food and medicine. Neighbors who had previously waved and smiled to each other every morning suddenly refused to look at each other as they locked their doors for the first time ever.

The Vega family was no different. Valeria's father had been one of the lucky few who had managed to get enough supplies to hold them over for a few weeks. They kept the curtains drawn day and night to cover up the boarded windows, and played music to drown out the intermittent sound of gunfire. Val's mother had strictly forbidden anyone to turn on the TV, especially the news.

And when Val's grandmother got sick, everyone treated it like a normal stomach bug.

"*Mamá made caldo de pollo, Abuela,*" Val said as she placed a tray at her grandmother's bedside. She'd been sick for nearly three days, unable to keep anything down despite the family's best efforts to make her every gentle food and stomach-settling tea they could think of. None of it went to waste—Val's brothers made sure of that, with their bottomless pit stomachs—but it didn't stop Val from staying awake at night, thoughts of her grandmother dry heaving in the other room keeping her from even considering sleep.

Voice scratchy, Abuela whispered, "Gracia, mija. Now, let me be. I need my rest."

"Please try to eat," Val whispered.

Abuela didn't move. She looked so small huddled under the blankets, her body frail like a baby bird's. Her long gray hair was tangled and unkempt—Val had offered to braid it for her, but she refused.

"Val!" a voice called from the kitchen. "Dinner!"

Val leaned down and softly pressed a kiss to her grandmother's cheek. "Te quiero, Abuela. Feel better."

At dinner, the Vegas said grace before digging into the rest of the caldo de pollo. Val's older and younger brothers wolfed it down so fast their mother had to snap at them to slow down or they'd choke. Val, meanwhile, nibbled at the chicken, trying to keep her breathing even. Even the scent of it had begun to make her stomach churn, and she had to bite back a gag with each bite.

While her mother was busy scolding her siblings and her father was glancing at his phone, Val took the pieces of chicken from her soup and passed them under the table to Sunny, the family's pit bull mix, who gratefully swallowed them without hesitation. Thank god Sunny was there, otherwise Val never would have gotten away with the meager amounts of food she'd managed to choke down the last few days.

Val cleared her throat, saying, "I'll be right back."

Her mother waved her away, clearly distracted by lecturing her brothers about proper table manners. Val left her spoon in the bowl, then tucked in her chair and headed down the hall toward the bathroom. The sound of her family chatting plus the soft melody of her mother's music was enough to almost make it feel like any other family dinner, even with Abuela sick in bed. It was like her mother had said when whispers about the Hollowing had first begun: that's a problem for other people, not us.

Val closed the bathroom door behind her, locked it, and turned the shower and sink on full blast. Then, when she knew the sound would be drowned out, she lifted the toilet seat. Hunching over it, she coughed up bile, black and oily, spattering viscous droplets across the toilet bowl.

Just like she had for the last three days straight.

Tears streaked Val's cheeks as she weakly spit the leftover taste of chicken into the toilet. Softly, she pressed her fist into her mouth to muffle the sound of her sobs. Her shoulders shook, chin wrinkling as her face crumbled. She kept one hand on the table to brace herself, vision swimming. Steam began to rise from the shower, filling the room and sticking to the mirror. Good—she didn't want to see her reflection like this. She'd been avoiding it for days.

"Dios te salve, María, llena eres de gracia: el Señor es contigo," Val whispered, repeating the Hail Mary just as she'd always been taught to recite it. Her voice caught as she whispered it, clasping her hands together.

She repeated the prayer twice more all the way through. On shaky legs, she stood, then flushed the toilet, turned off the shower, and washed her hands. Splashing cold water on her face, she took one, two, three deep breaths to steady herself.

"You're okay," she whispered to herself. "You're fine."

A few minutes later, she returned to the dinner table to find her *family still poking fun at her brothers. As she pulled out her chair, her mother shot her a small smile.*

"You all right, baby? You look pale."

Val nodded, plastering on her best smile.

"Fine, Mamá." She sat down, scooting her chair in. "Thank you for dinner. Delicious as always."

She picked up her spoon and dipped it back into her soup.

By the time Val and Jasmine made it back to the hotel room, they'd been hanging out with the No Flash Photography boys for almost three hours.

"How did you manage to not tear their throats out?" I grumbled to Jasmine, who was fresh out of the shower and finishing her skincare routine on her bed. Val was still in the bathroom, loudly singing one of No Flash Photography's songs. She'd just turned the water off, which had been the only thing drowning her out.

Jasmine shrugged, rubbing in her moisturizer. "Wasn't easy, trust me."

"Wikipedia says Eli's twenty-four," Celeste said, pointing to her laptop screen. "So he was eighteen when Val was *twelve*."

"Ew," I muttered. "Do you think she knows that?"

"No point stirring the pot when Val's ready made up her mind," Jasmine said, dotting a different skin cream under her eyes. "Trust me, I tried. I got an elbow in the sternum."

As if on cue, the bathroom door popped open, and Val strode out in satin pajamas with her dark hair in a braid.

"Heya." Still whistling the tune of the song she'd been

singing, she came straight to mine and Celeste's bed and lifted the covers. "Scoot."

"It's *my* bed," I argued. "You have your own!"

Val squeezed her way in anyway. I had to practically shove myself into Celeste, who was chuckling the whole time, to make room for her. Val snuggled against me, kissing my cheek before pressing her nose to my throat. While I grumbled out a curse, she said, "Don't pretend you hate cuddling. Jasmine, get over here."

"Come *on*—"

Jasmine screwed the top onto her moisturizer bottle before sliding out from under her covers and climbing between ours. I all but had to climb into Celeste's lap to make enough room for her. Jasmine wrapped her arms around Val, spooning her. Val giggled while I let out a guttural groan.

Meanwhile, Celeste smiled, closing her laptop and setting it down on the bedside table. She rolled over onto her stomach and propped her palmed chin up on her elbow. This close, I could feel her breathing against my pinkened cheek.

"Hey Val," Celeste said, innocently batting her eyelashes. "Did you know Eli's twenty-four?"

Jasmine sputtered a laugh while Val huffed. "And I'm eighteen. It's not that weird—plus, he's cute."

"He looks like he spends all day chain-smoking outside of a 7–11 while waiting to buy minors booze," I argued.

"He's like if Pete Davidson had absolutely no sex appeal," Jasmine agreed.

Celeste snorted a laugh. "Or if a Four Loko had a magic spell cast on it to turn it into a real boy."

"Stop it," Val snapped while Jasmine buried her face into a pillow to cover up her cackling, Celeste and I snickering along. "He's really nice! *And* he invited us to two different VIP-only events at Desert Bloom, so he clearly wants to win you all over."

"With all that delightful talk of ghouls being monsters, how could we turn him down?" I said sarcastically.

"I'm not asking you to be friends with him," Val pointed out. "Just give him another chance. I really think it could be fun to hang out with those guys. I mean—think about it! Backstage passes, exclusive parties, free stuff, probably…"

"At what personal cost, though?" Jasmine argued.

Val rolled her eyes. "All right, all right. Point made. We'll talk tomorrow after we get some sleep."

"Which you're doing in your bed, right?" When neither Jasmine nor Val moved, instead curling up and closing their eyes, I added, "*Right?*"

The only response I got was Celeste giggling and clicking off the bedside lamp while Val and Jasmine pointedly ignored me.

It wasn't long before everyone else had fallen asleep around me, the sound of soft breathing the only thing in the room to keep me company.

I stared up at the ceiling, so tense I could barely move. Val had her arms around me on one side while Celeste's face was inches away on the other. Her hair was in a pretty pink braid that hung over her shoulder, loose strands glowing in the moonlight that poured over her face. Her eyelids fluttered just faintly in her sleep. She looked so peaceful.

Slowly, I let my hand reach for her face, where a single strand of hair was caught on her eyelashes. My fingers lingered in the air over her cheek, my heart beginning to race as I thought of tucking the strand behind her ear, then letting my fingers slide through her hair. The millimeters of air between our skin seemed to heat like an electric coil, shooting off sparks.

I jerked my hand back, wrapping my arms around myself. I stared as hard as I could at a water stain on the ceiling, begging my brain to shut up. Briefly, I wondered how long it would take me to bleed out if I jammed the hotel-branded pen on the bedside table into my femoral artery.

Fuuuuuuuuck me.

The gay crisis thing was new. Or at least it was regarding Celeste—I'd been out as bi for years, so that part wasn't a surprise. But I'd known Celeste since we were kids. One time, I watched her snort Pixy Stix in the lunchroom on a dare because she was too stubborn to let a boy get away with telling her she couldn't do something. You'd think that would be enough of a turnoff to dissuade me from wanting to kiss her, but no.

It all started three weeks ago during a game of Spin the Bottle at Cleo Jacobsen's graduation party. We'd been doing shots of Fireball when Cleo stole the empty bottle out of Josh Bellingham's hand and dropped it on the floor before shouting that everyone needed to sit in a circle. And three shots and two White Claws deep, who'd say no to that?

Immediately, the bottle landed on me. I gave Cleo a gentle peck, much to the delight of some of the nasty football boys crowded in one corner and the gasping surprise of some of the girls. It wasn't like my friends and I were the only queer kids at school, but we made up a very large fraction of them. Thankfully, aside from the unpleasant smell of vodka on Cleo's breath, it was a completely neutral kiss.

So when I spun the bottle and it landed on Celeste—who had curled her hair and had on a white minidress with a heart-shaped cutout over her collarbone—I laughed and smiled like it was any other random person. At least in this case, it would be a funny story later.

Except then she leaned forward and her hand was on my cheek, brushing backward into my hair as she leaned in and pressed her lips against mine. There was a tenderness to the way she held my cheek while her hair tickled the side of my face. The scent of vanilla swept over me as her lips parted and she gently sucked my lower lip, much to the gasping surprise of a few people in the circle. Her fingers tightened in my hair as I stiffened, eyes flying open.

She pulled away, grinning and gesturing to everyone else in the circle. "*That's* how you kiss in spin the bottle."

I hadn't stopped thinking about it since. Naturally, Celeste had been joking about it for weeks, clearly unfazed by the event that had sent me spiraling. It was absolutely maddening.

And now there she was, inches away from me, all of her makeup off and the shadows of her eyelashes dancing across her moon-lit cheeks. God, she even looked pretty sleeping. Back in middle school she'd been the sort of kid who only wore gray hoodies and baggy pants and hid behind her overgrown bangs. It was like one day she was completely invisible and the next she was the walking embodiment of neon light and cotton candy. If I'd known estradiol, spiro, and the ability to use liquid eyeliner correctly were that powerful, I'd have looked into it myself.

I sat up in bed, my hair a mussed wreck that stuck out on one side. Val grumbled in her sleep as I pushed her arms off me. After managing to crawl out of bed—barely avoiding kneeing Val in the head—I slipped on my shoes, then grabbed my phone, room key, and jacket off the chair where I'd abandoned them.

I needed some air.

I pulled the main door closed behind me as quietly as possible. The motel hallway was empty, the carpet a heinous shade of brown that had probably been sunny once. The closest smells I could associate it with were wet dog and Pine-Sol. One of the overhead lights flickered as I headed down toward the pool, praying it would be empty this late.

Thankfully, it was. I kicked off my shoes and sat down on the edge of it, dipping my feet into the water. Overhead, stars glimmered in the cloudless sky, no light pollution to obscure them. Refracted light danced at the turquoise bottom of the pool, rippling until my eyes blurred and my thoughts finally began to slow down. I leaned back on my hands and stared up at the sky, exhaling a heavy breath through my nose.

As much as I loved Celeste, the truth was I was a little relieved that there was a specific end date to our time together. I was moving to New York City in August to attend NYU's journalism program, and she was unsure of where she'd go since she wasn't planning on going to college—at least not yet. Being an influencer was nice in the sense that she could live anywhere she wanted, and at the moment she had no idea where that was. In my wilder fantasies, I like to imagine her coming to the city with me, the two of us renting a tiny apartment and carving out a quiet life together. But I was smart enough to know that was an absolute nightmare of an idea.

Because then I'd have to admit I had feelings for her, and I'd rather wither away in the desert sun until the vultures got me than do that.

Just as I let out a heavy breath and debated going back inside, a voice from behind me made me jump. I craned my neck to see the redheaded boy, Cole, who'd tried to introduce himself to me earlier, shoving his way through the doors to the pool with his phone wedged between his shoulder and ear. Based on the way he was looking at the ground, he hadn't noticed me.

"Yeah, I'm fine." He pressed a knuckle into the furrowed spot between his eyebrows as he began to pace. "Yes, made it to the hotel without any issues. We hung out with some girls tonight—no, ew, not like that."

Despite myself, I snorted, and Cole jumped.

Whoops.

Unsure of how else to seem less like a creep, I stood up and waved. "Hi—sorry. Didn't mean to scare you."

Cole's eyebrows rose, then fell, as he said, "I'll call you back tomorrow."

He ended the call and swallowed, his Adam's apple bobbing as he shoved the phone in his pocket. "Um. Sorry about that. I didn't think anyone would be out here."

"Guess we had the same thought." I grabbed my own phone off the ground and started to say, "The pool's all yours. I should probably go to bed anyway—"

"Wait!" Cole held up a hand, stopping me. He smiled awkwardly and made a weak little sound behind his teeth. "Look, I just—I wanted to apologize for Eli and the other guys earlier. They should have shut up once they saw you were getting uncomfortable."

"Oh. Yeah." I shrugged. "It's whatever."

Cole winced. "You've probably heard a lot of that, huh? Since the Hollowing?"

My eyebrows shot up. "Why…?"

"Oh god, that was rude too. I'm so sorry." Cole rubbed the back of his neck sheepishly. "When you got out of the hot tub earlier, I noticed your…claws. That must have been really shitty to hear Eli and the others ranting about ghouls with you *right there*."

I blinked, unsure of what to say to that. And here I thought I'd made a pretty slick escape. Clearly not slick enough for Cole, though.

"It's fine, really. Like you said, I've heard a lot of that since the Hollowing." I met his eyes—they were a pleasant shade of green. I guess he was sort of cute, in a nonthreatening puppy dog kind of way. "Did Eli notice?"

Cole shook his head. "He was a little busy staring at Valeria for that."

I snorted a laugh, which made the corner of Cole's mouth quirk up just slightly.

He added, "Sorry about that too. We're not exactly headliners, so hearing that a girl not only listens to our music but enjoys it was enough to make Eli more…over the top than usual."

"Trust me, Val wasn't complaining." I ran a hand back through my hair. "You know what? You seem like a decent guy, Cole. If Eli does invite Val and the rest of us to hang out with you at Desert Bloom, we should talk."

Cole's face warmed. "I'd like that. You seem cool too, Zoey."

"You remembered my name?"

"You're pretty memorable," Cole said with a sly smile. "Most girls don't almost eat my lead singer in front of me."

I bit back a laugh. "Touché."

He reached into his pocket, withdrawing his phone. "If you want, maybe we could exchange numbers? Stay in touch at the festival?"

"Totally." I took his phone and quickly sent myself a text before adding the name Zoey Huxley to his contacts list. I handed it back. "See you at the festival?"

"Yeah." He put his hands in his pockets.

"See you there."

four

"Hey, Celeste?"

Celeste didn't stir aside from a faint groan. She was snuggled deep under a pile of blankets on the bottom bunk in their cabin at Camp Everwood, her skin wet with sweat as chills racked her body. She and Zoey had been quarantined there for four days now—ever since that stomach bug had started going around. From what they heard from notes slipped under their door, nearly all of the sick kids and staff were starting to get better.

Except Zoey and Celeste.

"What?" Celeste finally managed to ask. Her face was buried in her pillow, muffling her voice.

"I wanted to save these until the last day of camp," Zoey started. She leaned over from the top bunk. She looked marginally better than Celeste, the hollows under her hazel eyes not quite so deep. "But maybe we should give them a try now."

"If you think I'm gonna dig through your bag, it's not happening," Celeste groaned. "Unless you want me to throw up black ooze all over the floor again."

"Okay, quitter."

There was an ungraceful thump as Zoey rolled off the top bunk and landed on the floor in a crouch. For a moment, Celeste lifted her head from the pillow, nearly gasping at her friend's sudden recovery. But then Zoey swayed, braced herself against the floor, and dry-heaved loudly.

"Dude," Celeste moaned, hiding her face.

"I'm fine," Zoey choked. She swallowed and shook her head. "Yep. Never better."

After a few more deep breaths, she gathered up the strength to crawl over to her duffel bag. She unzipped it and pawed through until she came upon something wrapped in crinkling plastic. She pulled it out and held it in the air with both hands in her best Lion King *impression.*

"You snuck Oreos into camp?" Celeste said, pressing a hand over her heart like she'd just acknowledged some great sin. Camp Everwood was the sort of crunchy-granola establishment that only fed the campers things that came from the ground, effectively outlawing processed foods. Celeste hadn't had a potential carcinogen in weeks.

Zoey beamed. "Sounds pretty good, right?"

Celeste paused. The two of them had tried tons of different foods over the last few days while trying to get anything to stay down. But that had all been healthy stuff—fruits, grains, pureed vegetable soups—that wasn't very appealing even when they weren't sick. The thought of pure sugar didn't churn Celeste's stomach, so that seemed like a good start.

Celeste nodded. "Let's split one."

Zoey scooted over to Celeste's bedside and crossed her legs. She plucked an Oreo out of the packaging and snapped it in half, weighing it in her palm for a beat. She handed the slightly larger half to Celeste, then tapped her half against it.

"Cheers," Zoey said, "to high-fructose corn syrup."

Celeste went to take a tiny bite, but at that moment, something sharp sliced her tongue. The taste of blood filled her mouth. Or—it seemed like blood, anyway. Warm, coppery, maybe a little bit sweet.

Celeste didn't remember blood ever tasting good.

Zoey's brow furrowed. "You okay?"

"I—" Celeste winced, then opened her mouth and stuck out her tongue for Zoey to see. "I-I cut myself."

Zoey froze.

"Zo? What is it?" Celeste's voice grew strained, her eyebrows furrowing. When Zoey didn't immediately respond, Celeste cautiously poked at the sharp something embedded in her gums with her tongue.

A…tooth?

No. Sharper than that. Half an inch long and jutting out where her canine should have been.

A fang.

Zoey gulped. "I think I should call a camp counselor."

"Zoey, hold on—!"

But she was already up, sprinting to the door of their cabin, face white as a sheet. Celeste moved to try and chase after her, but all she could manage was to fall out of her tangle of blankets onto the floor. She moaned and winced as her stomach lurched at the sudden jostling.

"Devin!" Zoey shouted through the open door. "We need help!"

Celeste's vision began to cloud. Her head throbbed, and the inside of her throat felt dry as sandpaper. The taste of her own blood in her mouth was the only tie to her body, the rest of it totally numb and hollow.

She gently sucked the cut on her tongue, blood wetting the inside of her teeth. Her stomach snarled. Her jaw twinged with pain as something sharp retracted from inside, filling Celeste's mouth with jagged points like broken glass.

"Zoey," she whimpered. "Something's...wrong."
She blacked out.

After my talk with Cole at the pool, I was finally able to fall asleep, largely by forcing my brain to focus on how cute *his* smile was instead of my best friend's. It wasn't much, but it was a nice distraction from Celeste smiling in her sleep. I woke up once in the wee hours of the morning to mine and Celeste's hands touching. Though, maybe that was just a dream.

The sun crested over the desert the next morning, warming the sand and stone that had grown cold overnight. The yucca and Joshua trees were the only hints of green among the rocks and scraggly brush that dotted the earth. I'd always loved the California desert, barren as it was. Something about the emptiness of it felt comforting. Sometimes I thought about how nice it would be to just lay on the rocks and soak in the sun like the tiny lizards I used to catch between my thumb and forefinger as a kid.

The sound of a cup being set down beside me snapped me out of my thoughts. Celeste stood at my side, gesturing to the table.

"Morning, sunshine. I got you coffee downstairs. They don't have any options for us at the continental breakfast, unfortunately."

"I'll be sure to add *lacking in flesh selection* to my Yelp review of this place," I said, grabbing the coffee. As I did, I noticed the time on the bedside clock. "You're up early."

"Yeah," Val groaned from my side, where she and Jasmine were snuggled deep under the comforter. They'd pretty much monopolized it all night long. "Go back to sleep, you weirdo. It's the middle of the night."

"It's *eight in the morning*." Celeste crossed her arms, sighing. "Look, if we want to make it to Desert Bloom in time to catch the opening acts, we need to leave in half an hour. So, consider this my wake-up call."

"Did you bring us coffee too?" Jasmine asked, still facedown in her pillow.

Celeste shook her head. "No, only Zoey. She's the driver, so she's the one who actually needs it. You two can just pass out in the back seat."

Only Zoey. My heart thumped traitorously.

Val groaned. She pulled herself up, rubbing her bleary eyes. "It's like you don't even love us."

"You'll thank me later." Celeste tossed the keys at me, nearly hitting me in the face. "Get to it, we're burning daylight."

Technically Celeste was right, but that didn't mean anyone was enthusiastic or even more than half awake by the time we all piled back into the Mini Cooper. I rested my forehead on the steering wheel while Celeste handed out packages of SynFlesh to Jasmine and Val. Val turned it down—as usual—saying she'd eaten while we were all packing up, while Jasmine bit into hers without hesitation.

Celeste held out a package to me. "SynLiver okay?"

"Mmm. Nothing hits quite like a cold liver in the morning." I took it from her. "Thanks."

Soon after, we were on the open road, the desert spread out in front of us for miles with no sign of civilization other than the pavement beneath us. Celeste stole the aux cord to play some upbeat music that we all sang along to. I rolled down the windows to let the air in, the rush of it warm against my face. I tapped my hand against the steering wheel with the beat, grinning. Two years ago, when everything had gone to shit with the Hollowing, I definitely didn't think I'd ever get to do anything like this again, much less with people I cared about so much.

Desert Bloom was a newer music festival, but it had already grown to the point where people thought it would only be a couple of years before it got as big as, or bigger than, Coachella. It had been on hiatus since the Hollowing, so when it was announced it would be happening this year, the Internet all but shattered into pieces. It had trended for a week straight, and it felt like every celebrity on the planet had posted the logo on Instagram.

All that amounted to tickets that were nearly impossible to get without very fast Wi-Fi, a ridiculous amount of money, and/or insider connections—we were lucky that Celeste had managed to snag not one, but three additional tickets from her manager.

"Okay, we need a game plan," Jasmine said halfway through the drive. She leaned forward, sticking her face between mine and Celeste's seats. "Where are we going first, who are we seeing today, and what are our plans for the evening?"

"We should leave our stuff in the cabin before we do anything else," Celeste said. "Then Blue October is opening at the Rabbitbrush Plaza—after them I'm thinking either Breakfast in Accra or Violet Harlow."

"So, basically, sad indie girls or…sad indie girls?" I pointed out.

Celeste scoffed. "Excuse you, Violet Harlow smashed a guitar during her Jimmy Fallon performance."

"While crying," I pointed out.

"She's a Cancer; they're all like that," Val said, her voice sound-ing far away as she gazed out at the desert. "Oh look, cows!"

We all paused to wave at the group of cows hanging out on the side of the road munching on brush, then Jasmine continued, "I wanna see Breakfast in Accra. At least you can dance to their stuff."

"Agreed," I said. "As for tonight…"

"Eli texted me this morning that he's going to an industry party and he wants us to come hang out with him and the band," Val said, shimmying her shoulders. "It's open bar and they're definitely not going to ID."

All of us went quiet for a beat.

Val sighed melodramatically. "You're going to let me go *alone*? Come on, it'll at least be something to do that isn't just wandering the festival grounds."

"There are definitely other shows happening tonight," Jasmine argued. "Ones that'll probably be a lot more fun than trying to make small talk with Eli's bandmates while the two of you stare longingly into each other's eyes."

Val held up her hands. "It's an industry party, Jaz! There are gonna be plenty of cool people to talk to."

"I'll go with you," I said, glancing at her in the rearview mirror before Jasmine could fire off a rebuttal. "Free drinks might make Eli bearable."

While Val seemed perfectly happy with that answer, Celeste and Jasmine both shot me wide-eyed looks. Jasmine's forehead wrinkled and Celeste hiked up her brows.

"*What*?" I asked.

"Did you forget the fact you literally ran away from him yester-day?" Celeste pointed out. I was thankful she left out the part about finding me ghouled out in the bathroom after I thought too hard about ripping his throat out.

"Yeah," Jasmine asked, crossing her arms. "What's your angle?"

I took a hand off the wheel to rub the back of my neck. "Look, it's nothing. I kinda talked to one of the boys last night and he was...decent. So I guess it wouldn't hurt to talk with him again—"

Val made a shrieking noise so high-pitched it was probably a few steps away from doubling as a dog whistle. "That is extremely important information, Zoey! Who did you talk to? When? And why the hell did you not say anything until now?"

I drummed my fingers against the wheel. "The redhead, Cole. But seriously, it wasn't a big deal. I ran into him while I was walking around the hotel and we chatted a little and exchanged numbers. That's it."

"You like him," Val said factually, a smug smile on her face.

"Uh, sure? As much as you can after a five-minute conversation."

"I'll come too," Celeste cut in before Val could continue pestering me. "Might be good for networking."

"*Networking*," I repeated with a shiver. "Horrifying."

"All right, fine, I'll come," Jasmine finally caved. "But y'all better not abandon me for some lame-ass guys—you know how I start befriending everyone in the bathroom once I've had a few drinks. I'll have a new friend group by midnight and I *know* we don't have room for that many people in our cabin."

"Touché," I chuckled.

It took us about two hours more to reach De Luz Valley, where Desert Bloom was taking place. It was near the border of California and Nevada, deep in the Mojave and far enough from civilization that it was a wonder our phones still got signals. The sun beat down on five different stages, their white roofs gleaming against the red and tan rock walls that surrounded the valley. A Ferris wheel was in the process of getting set up at the edge of the festival, near various tents selling food and art. Traffic control pointed us left to the other side of the valley toward the attendee lodging. Celeste had managed to get us a small cabin, one of the more exclusive non-camping options. It was certainly better than the alternative, which were hostel-like yurts that housed up to ten people in a single room.

The line of cabins hugged the slickrock rim of the valley, patches of cacti and sagebrush thickly rooted into the dirt around them. Ours was on the end nearest to the festival, and the sound of music carried faintly on the breeze. It was an A-frame, the outside painted white and the roof a pleasant yellow. I put the Mini into park out front.

"This is us," Celeste said.

"Damn," Jasmine whispered, craning her neck to get a better view of the cabin. She clapped Celeste on the shoulder. "You really outdid yourself this time, Fairbanks."

Celeste bit back a smile and blushed faintly as we all climbed out the car. While everyone gathered their bags, I popped the trunk and hoisted the flesh cooler—which I was now convinced had been sent from hell to kill me—out of the back with a grunt. Up ahead, Celeste went to the door and typed in the code.

"Little help?" I asked Val through gritted teeth.

"Oh! Sure!" Val smiled pleasantly. She looked over my shoulder and called, "Hey Jasmine, I think Zoey needs help."

"God, you're the worst," I groaned.

She giggled before taking the other half of the cooler. "Kidding, kidding."

The two of us carried the cooler up the stairs just as Celeste pushed the door open. As we headed inside, Val dropped her half of the cooler in the entryway, nearly yanking my arm out of the socket. I swore colorfully, but it was drowned out by the sound of her clapping her hands and chirping, "It's *so cute!*"

To be fair, she was right—it was cute. The inside of the cabin was decorated in that specific desert-boho style with a lot of macramé-hanging succulents and accents in a soft pink like the color of the sunset over the heat-soaked Mojave. The living room hosted two yellow velour couches and was connected to the sleek white-granite kitchen, sun filtering in from the massive windows. Three other doorways opened to a bathroom and two bedrooms, one with a set of twin beds and one with a king.

"Same sleeping arrangements as last night?" Jasmine asked.

"Sure," Celeste said before I could attempt to interject. She hooked a thumb to me and said, "Zoey and I can take the king bed."

A tiny sigh escaped my lips, but no one seemed to notice.

"I guess we can't cuddle before bed," Val said, wrapping her arms around Jasmine's waist. "So sad."

Jasmine, much taller than five-foot-nothing Val, turned and leaned down to kiss the top of her head. "There's always the couch."

While Val and Jasmine headed off toward their room, Celeste and I went to ours. She gently set her bag down on an armchair in the corner of the room before pulling open the curtains. Her outfit today was a bit more toned down than her usual—she probably wanted to avoid being noticed in crowds. Not that she was exactly the sort to blend in, what with the fact she was nearly six feet tall and had bright pink hair, but without a lot of her trademark clothing items it might be less apparent that she was *the* Celeste

Seasons, as her followers knew her. It meant we might not get stopped for pictures as much, or at least enough for us to not have to block out a solid hour of our time for it.

"You seem quiet," Celeste said, glancing back at me. She wore shimmery eyeshadow that brought out the gold flecks in her blue irises. "Something on your mind?"

I shook my head. "It's nothing."

Celeste's mouth pressed into a tight line. "Is this about the nightmare from yesterday?"

I opened my mouth to say it wasn't, but she quickly added, "Because I get it. Honestly, I do. This whole festival—this many people in one place—it freaks me out too. Obviously, we have plenty of SynFlesh but—"

"Oh," I realized aloud. "Are you worried about losing control?"

Celeste's eyebrows pressed together. "That's not what you were thinking?"

Definitely not, though I didn't think it was exactly the right time to talk about my stupid crush when my best friend was worried about going feral and eating helpless bystanders.

"I guess it's sort of always on the backburner."

Celeste's gaze fell to the floor. I should have known this would be the thing eating away at her. It always was.

My memories of when we'd first become Hollow were largely blurs. I remembered the day after we devoured Devin Han clearly, but things after that were harder to parse as the hunger came back. I know that the two of us, blood soaked and shivering, had walked deeper and deeper into the woods, trying to get as far from Camp Everwood as possible. We'd slept huddled together under a huge pine tree, wincing each time we heard the other's stomach snarl.

The only good thing about both of us turning into ghouls was that we didn't have any interest in consuming each other.

We spent two weeks in the woods together. While society unraveled around us—people locked inside their homes waiting to see if their hunger pangs turned into monstrous cravings—we slowly lost track of ourselves. For me, everything went dark after that first night.

While she'd never confirmed it, I had the sneaking suspicion that Celeste remembered it much more clearly.

"We'll be fine," I quickly said, going to her side. I reached out to touch her shoulder, but suddenly the thought of that made my fingers feel electric, so I pulled back. I settled for staring out the same window she'd diverted her attention to. "We've got each other, right? We'll look out for each other like we always have."

Celeste chewed her lower lip.

I quickly added, "We're not monsters, Cel."

Something about the shadow that darkened her expression told me she wasn't so sure.

five

*L*os Angeles was one of the first big cities to feel the full extent of the Hollowing, and Jasmine had a front-row seat.

She was on a trip with her twelve-year-old brother, Isaiah, to visit her grandmother just before it happened. Ruth Owusu lived in downtown Los Angeles in a fancy high-rise that looked out across the valley and all the way to the ocean. Ruth was the sort of grandma who made Jasmine a cosmopolitan every evening while they watched TV and liked to show her and Isaiah around all of the Old Hollywood landmarks she loved in her youth. For the first few days of the trip, they had a great time sipping cocktails and seeing the sights.

It was around day five of the trip when the air in LA changed. It was a hot, sweltering summer, but that day was pleasantly warm and overcast. Problem was, the clouds had a strange, faint green aura to them—sort of like what they looked like before a tornado. But this was different. The shift started with people getting nervous, wondering what could possibly make the sky look like that. Moreover, what was making the sky look like that across the entire planet.

And then people got sick.

"Jaz," Isaiah had whispered from the other side of their grandmother's couch. Ruth was passed out in an armchair, snoring faintly while the TV played one of her favorite old movies. Careful not to wake her, Isaiah added, "Look at this."

He held out his phone to her. Raising an eyebrow, Jasmine took it, pressing play on the video.

"Reports of violent attacks have skyrocketed in the far north, where the meteorological anomaly now called the Green Veil first appeared," a newscaster said. "Scientists in northern Canada shared the following video from a research site. Viewer discretion is advised."

The clip shifted to a grainy video of a darkened hallway. A figure staggered down it, their voice little more than a keening whimper. Their head was cocked at a strange angle as they slowly approached whoever was filming.

"Tara?" a voice asked. "Are you okay?"

They stopped. Swaying and unsteady on their feet, they slowly angled their face up to the light. The veins around their eyes were inky black, mouth slack and sharpened teeth dripping with black bile. Their skin looked sallow and pale, and Jasmine could nearly make out the shadow of a skull beneath the skin.

The person recording cried, "What the fu—!"

They dropped their device, which clattered to the floor. The camera pointed at a wall as the sound of screams sharpened and echoed. Something snarled, and a spray of blood spattered across the wall. Just as soon as it had started, the screams stopped.

The footage cut out.

Jasmine passed the phone back to Isaiah, silent at first. Finally, she said, "Don't watch shit like that. You'll give yourself nightmares."

"That was a real video," Isaiah argued. "How are you not freaking out? An actual zombie apocalypse is about to hit—"

"Nuh-uh. Don't say that." Jasmine shot him a narrow-eyed glare. "Stuff like that doesn't happen in real life, all right? It's just—"

At that moment, their grandmother's eyes flew open. She pressed a hand over her mouth as she was suddenly racked with a coughing fit that shook her shoulders and rattled her lungs. Jasmine hopped up, going to her side to gently rub her back.

"Nana?" she asked. "You okay? Can I get you some water?"

"I—" Ruth coughed again but managed to inhale a couple of shaky breaths. "I'm fine, sweetheart. Don't worry about me."

But when she pulled her hand away from her mouth, the light caught a smear of something dark, viscous, and oily on her palm.

Once we'd done a little basic unpacking at the cabin, our first stop was the opening show at Rabbitbrush Plaza, one of the larger festival stages. The plaza's tentlike roof protected everyone from the sun, but that didn't stop the heat from creeping in and causing the air to swirl with the scent of sweat and perfume. I hadn't actually given much thought to how crowded it would be, seeing as I hadn't been to a concert since the Hollowing. But bodies were packed into every free space, glitter sparkling on their sweat-soaked skin while they swayed to the music.

The band, Blue October, was the sort of music I put on in the background to do homework, but their live presence was immediately more electric than it had ever been through my computer speakers. Val held up her water bottle and twisted left and right to the music while Jasmine bobbed her head and smiled. Celeste chewed her lower lip for the first few songs, arms crossed as she tried to angle herself away from the swaying crowd.

I reached out, touching her arm. "Hey. Get out of your head."

She blinked. "I—"

"If you were going to snap," I said, keeping my voice low enough that no one dancing nearby could hear, "it would have happened already. Right? It's okay."

Celeste hesitated. She glanced around at the crowd, her shoulders slowly beginning to sink from where they'd been tensed by her neck. "I…"

As if to punctuate that thought, Val grabbed Celeste and me by our hands and pulled us closer to where she and Jasmine were shoulder to shoulder and bouncing to the beat. I let out a breath through my nose and joined them, tension melting out of my muscles and joints. Celeste also seemed to unclench a bit, letting herself brush against us as she swayed. The guitarist played a gentle tune, plucking the strings while the lead singer held the vintage mic wrapped in fake flowers and warbled a tune that was bright and calm all at once, like a breeze on a summer afternoon.

It had been long enough. We deserved time like this.

Blue October closed out with a fiddle-heavy number that had the crowd jumping up and down like it was a rock concert instead of the sort of indie folk that was easy to fall asleep to. The sun began to dip behind the rock walls that lined the valley, painting the sky in shades of pink and orange, just as the set came to a close. Val threw her arms around Celeste and me as we shuffled out with the crowd, smiles on our faces.

"You know, the festival website said that one of the food vendors makes SynFlesh that's seasoned and cooked or fried like regular meat," Jasmine said. "Might be nice to send Patricia a picture of something a little different for once. We could grab dinner before the next show?"

Celeste tensed. "I'd love to, it's just…eating SynFlesh in public like this…"

"Ooh, right." Val rubbed the nape of her neck. "I forgot your viewers don't know you're…"

"Being trans gets me plenty of shit from random people on the internet," Celeste said in a low voice, scanning the crowd as if expecting to find someone watching her. "If I threw in *ghoul* on top of that, I'd probably hemorrhage viewers. Turns out moms don't want their daughters learning how to contour from a cannibal."

"Hey, come on, no c-word," Jasmine snapped, shooting her a look. "We'll go back to the cabin. I bet we can even heat up those SynLivers to be almost palatable."

"And then we can go to the No Flash Photography show," Val said with a grin. She hooked her arm around Celeste's. "You'll do my makeup for that, right? Maybe you could draw the little sunflowers on my cheeks like you did on your stream the other day."

The two of them continued discussing potential makeup options while we all started toward the cabin. The crowd was still thick, even as we left the festival grounds, and only began to thin when we were halfway down the road to the cabins. The smell of stranger's bodies dissipated, replaced with dust in the air, someone barbecuing, and—

I paused. For the briefest second, I'd caught a scent—one that I hadn't smelled in nearly two years. But it was acrid enough to make my nose wrinkle just like it had back then.

"Do you smell that?" I cut in while Celeste and Val debated whether or not a summer or spring palette was better for Val's skin tone.

The others exchanged glances. Jasmine said, "What do you mean?"

I inhaled again, catching it just faintly. It was nearby and seemed to be coming from the towering wall of rock that loomed behind the rows of cabins.

I turned and took off, leaving my friends to shout after me in confusion. The dirt crunched under my feet as I wove between two cabins, forehead wrinkled. That smell—there was no way. That part of the Hollowing was over. How could—?

I skidded to a halt, maybe thirty feet from the rock wall. It was a mix of red and tan sandstone, lichen clinging to the side of it where rains had left dark marks like mascara tracks down the side of the cliff face. There was a patch of cacti poking out of the parched earth, spines thin and menacing. I carefully knelt down in front of it.

There, among the spines, was a pearly white bone.

The others caught up to me just as I found a stick to move the bone with.

As I nudged it free from the cactus patch, Jasmine asked, "What the hell is that?"

"Dunno. Looks kind of like a radius." As the bone rolled to a halt, I held my own arm out for comparison. It was roughly the same length. "Look at the end of it."

Celeste knelt down beside me. Her head tilted to the side as she whispered, "That almost looks like…"

"Ghoul bile," I said. "And it's still wet. I could smell it from the road. Looks like it's been chewed on a bunch too."

"Must be an animal bone, then," Val said, hands on her hips. "Ghouls wouldn't be throwing up bile if it was human."

"Why the hell would a ghoul be trying to eat an animal out here?" Jasmine asked.

"Desperation?" Celeste offered.

While the others continued to debate, I let my eyes start to wander. I wasn't sure what I was looking for—more bones, maybe. Something to signify what exactly this was. But the desert was quiet, nothing but the faint sound of the festival carrying over on the wind. Until I spotted a narrow crack in the rock wall, just large enough for a person to fit through.

For a brief second, I thought I saw a pale, skeletal face staring me down from inside.

The next time I blinked, it was gone.

"Did you see that?" I asked.

The others glanced up. Celeste said, "See what?"

I bit the inside of my cheek. Maybe I'd imagined it. It didn't make sense for a feral ghoul to be lurking out here. SynFlesh was readily available—there was no reason for someone like us to be hiding out in the desert. No reason for them to be chewing on bones that made them sick.

I shook my head. "Nothing, sorry. I'm overthinking it. It's the desert—there are animal bones everywhere. Maybe it's just something else that smells kinda like ghoul bile."

"Exactly." Val nodded to the road. "Now, come on. If we don't finish dinner soon, we'll be late for Eli's show."

Val turned and took a few steps toward the road before pausing to let us catch up. Jasmine quickly followed, and Celeste was soon up as well.

I lingered for a moment, staring at the bone.

"Zoey?" Celeste asked.

"Sorry." I straightened up. "Coming."

six

While the prevailing attitude when the Hollowing first began was that Hollow people were incapable of rational thought or emotion, time has proven that this belief is false. Your Hollow child, if kept happy and fed, can live a life very similar to the one they led prior to the Hollowing. You can look forward to all the same milestones as before, from the first day of school all the way to graduation. With your support, anything is possible!

That said, it's important to remember that accidents happen, especially when children are too young to understand the consequences of their actions. While it may seem extreme at first, we recommend that parents, caregivers, and teachers of Hollow children always keep some form of compliance weapon on hand. Visit our website for exclusive deals on child-safe tasers, pepper spray, and stun batons—the humane way to wrangle your hungry little one.

—Excerpt from *Your Hollow Child and You: A Guide to Strange Appetites*

*A*fter a quick SynLiver dinner, we spent the evening at the No Flash Photography show. It was at a much smaller stage on the other side of the festival, and there were probably only a hundred or so people in attendance. Their music was a bit whiny for my taste, and it was clear they hadn't gotten used to playing on stage together. Eli dominated the stage with almost no interaction with the others, not even taking the time to introduce them. He had a good stage presence, at least, so it was entertaining if nothing else. We made it to the front row easily, and Eli spent most of the set winking at Val. In a way, it was sort of cute how into her he seemed to be.

Even if he was a total dick.

After the show, we had another hour to kill before the after-party, so we all headed back to the cabin to get ready. Celeste unloaded her sparkling tackle box full of makeup and set to work on Jasmine while Val thumbed through the music on her phone. She settled on her summer playlist, which was bright and pop-y and exactly what I needed after listening to Eli whimper into a microphone for an hour.

"Are you committing to fake lashes or no?" Celeste asked as she brushed sparkling shadow beneath Jasmine's eyebrows.

"If there's any chance I'm gonna run into someone famous, you damn well better believe I'm wearing lashes," Jasmine replied, her back perfectly straight while Celeste tilted her chin up.

"Is this too much?" Val asked, coming out of her room wearing cuffed and ripped loose jeans and a yellow crochet crop top. She gestured to the top specifically.

"Who gave you permission to be this sexy?" Jasmine said, cracking one eye open while Celeste prepped to glue lashes to her other eye.

Glancing over her shoulder, Celeste added, "I need you to stop being so beautiful because it's actually hurting my eyes."

"Angels weep knowing they'll never look that hot without a bra on," I agreed, resting my chin in my palm.

Val fluttered her eyelashes. "You're too kind. Now, whose hair am I doing first?"

"Dibs!" I said.

Val wound up braiding the front sections of my hair into a halo that joined at the back of my head. Once she and Celeste had attended to everyone, we each took a shot of vodka and headed out.

The party was taking place at a pavilion just outside of the festival grounds. The event planners had set up a fence around the space, which was decorated with twinkling lights strung above in crisscrossing rows. The four of us waited in line for a few minutes before Val offered her name at the front and the bouncer stepped aside to let us in.

The place was packed. People dressed in expensive but casual clothes pressed close together, chatting under the lights. There were a few food trucks, plus a pop-up beer garden and another bar where more impossibly beautiful people were gathered. A dance floor was lit up in rainbow lights near the far edge of the fence, while nearby outdoor couches were gathered around wicker tables. Waitstaff walked around with trays of food and drinks. Val flagged one down and stole four flutes of champagne, one for each of us.

"Cheers," she shouted over the music—something synth-heavy and fast. "To Desert Bloom."

"And to finally getting the hell out of Aspen Flats," Jasmine agreed.

We all cheered, clinking our glasses together before taking sips.

The taste of champagne nearly made me gag, but the bubbles left a pleasant effervescent feeling on my tongue. It almost made it bearable.

"Okay, game plan." Jasmine clapped her hands together. "Where are we going?"

"I want to look for Eli," Val said.

"I'm going to attempt networking," Celeste said.

Jasmine nodded and opened her mouth to say something, but before she could, I cut in, "I—I think I'll go with Celeste."

Jasmine sputtered a laugh. "Since when do you care about rubbing shoulders with influencers?"

I felt my face pinken. "I mean, it never hurts to have industry connections. If I want to be a journalist, it can't hurt to have friends in high places, right?"

Celeste bit back a laugh. "It's hard to imagine you... schmoozing."

"Well, good news. I'm about to schmooze the pants off these people."

Jasmine and Val both scoffed, locking eyes but not saying anything else.

"Meet back here in half an hour to debrief, then?" Celeste asked.

Val nodded and Jasmine said, "Works for me."

Suddenly, I felt something touch my hand, and much to my heart-pounding surprise, Celeste had woven her fingers into mine.

"Come on," she said. "Let's see who we can find."

The party continued to grow around us as Celeste introduced herself to other influencers who lit up upon recognizing her. I stood off to the side, scrolling through my phone while she exchanged gripes about algorithms and monetization with other girls who had the same polished aura as her. The difference, of course, was that while a lot of those girls looked nice in whatever they threw on, they'd never have the intentionality Celeste did. Her outward expression was like a block of marble that she took the time to carve tiny, purposeful details into every day. Each outfit and every delicate swoop of makeup served a purpose in the greater story she was trying to tell.

It was one of the things that had helped her online fame grow so fast, and one of the things that made my heart race when I thought about it too hard.

"Zoey—hey!"

I snapped out of my trance long enough to see Cole approaching. He had on black jeans and a T-shirt with the No Flash Photography logo: a broken camera with a flower growing out of it. He swept his messy red hair back and smiled.

"You made it," he continued as he came to a stop in front of me. Celeste and I had managed to get a seat on one of the wicker couches, where she was currently sitting in the middle while chatting with another influencer she knew from Los Angeles. If she noticed me scooting over to make room for Cole, she didn't say anything.

"Of course." I held up my champagne flute. "Never turn down an opportunity for free drinks, right?"

"Are you old enough to drink?" Cole asked, biting back a smile.

I felt my face turn red. Quickly I lied, "Of course I am. I'm—I'm a senior in college. I go to NYU."

Cole chuckled and lowered his voice. "Listen, it's okay—I'm

underage too. Industry parties never care how old you are. If you're on the list, you can pretty much do whatever you want."

"O-Oh." I chewed my lower lip. This was, admittedly, the first time I'd been to an event like this. Celeste had been to a few, and I'd heard about them from her, but all of a sudden, it occurred to me that there was an entire set of social rules to this sort of thing that I was totally unaware of. My stomach churned as I thought about whether or not that meant I'd already done something wrong and not even noticed. *Christ, I'm out of my depth.*

"That's, ah—good to know."

"That would be cool if you were going to NYU, though." He gazed distantly toward the dance floor, watching the swirling green, pink, and blue lights shine down on the gyrating bodies. "My sister wanted to go there."

I shifted in my seat, keeping my gaze on my hands. "Well— that's not technically wrong. I am going to NYU—I just haven't started yet. I'm majoring in journalism."

"That's cool," Cole said. "Why journalism? Do you like to write?"

I blinked. It wasn't a question anyone had really asked me before. When I told my friends that I wanted to go to school for journalism, they'd all just congratulated me on finding a path out of Aspen Flats. Which, to their credit, was better than my parents—all they'd done was agree to help me pay for part of my tuition, so long as it got me out of their house.

I cleared my throat, pushing that thought out of my mind. "Um—yeah. I'm interested in investigative journalism. Y'know, the in-depth pieces that go all the way to the top. I like getting different perspectives so I can figure out what's going on in people's heads and understand the full story as much as I can."

"Without having to share what's going on in your head?" Cole guessed.

I snorted. "I guess if you want to get psychoanalytic about it, sure."

Before Cole could say anything else, a voice from behind us cried, "Hey! Zoey, Celeste!"

We both turned to find Jasmine sprinting toward us, gasping for air.

Celeste cocked an eyebrow. "Everything okay?"

Jasmine wheezed. "Val"—she inhaled sharply—"needs our help."

My hackles immediately went up. "What happened?"

"Ran off." Jasmine pointed out toward the desert. "That way. She looked…" Jasmine glanced at Cole, then leaned in to just Celeste and I and mouthed, "Hungry."

I took in a sharp breath and cursed.

"Cole, um." I quickly offered him an apologetic smile. "Sorry, we have to go. But—I'll be in touch!"

I barely heard his response, though, because I'd already taken off running for the exit. A couple people turned to look as I sprinted by, furrowing their brows. The chunky high-top sneakers I had on didn't exactly make for the best running shoes, but that didn't stop me from getting to the gate in seconds flat.

Nearly as soon as I passed the bouncer, the breeze changed, and a familiar scent hit me.

Fresh blood.

Jasmine froze beside me. "You smell that?"

"Damn it, Val," I muttered. The smell was coming from the east, away from the festival grounds and deeper in the desert.

I took a step in that direction, but Celeste caught me by the arm.

I spun. "What are you doing? Val needs us—"

"That's not her blood," Celeste said. She glanced over her shoulder—the only person nearby was the bouncer, who was at least ten feet back and busy scrolling through his phone. "We'd be able to smell if it was a ghoul. That's human blood." Celeste shook her head. "What I'm saying is if we go now, it could…cause a frenzy."

"Then let's stop her," I shot back. "Hopefully before she eats something vital."

Celeste's mouth tightened into a line. "You're putting a lot of faith in your self-restraint."

"And you're not putting any in yours." I nodded to Jasmine. "Come on. We might be able to help."

Jasmine glanced between us, muttered a curse under her breath, and said, "Shit, fine."

The two of us hurried forward and, after a moment, Celeste swore and followed.

To a normal person, the scent of blood from this distance would have been undetectable. But ghouls were a little like sharks—we could pick out human blood from an impressive distance. So the scent was easy to follow, but the trouble was mentally willing my fangs and claws to stay in place with it perfuming the air.

"There," Jasmine said, pointing to the ground. There was a clear divot in the dirt, the tiny plants growing out of it snapped and hanging limply. "Something got dragged through here."

Celeste touched the trunk of the juniper tree beside it. Her fingers came away red.

Her nostrils flared as she inhaled the scent of it. A muscle in her neck twitched as her lips parted and her fingers slowly started to drift toward her mouth.

"Celeste," I snapped. "Don't."

Her eyes glinted in the moonlight. She quickly rubbed the blood back off on the tree, shaking her head. "Sorry. Sorry, I—"

"Over there!" Jasmine cried, pointing to a tall patch of brush. "Look."

We rushed to where she'd pointed, skirting the corner only to find a grisly scene.

There in the dirt with her back to us was Val. Her hair was still in the perfect beachy waves she'd sprayed into place before we left, and her back was straight. She sat cross-legged, like a child in a class circle, while her hands reached for something in front of her. My heartbeat immediately began to race, blood rushing in my ears.

It was a corpse.

His stomach torn open, pink entrails spilling out into the red dirt beside it. Blood pooled beneath him, inky black in the moonlight. His pale skin was waxy, lips tinged blue. His throat had been torn open, exposing the soft flesh of his esophagus.

I recognized him. It was one of the No Flash Photography boys—the one who had agreed with Eli that ghouls were monsters to be kept locked away from the rest of society. Not Cole, not Raj—*god what was his name?*

That's when I noticed the way one of his eyes stared dimly up at the stars. The other, however, was gone, leaving nothing but a ragged, torn socket.

"V-Val?" I managed to stammer.

She twitched slightly. There was a faint crack from her neck as she turned to look at me. Her body was curved at a strange angle, like her spine had gained the ability to bend just a bit too much. Her eyes were bloodshot and surrounded by black veins.

She licked her red-stained lips, looking like she'd eaten a Popsicle too messily without noticing.

Her bloody lips pulled into a grin, revealing two rows of jagged fangs. She opened up her mouth and her long tongue flicked out, wrapping around the sphere in her hand.

She bit down on the boy's torn eyeball, then swallowed it.

My stomach snarled.

I clapped a hand over it. "No, no, no—"

But the next moment, a low growl came from beside me. Suddenly Jasmine was on top of the boy, ripping off his bloody cheek with her claws and shoving the soft flesh into her mouth. Her shoulders tightened as she tore at his face again, making a horrible slurping noise as she lapped at the blood on her hand.

"Zoey," Celeste said through her teeth. "Damn it, we gotta get out of—"

Her voice faded out. The smell of blood seemed to permeate every inch of my consciousness. I could taste it in the air, rolling over my tongue until saliva nearly dripped from my lips. My fangs descended all at once, and my jaw grew pliable to accommodate them. My fingers twitched as claws pushed out over my nails, sharpening to wicked points.

A snarl escaped my throat and I threw myself at the body.

seven

I hadn't eaten in six straight days. Not since devouring Devin Han.

After a week in the northern California woods, Celeste and I had found a hunting cabin covered in moss and ivy. It was the first sign of civilization we'd seen in days, and we ran for the door as soon as we spotted it. It swung open easily, revealing a dust-covered living room filled with musty old furniture. The wood floors creaked under our feet as we shuffled inside. Instantly, I collapsed to the floor, moaning softly.

Celeste knelt down beside me, softly brushing my cheek with her clawed fingers. Her face had grown gaunt the last few days, her skin sallow and marred with dirt and scrapes. Nearly a week without her prescription also meant the peach fuzz on her upper lip had grown in. Not that it was easy to see under the old layers of caked-on blood.

My stomach had stopped growling days ago. Now, it just felt like a black hole, slowly consuming the other parts of me. I could feel each of my ribs when I wrapped my arms around myself. I'd never gone hungry before, but now it was the only thing I could think about.

Time had begun to flow in strange ways. Some moments I would close my eyes in the afternoon and open them again in the dead of night, and others seemed to be trapped in amber, struggling to move inch by inch. The next time I awoke after falling to the floor of the cabin, Celeste was asleep beside me.

And someone was trying to open the door.

I jolted up, lips pulling back from my fangs in a snarl. My heart slammed, and even from behind the door, I heard the sound of a heartbeat and smelled something sweet. Something…human.

My empty stomach growled. It ached like something was carving my organs out from the inside.

As soon as the door opened, I dove. The man on the other side cried out and tried to slam it on me, but I caught it and wedged my foot between us. My teeth snapped at the air while the man cursed, desperately trying to close the door. My clawed fingers wrapped around the edge of the wood, scraping so bits splintered off and fell to the ground.

Celeste keened, an inhuman, sharp sound, before she leapt forward and joined me. With both of us, we were strong enough to take him on. I could practically feel his sinew in my teeth, tearing apart like tissue paper—

There was a horrifying crack as something exploded, and Celeste fell beside me.

I screamed.

The man cocked the pistol he'd finally been able to get ahold of. "If there's anything human left in you, girlie, I'd back off before I shoot you too."

I glanced down at Celeste. She was whimpering, grasping at her shoulder. Blood began to bloom from the bullet hole, soaking the soft pink fabric of her shirt.

"Good girl," the man said, pointing his gun directly at me. "Now you *get back inside while I call for help. Don't you dare try anything or your friend is gonna bleed out here."*

I growled, low in my throat, but didn't move. Some tiny sliver of my mind understood what he was saying and the threat in it, but it was fighting with the screaming urge to dive on him and rip out his throat.

"That's right," he muttered. "Back up. I bet you want to get out of these woods, huh? Keep you and your friend alive?" Still holding the gun, he nodded to the bag on his back. "I've got a satellite phone in here. You just have to stay sane enough to let me use it."

Stay sane. Stay sane.

A piece of me screamed out to listen. Finally, this was our chance to survive. To get out of these woods and go home to our families. To not be starving to death moment by moment.

But god, I was hungry. I was so, so hungry.

"Good." The man lowered his gun. Very slowly, he began to shrug off his massive backpack. "Now, we're gonna get you some he—"

He didn't get the next word out, because the second he took his eyes off me, my teeth were in his neck.

I woke up with a gasp.

The first thing I noticed was how cold it was. The ground was rocky, dirt scraping under me as I reached a hand up to touch my face. As I tried to catch my breath, I realized something warm was wrapped around me from behind. I twisted my neck around to discover Celeste, face smeared with red, nuzzled against me with her arms around my middle as she slept.

Which might have been a nice surprise if it weren't for the fact that we were in a cave covered in blood in the middle of the desert with a gnawed-on corpse a few feet away.

"*Fuck*," I muttered.

Celeste made a sleepy sound and nestled her face into my hair. "Shh."

"Oh, sorry, I didn't mean to interrupt your beauty sleep," I hissed. "But you might want to open your eyes for a minute because we are *royally* boned right now, Fairbanks!"

She groaned and blinked, and immediately I felt her tense—first at the realization that we were spooning, and then the realization that we were spooning in a cave with the corpse of a guy we ate a few feet away.

"Oh, no," she breathed.

"Great, you're up," a voice came from the entrance to the cave. Jasmine stood with her hands on her wide hips while Val hovered beside her, sniffling and rubbing tears from her cheeks. "We were just discussing what the hell we're gonna do about *this*."

She gestured to the body on the ground. His clothes were torn ragged, and most of his flesh had been stripped away. Tooth marks left dents in his pearly white bones. Very little was left of him, aside from part of one of his legs and some of the skin over bonier bits that wouldn't have had enough flesh beneath to interest us.

I sucked in a hissing breath through my teeth.

"I'm so sorry," Val said, voice thick as she fought back tears. "God, I'm *so sorry* you got pulled into this. Kaiden didn't deserve—"

"*Kaiden*," I repeated under my breath. "That was his name."

Celeste shot me a sharp look. Through her teeth, she whispered, "Zoey, we just *ate him*. Have a little respect."

Meanwhile, Val let out a sob and sank to the ground, putting her face in her hands. Jasmine knelt beside her, rubbing her shoulders and hushing her. Tears dripped down Val's face, mixing with the blood and dirt still stuck to her cheeks.

"God, I-I'm such a monster. One minute I-I was drinking with Eli and Kaiden and Raj and the next I…I just lost control. I have no idea what came over me."

"But you ate at the cabin right before the party," Celeste said. "How could this happen?"

Val held her hands out, fingers splayed. "I don't *know*. It just… came over me. One second, I was fine, and then I felt like I was going to die if I didn't eat something. I tried to run, but Kaiden followed me and…"

She took a shaking breath before she sobbed again. Jasmine wrapped her arms around her, gently stroking her hair. Val leaned on her, pressing her face into Jasmine's shoulder while she cried.

"That doesn't make any sense," Celeste muttered. She turned to me. "Has that ever happened to you?"

I shook my head. "Never."

"So we know it was weird," Jasmine started, "but that's not exactly gonna get us out of, you know, *prison for murder*." She pointed to the corpse again. "If anyone finds this, we are supremely screwed."

"We didn't do it on purpose," I pointed out quietly.

Even as I said it, though, the words felt flimsy. As I stared at the corpse in front of us, I couldn't help but see the bodies of Devin Han and the hunter in the woods that I'd killed. Those men had been picked clean in the same way, and I remembered the taste of them just as vividly as I did the boy in front of me. Devin's blood on the ferns, the hunter's jaw slacked in a permanent scream—and now Kaiden's empty eye sockets, night-dark hollows that seemed to burn their dead gaze into my skin. I remember once seeing a piece of art that said the people you love become ghosts inside of you.

What I realized now was that it was true of the people you killed too.

Jasmine's voice came out soft, barely loud enough to overpower Val's weeping. "If people find out about this, it will ruin every single plan we have. Our lives will be over before they can even start."

"What are you suggesting?" Celeste asked.

Jasmine exhaled, tucking her braids behind her ears. Like the rest of us, she was bloodstained, though her black jumpsuit did a better job of hiding it. After a moment, she steeled her expression.

"We need to cover this up."

Val whimpered while I pressed my palms into my eyes so hard I saw red starbursts behind my eyelids.

The last two times I'd eaten someone, it had been during the Hollowing. When things had begun to settle down after the initial outbreak, most ghouls wound up in facilities or on house arrest for the safety of others. But when SynFlesh began being distributed and ghouls could access food without having to be delivered flesh harvested from cadavers, people started to wonder if it would be possible for ghouls to rejoin society—even the ones that had blood on their hands. Soon, a law was passed saying that ghouls wouldn't be charged for murders that took place during the Hollowing, using similar language as laws related to pleading insanity. Granted—it wasn't exactly the same, seeing as those who plead insanity didn't exactly walk free, but the reasoning was close: feral ghouls didn't have the capacity to understand that their actions were illegal.

Problem was, that didn't apply anymore now that SynFlesh was readily available. Murders by ghouls now were treated the same as murders by any other person.

Which meant that Val could be charged for Kaiden's murder, and the rest of us would be charged with desecrating a corpse at best, and accessories to murder *and* desecrating a corpse at worst.

Celeste exhaled and nodded, pulling her knees in closer to her chest.

My fingers twitched to reach out for her, to put my hand on her knee and rub slow circles into the skin with my thumb, but the oily ball of guilt in my stomach kept me paralyzed.

Celeste finally said, "Jasmine is right. There's no way my career could survive something like this. And you guys"—she looked between us—"would never be able to go to college with this on your record. We don't have any choice."

Val sniffled. "It's my fault, though. I should take the fall."

I pursed my lips, mind straying back to my last kill in the woods. In a way, it did have something in common with this one. So maybe…

"Not necessarily."

Everyone turned my way, eyebrows raised.

I held a hand out toward Val. "You said that you were suddenly overcome by the urge to kill, right? So it sounds like you went feral, which shouldn't have been possible if you just ate an hour before."

She sniffled, rubbing a tear away. "I—yeah. It felt just like back during the Hollowing when I hadn't eaten for…a week, almost."

I nodded. "Right. After the Hollowing, when I finally got out of the woods, I spent months straight doing nothing but research-ing ghouls. It's how my brain works—if I can teach myself enough about something that scares me, it won't be as scary anymore. So I know that there's no way you could have gone feral out of nowhere with no provocation. Something had to have triggered it. We just have to find out what it is."

Val wiped her cheeks. "You…you really don't think it was my fault?"

I shook my head. "I don't think this was any of our faults. Even if we did technically eat Tatum—"

"Kaiden," Celeste corrected, palming her cheek wearily.

"*Kaiden*," I amended, "I know that we're not the sort of people who would ever choose to do this to someone on purpose."

"That's not going to hold up in court," Jasmine muttered.

"Right. Which is why we might need to…buy ourselves some time." I stood up. "At least until we have proof that something happened to Val to make her go feral."

"What are we supposed to do with him in the meantime?" Jasmine asked, hooking a thumb toward the body. "We can't exactly *Weekend at Bernie's* a guy with barely any meat left on his bones, Zo."

"Definitely not." I pointed out at the red rocks, still shrouded in predawn darkness, and shrugged.

"But we can hide him somewhere no one's gonna look."

With the clock ticking until sunrise, Celeste and I split corpse-carrying duties while Jasmine, whose black clothes meant she could more easily clean off than the rest of us, took my car keys and headed back to the festival grounds to get the Mini. Not long after, we met her on the road, tossed Kaiden's body in the trunk, and started gunning it toward the first abandoned mine shaft I could find online. God bless the gold rush for leaving California absolutely littered with them.

The car ride was mostly silent, the only sound Val's faint sniffles in the back. Jasmine gently rubbed her back, whispering to her.

"We're going out of cell phone service," Celeste noted as we drove.

"Maybe for the best?" I offered. "Patricia doesn't need to track us to an abandoned mine."

"That's the problem," Celeste said. "She's going to get a ping saying we went out of tracking range. She's going to want an explanation."

"Oh, shit—*Patricia*," Jasmine groaned.

"Maybe we woke up early and wanted to watch the sunrise somewhere scenic?" I offered, gesturing to the clock, which was nearing 5:00 a.m. "People do that, right?"

"Um, yeah—old people and rich trust fund freaks who choose to live in camper vans full time," Jasmine muttered.

"I wake up at five all the time," Celeste pointed out, sounding a little offended.

"You text her then," I said. "She might actually believe you orchestrated this. If any of us do it, she'll send the cops after us before we can even dump the body."

In the back seat, Val whimpered loudly.

I winced. "Sorry, Val."

There was a long, awkward pause as Celeste pulled out her phone to send Patricia a message through HollowLife and Val squeezed her eyes shut, hanging her head so her hair fell in her face. I mentally cursed myself for bringing it up.

Finally, so quietly I almost missed it, Val whispered, "I've never killed a human before."

A beat of silence passed as Jasmine, Celeste, and I all exchanged glances. It wasn't often that we talked about the Hollowing in general, but Val had never once brought it up. She did her best to avoid it, changing the subject whenever anyone mentioned it.

"Not even during the Hollowing?" Celeste asked.

"There was…" Val bit her lip. She kept her eyes on the floor. "No. Not even then."

Jasmine squeezed her arm, but didn't say anything. Part of me was tempted to chime in, to say something supportive—but what was there to say? That ever since I killed that hunter in the woods it had felt like he was always watching me from inside of my own head? Like eating him had somehow made him a part of me that I could never get rid of, no matter how much melatonin I took at night or how many times therapists told me that it wasn't my fault what I was? That it always felt like part of me—part of my humanity—had died with him?

I bit into my cheek, staring hard at the road in front of me.

There was nothing to say.

We reached the mine shaft just before sunrise. There was a grate in front of it, but that was no struggle for us. With all four of us, we were able to pull it out of place easily. Eating SynFlesh meant that any of the heightened abilities that came along with being a ghoul—enhanced strength and senses, mostly—were no longer present. But after consuming a fourth of Kaiden's body, I didn't even break a sweat.

The four of us all peeked down. The rocky shaft went straight into the ground, a dark void that swallowed the lights from our phones. A faint dripping sound echoed up to us, but I didn't see a water source. There were some metal reinforcements on the sides of the shaft, but they were so rusty it was clear that no one had touched this place in a long time.

Celeste and I started scooting the body toward the edge when Val said, "W-Wait, hold on."

I nodded toward the sky, which was just barely beginning to lighten. "We don't have a lot of time here, Val."

"I-I know, it's just," she shuffled her feet, turning herself away to avoid looking at the body. "This is someone's son we're throwing down there. Shouldn't we, I dunno, say a few words?"

I flicked a strand of sweat-soaked hair out of my face. "You're serious?"

Celeste cleared her throat. "No, no—Val's right. I think it would be good if we at least did something quick. Y'know, for all our sakes."

"Not a lot of point in saying grace if you already ate the damn meal," Jasmine muttered.

Val chose to ignore her. "You know what? I'll go first." She took a deep breath and closed her eyes. "Kaiden, I'm so sorry things have to end like this. You were a senseless victim, and I'm sorry."

"Um—amen?" I offered.

"I'm sorry we couldn't help you while you were alive," Celeste said, looking down at the body. "But I promise we're going to try to figure out what happened so your death isn't wasted."

Val nodded. "That was really nice, Celeste."

I cleared my throat. "I'm sorry I didn't remember your name earlier—that was, um, messed up that it took me eating you learn that." I winced. "That was bad. Um—sorry, man. I'll make it up to you?"

"*A* for effort," Celeste whispered.

"This whole situation sucks, and I am ready to take a shower so, uh, sorry, Kaiden," Jasmine said. She exhaled. "I hope wherever you are now is better than this."

"Okay." Val set her shoulders, then clasped her hands as if in prayer. "Good. Thank you."

There was a pause as Celeste and I exchanged glances, unsure if that was our cue to toss him. Beside me, Jasmine whispered, "Just do it."

Celeste and I shrugged at each other, then each took our end of the body and swung it over the edge of the mine shaft.

There was a faint *splash* a few moments later.

I winced.

Jasmine straightened her braids and exhaled a breath. "All right. Let's get out of here."

The others nodded, slowly straightening up to head back to the car. I offered one last parting glance down the mine shaft and felt my stomach clench. Even if my only interaction with Kaiden before that had been him calling ghouls monsters who belonged in cages, that didn't mean he deserved what had happened to him. Val was right—he was a senseless victim. Just like Devin Han and the hunter in the woods.

One more person's blood on my hands.

I whispered one more apology to the air before I headed back to the Mini Cooper.

eight

When Celeste awoke outside the hunting cabin, she was covered in blood.

She still tasted the hunter's flesh on her tongue as it settled in her stomach. The worst part was just how good it felt, how for the first time in days she was more human than monster, her brain rewiring itself toward thoughts of escape instead of just the same gnawing desperation for sustenance that had haunted her nonstop.

She sat up with a start. The redwoods stood like judging sentinels around her, massive enough to block out most of the sunlight. Her breath whistled through her teeth as it all came back to her. Right—she was in the woods, miles from Camp Everwood. She had been for nearly a week.

Celeste wiped the back of her hand across her mouth, smearing it with blood. The smell of it was everywhere. But instead of metallic and sharp, it was sweet, almost like fruit juice. She held her palm to her nose and inhaled.

Immediately, her mouth began to water.

She wrenched her hand away. Focus, Celeste.

On shaky legs, like a newborn fawn, Celeste stood. The forest was silent around her. No birdsong, no creatures rustling in the brush—nothing. It was like they knew to be afraid of her.

"Zoey?" Celeste called, voice nearly cracking as she did. She cringed at the sound of it, gravely from days of not speaking. She cleared her throat. "Where are you?"

A faint groan came from behind her. Celeste whipped around to find Zoey, face hidden in her blood-and-dirt-smeared arms, curled up beside the corpse of the hunter. He'd been almost completely stripped of flesh—all that was left of him was the entrails, a bit of his face, and his feet inside his boots.

The back of Celeste's throat tightened. She blinked and two fat tears snaked down her cheeks, carving out tiny tracks through the blood on her skin.

"No," she whimpered, falling to her knees. Her shoulders began to shake as sobs overtook her. "No, no—please, not again—"

She reached out to try and wake Zoey, but a hot stab of pain in her shoulder made her wince. Clenching her teeth, she carefully reached up with her other arm and touched the spot that hurt. Her fingers came away with more blood. This, though, didn't smell like the hunter's blood.

He'd shot her.

Celeste rubbed her shoulder again. All things considered, though, it wasn't bleeding very much. Which struck her as off. But as Celeste flexed the muscle, it didn't hurt nearly as much as she expected it to. How was that possible?

As she rolled her shoulder in the socket, something suddenly fell out of it. For a moment, she thought maybe it was a button that had popped off her jacket.

But then she saw the bullet lying on the ground. And when she touched the wound again, it had stitched itself closed.

What the hell?

"Celeste?" Zoey moaned. She barely stirred.

"I'm here," Celeste said. She reached out, gently running her fingers over Zoey's arm. "It's okay."

"I don't know how long I can do this," Zoey whispered. "I just... wanna go home."

Tears pricked in Celeste's eyes all over again. Before the specter of starvation overtook her, she'd spent a lot of time thinking about her mother while she and Zoey wandered through the woods. Even before Celeste had transitioned, her mom had always said she was the Lorelei to Celeste's Rory, more of a friend than a parent when it came down to it. Aside from Zoey, she was the person Celeste always went to whenever she needed to get something off her chest. Now, though, Celeste wondered how her mother would ever look at her the same when she had the blood of not one, but two men on her hands.

If her mother even thought she was still alive.

Distantly, she remembered something the hunter had said before Zoey attacked him. I've got a satellite phone in here. You just have to stay sane enough to let me use it.

Celeste found the hunter's bag a few feet away from his body. While Zoey quietly began to cry, curling deeper and deeper into herself, Celeste dug through his things. She found clothes, water, food—for a second, she wondered if he'd lied about having a phone.

But then she found it. It was clunky and black—it looked more like a walkie-talkie than any phone Celeste had ever seen. With shaking fingers, she slowly typed in her mother's cell phone number and held the phone up to her ear.

After a few rings, Wendy said, "Hello?"

"M-Mom?"

Immediately, a sob ripped free of Celeste's throat.

"Celeste?" Wendy said her name like it was something precious, like saying it too loud could shatter it into a million pieces. "Baby, is that you?"

"Mom, I'm so sorry." Celeste choked on a sob. "I didn't mean to hurt anyone, I swear."

Before she could stop herself, Celeste was confessing everything that had happened. Killing and eating Devin, wandering in the woods for days on end, being shot and eating the hunter. She cried the whole time, her throat going raw as the words tumbled out. She covered her face with her free hand, struggling to catch her breath between sobs.

"Where are you now?" Wendy asked.

"A hunting cabin." Celeste sniffled. "We're okay, I swear. We can just stay here until we get better—"

"No, Celeste. I'm going to send someone to come get you." Celeste heard a chair creak on the other end of the call as Wendy stood up. "You're coming home, okay?"

"No!" Celeste shook her head, tightening her fingers around the phone. Her chest rattled as she sucked in a shaking breath. "I-I can't— Mom, I killed someone. I can't come home."

"The hell you can't. You're my daughter, and I'll be damned if I let you starve to death in the middle of the woods."

"Mom, please—"

Wendy cut her off. "You do whatever you need to do to survive, baby. I'm coming to get you."

The line went dead.

Not long after that, Celeste learned that Wendy wasn't kidding. Forty-eight hours after Celeste called her, a search party found them still huddled in the hunting cabin. Their clothes were torn and stained, blood dried to rust-brown smears across their faces and hands. Night *had fallen when the search party burst in through the doors, flashlights swinging wildly as they landed on the girls.*

"Muzzles," one said to another. "Now."

Three men descended on them. Celeste didn't fight back as they secured a cagelike muzzle over her mouth—she was too tired, too weak, too desperate to get out. Zoey, however, snapped at them, cursing when they braced her arms against the wall to hold her back. She stopped, though, when they started to explain they were there to bring them home.

The trip out of the woods was mostly a blur. It was a short hike to where they'd managed to land a helicopter. Distantly, Celeste wondered how much this would wind up costing her mother. If things were even close to as bad in the rest of the world as it had been at Camp Everwood, she had to imagine that it hadn't been easy to find rescuers.

She fell asleep in the helicopter not long after takeoff. It turned out that days upon days of just trying to survive meant that the lingering fatigue in her bones was too much to fight the second she felt safe again. She managed to stay asleep the entire time, barely waking up when they landed and loaded her onto a stretcher to bring into the hospital.

When she really, truly woke up, she was in a hospital bed, and sunlight was streaming in through the window.

She winced, holding up a hand to block out the light. Her entire body ached, like every bone and inch of skin was bruised. She had an IV attached to one arm, and she was uncomfortably aware of the cannula sticking into her. Her throat felt scratchy and dry, and there was something heavy on her face.

Absentmindedly, she touched it and discovered the muzzle was still on.

"Celeste?" a familiar voice asked softly. "You awake, baby?"

Celeste turned her head toward it. "Mom?"

Wendy Fairbanks shot up from her chair and flew across the room to throw her arms around her daughter. Immediately, she began to sob, holding Celeste so tightly it made her already sore body tense in protest. Celeste's eyes welled with tears as she held her mother, and she hiccuped a sob.

"I was so worried about you," Wendy bawled. She smoothed down Celeste's blond hair, tucking it behind her ear. "When your camp counselor called me to let me know you were sick I started panicking and then phone lines started going out, and I didn't hear anything for days and then when they did call, you'd gone missing—"

A knock on the door cut her off before she could finish. It swung open and a nurse stepped inside, carrying a small plastic-wrapped piece of… something *in her hand.*

At the sight of Celeste, she said, "Oh! You're awake."

Celeste and her mother exchanged a look. The nurse pulled out a sliding table on the side of Celeste's hospital bed before placing the plastic-wrapped something—meat?—on top. She took a hopping step back, forcing a smile to cover up an emotion Celeste couldn't place at first. She squinted.

Ah. There it was.

Fear.

"We were able to get a shipment of"—the nurse swallowed—"suitable food."

Celeste blinked. She reached over to the table and picked up the meat. It didn't look much different from beef, the flesh marbled with fat like a normal steak. Cautiously, she held it up to her nose and inhaled.

Immediately, her mouth began to water at the sweet scent.

"Is this…human? How—?"

"A lot has changed since you left," Wendy said gently. "You and Zoey aren't the only ones who got sick."

The nurse nodded to herself and stepped toward the door, saying, "I'm going to grab a doctor. He can talk you through everything. Oh and—just hit the call button if you need someone to remove the muzzle so you can eat."

The nurse quickly slid out the door, all but shaking in terror.

Celeste swallowed thickly. She chose not to linger on that for too long. Instead, she asked Wendy. "Where is Zoey? I–Is she all right? Is—?"

"Shh, it's okay." Wendy took Celeste's hand, using her free one to brush Celeste's hair back again. "Zoey's just fine. After they got her patched up here, she was transferred to a...facility for other young people with the same affliction. One close to Aspen Flats."

"Am I going there too?"

Wendy shook her head. "No, I couldn't—you're coming home with me. We'll have to make some adjustments but...we'll be okay. I can handle it."

Celeste cautiously touched the muzzle again. Tears welled as the back of her throat tightened. "Mom, I don't want to hurt you."

"And you won't." Wendy squeezed her hand. "You'll be just fine so long as we make sure to keep food for you in the house, and I already signed up for the weekly meat distribution for Hollow people that the local hospital is putting together—"

Celeste cut in, "Hollow? What does that mean?"

Wendy went quiet. Her eyes welled again, and she tore her gaze away, looking at the floor. After a long pause, she said, "The doctor can explain it better than I can."

Celeste's stomach dropped. Never once, not in her entire life, had her mom ever winced away from something she found uncomfortable. She

*was the sort of person who always tried to sympathize, to talk it through
until she could wrap her mind around it. She'd always owned her igno-
rance, thinking of it as the first stepping-stone to understanding.*

But now, she was quiet.

And the silence was the loudest thing Celeste had ever heard.

After we got back from dumping Kaiden's body, we decided our
best bet was to return to the scene of the crime.

With the sun slowly climbing in the sky, lighting up the red
and tan rock walls that surrounded the valley, the four of us set out
for the pavilion that had hosted last night's event. Our goal was
simple: see if we could find evidence of *something* that could have
caused Val to go feral, whatever that may be.

The festival grounds were mostly quiet—it seemed most people
were sleeping in, which made sense since the first shows wouldn't
start until after noon. We passed a couple of people jogging or filming themselves walking around in designer outfits, but overall, the
place was practically abandoned compared to yesterday. It felt eerie.

It was also jarring because—thanks to eating human meat—
suddenly I could hear every whispered conversation we passed.
Within five minutes I heard about someone's agent dropping them,
another person whose recent YouTube video had been demone-
tized, and a girl who thought her partner was cheating on her.

There was one conversation, though, that gave me pause.

It was a younger guy, in his early twenties, who was in the
middle of a phone call as he walked by us. He had on a tie-dye
shirt that indicated he was a member of the festival staff.

In a hushed voice, he told the person on the other line, "Yeah, Sophia didn't show up for her shift this morning, and Bennie is freaking out because he thought he saw some shit outside his tent last night. I swear to god, those mushrooms you brought had to have been laced with something."

I paused, glancing over my shoulder at him.

"No, like, an animal or…something," he added. "I don't know, ask him yourself! I'm not the one hallucinating monsters outside my tent."

He got too far for me to hear a few moments later.

"Zoey?" Celeste asked, pausing beside me.

I blinked, pulling away like I might take a step to follow him. "Did you hear that?"

"Yeah, sounds like those guys had a bad trip. Not a particularly notable experience at a music festival." Jasmine, who was a solid five paces ahead with Val at her side, held her hands out and gestured for us to follow. "Come on! Time's wastin', ladies."

Celeste and I exchanged a look but didn't say anything. I squared my shoulders and jogged to catch up.

It wasn't long before the pavilion came into view. It was infinitely less charming in the daytime. The lights that had cast a soft ambiance on the place last night were out, taking away a lot of the effect of the outdoor furniture and the bar, both of which looked dingy. Loose cups still littered surfaces, and the trash cans overflowed.

"Oh good," I said. "They haven't cleaned up yet. We might still be able to find something."

The entryway that the bouncer had been in front of last night was now blocked by a locked gate. The four of us exchanged glances, eyeing the thin padlock as we approached.

"Either we break it, or we climb the fence," I muttered.

"It's broad daylight," Jasmine pointed out. "We can't hop the fence."

"Breaking the lock is also going to draw attention," Celeste pointed out. "We'd need some of those heavy-duty pliers or—"

Jasmine held up a hand to stop her. "Hold on, I have an idea. Keep an eye out for a second, will you?"

"What do you want us to do if someone comes?" Val asked.

"Distract them, obviously." Jasmine gestured to Val's light blue sundress, which hung just above her knees. "Val, you've got natural charisma going for you. Just strike up a conversation or something."

"What about us?" I asked, gesturing to Celeste and me.

Jasmine nodded. "Good point. Celeste, you can help too."

"You are such a c—"

But Jasmine just turned and headed toward the gate, not staying to hear me cuss her out.

Val said, "Here—let's pretend to take a selfie. We can keep an eye on Jaz behind us and still see anyone walking by in front."

"Smart," I said.

Celeste and I squeezed in with her, smiling as she held her phone out. Celeste leaned against me, practically pressing her cheek against mine while she smiled. My reflection in the phone screen turned wide-eyed and pink as she put her arms around Val and I on either side of her. Every hair on the back of my neck stood to attention, and the places where our skin touched made the nerves beneath feel like sparking exposed wires.

A jogger passing by glanced at us briefly but didn't look long enough to care that Jasmine had the padlock in her hand. Out of the corner of my eye, I watched her grit her teeth and squeeze the latch.

The metal snapped against her hand.

She pulled it off the gate and stashed it in her pocket. With a sharp nod of her head, she gestured for us to follow, eyebrows raised and forehead wrinkled.

I went to move, but Val said, "Wait, this actually is kind of a cute picture."

"Let's try not to create even more evidence for a future trial," I said, ducking out from under her arm and heading toward Jasmine. As subtly as I could, I rubbed the place where Celeste had been touching me, trying and failing to hide my blush.

Jasmine slid the gate open and held it, quickly ushering us all inside while she kept an eye out over our shoulders. She quickly shut it behind us, exhaling a breath.

"Let's try to be fast," I said. "We don't know when the cleanup crew is gonna show up."

Celeste nodded. "Right. Val, what did you do when you first got here?"

"Came in through here," she said, pointing to the gate. She palmed her cheek. "Then went to that couch over there."

We followed her to it. The outdoor couch's pillows were on the ground, and the wicker arms were covered in empty cups. Some used napkins littered the table, plus crumbs and a stubbed out joint.

I picked it up. "Did you smoke this?"

Val shook her head. "No. Eli, Kaiden, and Raj split it. I don't like getting crossfaded."

"So not the weed," Celeste clarified. Her eyes wandered to the napkins and crumbs on the table. "Val, did you eat anything?"

She shook her head. "No. There were no SynFlesh options, and even if there had been, I didn't want to risk eating in front of the boys."

"So that means whatever caused you to go feral must have been something in the air..." My gaze wandered to the arm of the couch, with the crowd of cups still teetering on the edge. "Or something you drank."

Val chewed her lower lip. Softly, she picked up one of the cups with a lipstick stain on it—the same shade of dusty pink she'd been wearing last night. "Right before it happened, I was drinking something called a Groupie. Eli thought it was funny and got it for me."

I chose to ignore the way that statement made my skin crawl. "What was in it?"

"Um—tequila? Something pink?" Val's nose wrinkled as she struggled to remember. "It was on a drink menu taped to the bar."

"Let's check that out," I said. "Maybe there's some weird ingredient that could have interacted with your system poorly."

"Like what?" Val asked.

Celeste shrugged. "I can't drink grapefruit juice or it cancels out the medication I take for anxiety. Could be something like that where it's just a totally random ingredient that has an impact on specific enzymes."

"Like an appetite stimulant just for ghouls?" I guessed.

Jasmine nodded. "It's possible. Ghouls have only been around for two years—maybe there's some kind of substance we don't know about yet that could do that."

"Let's go check out the bar," I said. "Come on."

I straightened up from the table and started toward the bar. It was L-shaped, with a dark countertop and a vague cowboy theme as hinted at by the cow-print barstools and the lasso on the back wall. Menus on faux-aged paper were laminated and taped to the bar top, decorated with little images of horseshoes and written in a bold font.

I pointed to the description of a Groupie. "Okay. So that's tequila, prickly pear syrup, triple sec, lime juice, and a sparkling lava salt rim. So basically, just a fancy margarita."

Jasmine started to mutter, "The hell is sparkling lava salt?"

Before I could respond, though, a faint burble of voices made me freeze.

"Damn it, someone's coming," Celeste whispered, blue eyes locked onto something over my shoulder. "Hide!"

Jasmine immediately launched herself over the bar and slid across the top of it, landing in a crouch on the other side. Celeste, Val, and I followed, barely avoiding landing on top of each other. I hit my knee on something on the way down and had to slap my hand over my mouth to stop myself from yelping. Pain surged up my leg and I bit into my lip.

"You heard about what happened to the guys who were supposed to clean this up last night, right?" the man coming around the corner said. He was dressed in a boiler suit and had his hands on his hips—he must have been a custodian. "Skipped out before the end of the night. Didn't even have the decency to tell anyone they were leaving or where they went."

Two other men came in behind him, muttering their agreement that the missing staff were bastards, before they spread out to start collecting dirty dishes. I let my eyes wander to the gate where they'd come in—it had been left ajar at the back of the pavilion. A truck with a cleaning service logo was parked on a concrete slab beyond it.

I tapped Celeste's shoulder and nodded toward it. "Come on. We can sneak out that way."

She started to nod at the same time Val grabbed something from one of the shelves behind the bar. It was a tiny mason jar full of silvery powder. A handmade masking tape label read FOR GROUPIES.

She ran her finger across the edge of it, picking up a streak of silver. Carefully, she lifted it to her nose and smelled it, brows furrowed.

Immediately, Val's face went blank. The jar fell from her hand, clattering on the ground and rolling under the bar. The veins around her eyes suddenly began to protrude, stained pitch black beneath her tan skin. She pressed a hand over her mouth as her fingernails began to extend into wicked claws.

Oh no.

I hauled Val up by her elbow. Her shoulders were tensed, sharpening teeth gnashing as she fought against whatever the powder had done to her. Celeste and Jasmine popped up behind us and started sprinting toward the exit.

I dragged Val behind me, not even looking over my shoulder. It didn't matter if those men saw us so long as we got out in time not to claim any more victims. We could run faster than them, we could get out—

"The hell?" one of the custodians said, maybe ten feet behind us.

At the sound of his voice, Val's head whipped around, hair flying with her. She yanked at my grip, jagged teeth bared. Her eyes bugged out, a low rumble building in the back of her throat while she thrashed. Her arm began to slip through my hands.

My heart stopped.

Just then, Celeste caught up to us. The second Val was free, Celeste wrapped a hand around her wrist, holding it in a vise grip. I snagged her other arm and, with the two of us both pulling her, she stumbled back.

It was enough to snap her attention away from the men. Jasmine shouted for us to hurry up as we darted the final few feet through the gate, hearts pounding.

We kept going until we were well out of the way of the pavilion, the men's voices dissipating behind us. Gasping for breath, we ducked behind a thick rabbitbrush bush.

Me, Celeste, and Val fell to the ground on our knees while Jasmine craned her neck to see over the bush, making sure we weren't followed. Meanwhile, Val squeezed her eyes shut, hissing breath escaping between her sharpened teeth. Her chin tucked against her chest and her shoulders shook.

"It's—" she whimpered, "it's happening again—"

Celeste said to Jasmine, "Unzip my backpack—I brought extra SynFlesh just in case."

Jasmine nodded and unzipped the heart-shaped backpack hanging off Celeste's shoulders. She withdrew the wrapped SynFlesh steak and quickly tore the plastic off with her teeth.

Val snatched it out of her hands before she had a chance to even unwrap it fully. The three of us politely looked the other way as she unhinged her elastic jaw and swallowed it whole.

We were all silent for a brief second before Jasmine asked, "What the *hell* was that?"

"You okay?" Celeste asked, loosening her grip on Val's wrist.

Tears shone in Val's eyes, but she nodded. The dark veins slowly started to fade, and her fangs retracted into the normal shape and size of her teeth. Sniffling, she said, "That was exactly what happened last night."

"Guess we found what made you go feral then," I muttered.

Val nodded to herself. "They added that to the lava salt rim on my drink last night. Must be...edible glitter? It tasted like...mint, almost."

"Mint?" I repeated.

Jasmine's eyebrows shot up. "I'd say we should go back and try to take it, but clearly that's a bad idea."

"I've never heard of mint doing something like that to ghouls," Celeste said, tapping a shiny acrylic nail against her chin. "But considering the ingredients list, something minty seems like a weird thing to add to that drink."

"So the question is whether or not the drink was just a normal cocktail with weird ghoul-specific side effects," I said, "Or if someone was purposely trying to create some kind of frenzy by giving it out at an event that at least a few ghouls might be attending."

Everyone went quiet for a moment, letting the statement sink in. If someone was targeting ghouls, that made us the victim. If it was a mistake, it only proved what all the anti-Hollow people said: We were monsters who could snap at any moment.

"Woof," Jasmine muttered.

At that moment, Val's phone buzzed. She reached into her pocket and pulled it out, fingers tightening around the succulent-patterned case. She winced as soon as she saw the screen.

"Oh, no," she said. "It's Eli. He's asking if I've seen Kaiden."

Jasmine clapped her hands together. "Well. It's been nice knowing you, ladies, but we are, unfortunately, screwed."

"We don't know that yet," I snapped. "Val, tell Eli that you felt sick and went home early. That'll throw him off for a bit. Then we can go back to the cabin and research to figure out if anyone knows about this weird mint substance."

"What if those custodians call security about us?" Jasmine asked, crossing her arms.

"We'll cross that bridge if we come to it," I said. "For now, let's focus on what we have."

"I don't think we have much time to find answers," Val whispered.

I set my jaw and squared my shoulders.

"Then I guess we better get started."

nine

*F*or five days, Jasmine watched her grandmother's condition deteriorate.

It had been easy to hide at first. With Ruth mostly sleeping in her room, Isaiah didn't have to see the way that the hollows under her eyes had begun to deepen as the hours without eating stretched into days. But then, four days in, Isaiah had watched in horror as Ruth hunched over the kitchen sink, throwing up the saltines Jasmine had forced her to swallow. The bile had a distinctive black, sludgy quality to it as it splattered into the sink basin. Jasmine had stood nearby, rubbing her grandmother's back. Isaiah was only twelve, and Jasmine wasn't about to let on that he could be in danger.

"Nana just had too many cocktails last night," she'd promised him, patting his shoulder. "No big deal."

But that night, Jasmine waited until Isaiah was asleep, then used all of her strength to drag a couch from the living room to in front of her grandmother's bedroom door. She'd woken up the next morning to the sound of inhuman shrieking and banging. Isaiah had shuffled out of his room bleary-eyed, rubbing his forehead and asking what was wrong with Nana.

Jasmine had rushed him out the door, with barely enough time to get his shoes on. They grabbed the essentials before making a run for it.

What they found was a downtown Los Angeles eerily devoid of life. The mayor had issued a shelter-in-place order a few nights before, and it was clear that residents were taking it seriously.

Jasmine didn't know exactly where she was taking Isaiah. All she knew was that they needed somewhere to sleep for the night. They tried a few hotels, but they were all guarded by men wearing camo—Jasmine wasn't sure if they were National Guard or just random guys the hotels had hired—with guns slung over their shoulders who told them to go elsewhere. When Jasmine pointed out they weren't supposed to be outside at all and needed a place to shelter, the men informed her that was her problem, not theirs. Each time Jasmine saw a cop, she pulled Isaiah along, jogging out of view before they could be spotted.

She had to get them somewhere safe before night fell. Otherwise, they'd be face-to-face with all the gunfire she'd heard night after night from Ruth's high-rise.

Just as the streetlights were starting to flicker on, the siblings came upon a building under construction. There was a tall fence around the perimeter, and it looked like all the doors and windows had been installed.

It would have to work.

"Come on," Jasmine said, wrapping her hand around the chain link. "We can sleep here tonight."

Isaiah's big brown eyes rounded. He still had a baby face, despite having shot up to be almost as tall as Jasmine over the course of the summer. "But—is it safe?"

"There's a big fence and doors that'll probably lock, so safer than being out here with the cops and the ghouls." Jasmine gestured for him to follow. "Come on. I'll help you over."

The two of them climbed the fence, Isaiah's arms shaking as he pulled himself up. Jasmine landed on the other side and helped him down after her. He paused at the bottom of the fence, and Jasmine gently squeezed his shoulder.

"We're gonna be fine," she told him. "Promise."

He nodded softly and followed her.

They were able to get in easily enough—all Jasmine had to do was break a window, and she was able to unlock it and slide it open for them to climb through. Most of what was inside was tarps and painting supplies, along with some abandoned bottles of water and energy drinks.

Jasmine fashioned the tarps into makeshift beds for both of them in one of the rooms at the side of the building. It wasn't exactly cozy, considering the place had concrete floors and no electricity, but it would work.

While Isaiah curled up under a tarp, Jasmine stood and said, "I'm going to look around for a flashlight. I'll be back."

He didn't respond, which wasn't a huge surprise. Isaiah hadn't said much since they fled their grandmother's apartment. A couple of times, Jasmine had caught him dabbing at tears that he quickly hid from view.

Poor kid, *she thought, stepping out of the room and closing the door behind her. She lit her phone flashlight, grateful she at least had that for the time being.* I gotta get him home before…

She winced. The hollow feeling in her stomach ached, and she put a hand over it as it growled.

Jasmine pressed her lips together, squeezing her eyes shut. She wasn't sure how much longer she could stand to be around her brother, with his rabbit-quick heartbeat that made the back of her throat burn and her stomach twist with hunger. It had been days since she'd eaten anything, and all she could think about was how easy it would be to sink her teeth into her brother's throat.

She shook her head. Pull it together. He needs you.

She held her flashlight aloft. The shadows of paint cans and stepping stools cast spindly shapes on the walls that flickered as she moved from room to room. Outside, the wind had begun to pick up, and the bones of the building groaned as it whistled by. As she walked through them, her footsteps echoed. Her heartbeat quickened, and a cold sweat broke out on the nape of her neck.

Near the back of the building, she found a duffel bag propped up against the wall. Immediately, she dove to her knees, ripping the zipper open. She pulled out a couple sets of clothing, some tampons that she pocketed for herself, a couple snack bars for Isaiah, a small first aid kit, and—

A massive flashlight. Perfect.

Jasmine stuffed her phone in her back pocket and clicked the bigger flashlight on. Its beam illuminated the room in front of her, wide and open like the rest of them.

This one, though, had one big difference.

The tarps were all bunched up and laid the same way that Jasmine had done for Isaiah in the other room. A couple more bags were lined up against the wall, and a camping lantern sat in the center of the room. One of them had an American flag patch, while another had a thick cross topped with an eagle head stitched onto it, and another yet was a yellow DON'T TREAD ON ME *patch. The hair on the back of Jasmine's neck stood on end. Her stomach twisted.*

They weren't the only ones who had decided to stay here.

Just then, a familiar scream rang out through the building.

"Isaiah!" Jasmine cried.

She dropped the duffel bag and made a run for the room where she'd left her brother. She accidentally kicked over a paint can as she ran, creating a clattering bang. The flashlight beam swung wildly as she rounded the corner and held it up to illuminate the room.

Standing with a gun aimed at her little brother was a white couple, a man and a woman, wearing camo and black clothing. The man who had the gun trained on Isaiah was bald, with a number of thick, black tattoos up one arm. One of them, unmistakable, was a swastika. They both reeked of cigarette smoke and liquor, and the woman seemed to sway a bit as she stood there.

"The fuck are you doing here?" she demanded, spinning to Jasmine. She staggered in place—definitely wasted. "This is our goddamn place. You're trespassing."

Jasmine held her hands up slowly. "Please. We—we're just kids. We didn't realize you were already—"

"They're probably ghouls," the man said, his finger twitching toward the trigger. Jasmine could hear his heartbeat, smell the sweet aroma of the blood rushing through his veins. "Thought you could ambush us, didn't you?"

"We're not!" Isaiah cried. Tears dribbled down his cheeks. "P-Please, we'll go—"

"Shoot 'em, babe," the woman said, her smile toothy and sideways. Jasmine probably would have been horrified if it weren't for the fact that the corners of her vision were starting to close in and something sharp had begun to unsheathe from her gums. "If they're ghouls, good riddance. And if they really are just kids—we can use them as bait when we go ghoul hunting."

The man trained his gun on Isaiah and chuckled. "Good call."

He never got a chance to pull the trigger, though. Because the next moment, Jasmine got ahold of his arm in her clawed hand and, in one fluid motion, snapped the bone like a twig.

The man and woman screamed at the same time. The gun fell out of the man's hand and hit the floor.

Jasmine kicked it in her brother's direction and shouted, "Isaiah, grab it!"

Isaiah scrambled to get the gun while Jasmine pushed the man so hard against the wall his skull cracked. Her lips pulled back from her teeth to reveal two rows of sharp fangs which, moments later, sunk into the man's throat. He screamed, only to cut off sharply as Jasmine tore his windpipe in a spray of crimson and thready sinew. The taste of it exploded in her mouth, sweet and warm like Fireball without the bite.

She swallowed the chunk whole.

"Jaz!" Isaiah cried. "Help!"

Jasmine's head swung around, blood dripping from her chin. The woman was on the ground now, grabbing for the gun while Isaiah struggled to hold on to it. Her broken acrylic nails barely missed sinking into his skin.

Jasmine threw herself at the woman. They rolled, the woman shrieking, while Jasmine got her hands around her throat. She sunk her claws deep into the woman's neck, tearing to sever the carotid artery. Red sprayed Jasmine and the wall behind her. Bloody froth bubbled from the woman's lips as she choked on her last breath.

She slumped down, dead.

The smell of blood quickly overwhelmed Jasmine's senses. Her stomach snarled and saliva filled her mouth. The still-warm scent of the woman's skin was enough to drain Jasmine of all but the tiniest bit of humanity.

"Go hide, Isaiah," Jasmine whispered through her sharpened teeth. "Take the gun and don't come out until I tell you."

Isaiah's eyes sparkled. "Jaz—"

"Run!" Jasmine shouted. "Now!"

Isaiah scrambled to his feet, hitting the ground running. It was all Jasmine could do to wait until he couldn't see her anymore before she gave in to the hunger.

She tore the woman apart.

Back at the cabin, everyone curled up on the couch and took out our phones. Apparently, Celeste's excuse to Patricia about going to see the sunrise had been a good enough lie—or Patricia simply didn't care enough to report it—because we didn't get any messages asking what we'd been up to that morning.

The heat outside began to leak in through the windows, and soon we all had our hair up and any extra layers of clothing taken off. Beside me, Celeste had on a casual white dress, the slim straps showing the star-shaped bullet scar near her collarbone.

For a flashing second, the hunter's face appeared at the forefront of my brain, stained with blood after I'd ripped out his jugular.

I averted my eyes, wincing.

Celeste glanced up. "You okay, Zoey?"

My heart shuddered. I hadn't realized I'd been staring at her. I buried my nose in my phone. "Sorry. Just zoning out."

On the other side of the room, Jasmine raised an eyebrow at me.

"Wait," Val said, straightening up in the velour armchair she'd curled up in. "Look at this."

Our phones all buzzed a moment later with a text from Val containing a link. I opened it, immediately confronted with an image of a man in a lab coat shaking hands with another man in a business suit. It was a news article from two years ago. The title read: BLACKWELL PHARMACEUTICALS CLOSES IN ON APPETITE SUPPRESSANT FOR THE HOLLOW.

"'Director Sterling Blackwell announced Monday that scientists were nearing the end of a study to find an effective appetite suppressant for those impacted by the Hollowing,'" Val read aloud. "'Utilizing the properties of a genetically engineered variety of spearmint, Blackwell researchers expect to put the product, Menthexus, on the market as soon as human testing is complete.'"

"I never heard of any sort of appetite suppressant for ghouls," I whispered under my breath. "Much less one called Menthexus."

Val nodded. My phone buzzed with another link and she added, "Probably because of this."

Another article popped up, this one bearing the image of a fiery plume of smoke rising from a building in the desert. The title read: BLACKWELL PHARMACEUTICALS RESEARCH SITE CATCHES FIRE DAYS AFTER WHISTLEBLOWER LEAKS INFORMATION ON FAILED HUMAN TRIALS.

"That explains it," I muttered.

"This facility was only ten miles away from here," Celeste said, her brows furrowed as she leaned in closer to her phone screen. "Looks like it's been abandoned since the fire."

"Sounds like they needed to cover something up," Jasmine said, eyebrows raised and arms crossed. "Something like a drug that stimulates ghouls' appetites instead of suppressing them."

"I agree. That's way too much of a coincidence." I copied the name of the facility into the maps app on my phone and had it plot a course. Celeste was right—it was only a few minutes away by car. Granted, it was a dirt road, which might add to the travel time, but I had faith in the Mini.

I looked up from my phone. "I think we should go check it out."

Celeste sputtered a choking sound. "By going to the old research site? Zoey, that's a terrible idea. We have no idea if it's even structurally sound enough to be explored, and even if it is, what would there even be to find? Any useful information is probably burned to a crisp."

I shrugged. "Do we have any other leads?"

"We could try to find who was bartending last night," Val suggested. "They might know where this weird powder came from."

"Why not both?" Jasmine suggested. "We can split up—two of us can head to the research site and two of us can try to dig up some information about whoever worked the party last night."

Val said, "Dibs on finding the bartender—exploring some burned-out research facility sounds terrifying."

"Ditto," Jasmine agreed. "That place is definitely gonna be haunted."

"I can go alone," I asserted, crossing my arms.

Celeste sighed. "No, you can't. I may not think it's a good idea, but I'm not going to let you go to some creepy old building by yourself."

I cocked an eyebrow. "Seriously?"

Celeste nodded. "Friends don't let friends get possessed by the ghosts of unethical human testing victims."

I tried and failed to withhold a smile. I knocked my foot against hers. "Fine, you win."

"One thing first," Val said. She yawned, stretching her arms up. "I am dead on my feet right now. Can we, like, get some sleep before we do more sleuthing?"

"A nap sounds absolutely fantastic." Jasmine stood. "The bags under my eyes could count as carry-on luggage. Let's reconvene in a few hours."

I covered my mouth to hide a yawn. "Deal."

It only took me a few minutes to fall asleep, so it felt like the moment I closed my eyes in bed, I opened them again in a dream.

I was in a white room. White tile floors, white walls, a white bed, a white chair, and a white toilet, shower, and sink in the corner behind a curtain. I sat up from where I'd been laying on the bed, rubbing my throbbing head. There was something gritty between my teeth and my mouth felt dry. Every muscle in my body ached like I'd been put through a meat tenderizer. When I looked down at myself, I had on a hospital gown with little pink flowers on it.

"Zo? You awake?" a voice asked.

I looked up. There was a glass door at the front of the room with a barred window. Through it, I spotted a familiar face staring at me from between the bars.

I hopped to my feet. "Dad?"

I took a few steps closer to the door, and his face immediately drained of color. Frank Huxley looked the same as he always did, with his thick mustache and salt-and-pepper hair. His pulse jumped in his neck. It was like I was an animal threatening to lunge at him.

He cleared his throat and forced a shaky smile. "Hey, kid. It's—uh—good to see you."

"What's going on?" I took another step closer to the door and nearly winced when Dad drew back an inch. "What am I doing here? Where's Mom?"

He rubbed the nape of his neck, casting his gaze sideways. "She, ah…she needs a little more time, sweetheart. She's still wrapping her mind around all of this."

Immediately, the back of my throat tightened. "Dad, I swear we didn't mean to hurt anyone—"

"I know, kiddo." He let out a small sigh. "The doctors told us you couldn't stop yourself. You were starving."

The images of Devin Han's skin tearing beneath my claws rushed back all at once. The way that the blood bubbled up from inside, the way it tasted when I shoved my fingers in my mouth.

I blinked and two fat tears ran down my cheeks.

"Dad, you have to get me out of here. I just want to go home. Please."

"You have to understand why that's not safe, Zo. I mean, look at yourself."

I started to say something else, but something cut into my lip. My teeth were sharpening and lengthening all at once, and when I reached up to cover my mouth, I found my hands clawed and covered in blood and stringy bits of viscera. I yelped, hopping back, just as I noticed a puddle of red at my feet.

"I can't take you home," Dad said, his expression lifeless, "because you're not my daughter anymore."

The puddle at my feet began to grow like the ground itself was bleeding out, thick crimson rising like an incoming tide. I tried to step away from it, but it swelled, consuming my feet and my ankles. Chunks of torn flesh bobbed to the surface of the rising pool of blood like ingredients in a stew—disembodied hearts and eyes and lungs. The smell of it was everywhere, coppery and sharp and just a bit sweet.

"Dad, please!" I begged. The blood rose to my chest, hot and sticky across my skin. "Help me!"

Just as the blood rose to cover my mouth, a sob choked my throat, and a distant voice said, "Zoey?"

I woke up, eyes slowly blinking open.

Nightmare, I reminded myself. *You're okay. Everything's okay.*

Celeste looked at me with a soft expression from the other side of our bed. She was sitting up against the pale wood headboard with a pillow wedged between it and her lower back. Her hair was in two messy braids that rested atop her collarbones, her bangs sticking up just slightly in a way that told me she'd just woken up as well.

"Is everything okay? You're—you're crying."

I reached up to touch my cheek and found it wet with tears. I quickly wiped them away with a fist, shaking my head. It ached, and I wasn't sure if it was from crying, lack of sleep, not drinking enough water, or all of the above.

"I'm fine," I lied, staring at the pink bedspread and slowly rubbing my thumb across the top of it. "Just a nightmare."

Celeste reached out and brushed a lock of hair out of my eyes. The touch was so feather-light, so gentle, that I almost started crying again.

"Care to share?" she asked.

I bit my lip and sniffled. "Maybe later. I'm just gonna get some air."

I slid out from under the covers. Celeste's eyes practically bored a hole in my shoulder as I put on sandals and headed toward the living room. I closed the door behind me before she could push any further.

Squinting at the brightness of the sun in the living room, I sighed as I pulled my loose hair into a small bun, trying to shake the image of my father's face from the forefront of my brain. That had been the beginning of what was now a long-standing pattern of my father refusing to look me in the eye.

I grabbed my phone from where I'd left it charging on a geometric-patterned side table in the living room and went to the sliding glass door at the back of the cabin. It led to a small deck, with a table and some chairs atop a green rug.

As I slid the door open, Jasmine turned from where she was sitting. She had on cat-eye sunglasses and a floppy sun hat. She was drinking something iced and pink, condensation dripping from the sides. A pitcher of it sat sweating in the center of the table.

"Afternoon, sleepyhead," she said.

I slid the door closed behind me. "What time is it?"

"Almost four." She gestured to the open chair beside her. "Take a seat. I made pink lemonade."

I pulled out the chair across from Jasmine and settled in, crossing my legs and tucking my feet under me. Jasmine took an extra glass she'd brought outside and filled it with lemonade, passing it to me. Absently, I took a sip, staring out at the marbled sandstone walls towering over the valley. A couple of hawks were circling overhead, flying around each other in what I assumed was some kind of territorial spat. Their talons were extended and slashing at the air, long enough that they were visible even from the ground.

I glanced down at my fingernails, knowing I could curl them into claws whenever I needed to.

In an odd way, it was a comfort. I'd always been a quiet, nervous child before the Hollowing. The world was big and dangerous, and as much as I tried to fight back against it, I was very rarely successful. I got picked on for being small, and the boys made a point of pushing me around because they knew that when I fought back, I couldn't actually do anything to hurt them. I was too small, too weak, too angry.

After the Hollowing, that changed. As much as it stung to see the way that my parents looked at me pale-faced and wide-eyed whenever they spotted my fangs, it was also oddly comforting. Because I wasn't just a weak little girl that anyone could hurt if they wanted. I was the monster that lurked in the night, and monsters didn't have to be afraid of weakness.

"Val's still asleep," Jasmine said, breaking through my thoughts. "She stayed up for another hour texting Eli. It sounds like they aren't too worried about Kaiden yet—apparently, he's not the most communicative guy. They just think he hooked up with a girl and is hanging out with her."

"How long do you think before they report him missing?"

Jasmine shrugged. "No idea. But if anyone tries to track his phone, they're SOL. I wiped the SIM card and then smashed it last night as soon as I woke up in the cave. It's down in the mine with him now."

"Good thinking."

A moment of silence passed between us as we both sipped our drinks, staring out at the desert.

Then, point-blank, Jasmine asked, "Have you been crying?"

I sniffed, clearing some of the leftover snot out of my nose. "God, is it that obvious?"

"S'okay. I cried earlier too." Jasmine watched a bead of condensation slide down her glass and over her thumb. "Not our finest day."

Kaiden's face appeared in the forefront of my mind again, eyeless sockets pointed toward the sky. My stomach twisted, and I wrapped my arms around myself.

Jasmine adjusted her sunglasses, sighing. She had on dark red lipstick to match the ribbon on her hat so she looked like an old-fashioned pinup girl. She wasn't usually the type to put that much effort into what she wore, and I couldn't help but wonder if this was her attempt at maintaining some level of normalcy—of control.

"I was thinking about what Val said earlier," Jasmine said, breaking the silence. "About how she's never killed a human before this. I guess I just assumed...all of us had."

I opened my mouth, then closed it. She was right—none of us liked to talk about what had happened during the Hollowing, when we were all desperate and confused and starving to death. When I was still at the facility for juvenile ghouls, we had required therapy sessions where they told us to think of the ghoul part of ourselves as something separate, like a different person who had done things we never would. Some people even gave it names, kind of a Jekyll and Hyde situation, so that they could say, *Oh, it wasn't me that killed that innocent person. It was someone, something else.*

I wasn't really sure how much I bought into that, but at moments like this, it bubbled back to the surface.

"I guess we've never been the sort of friends to compare body counts," I whispered, taking a sip. "At least not in the traditional sense."

Jasmine heaved a sigh and settled back into her seat, letting the sunshine soak her skin. "For what it's worth, I've got two."

My eyebrows shot up. Back in school, Jasmine and I were good friends, but we weren't exactly the sort to have heart-to-hearts. Both of us were reserved enough that we kept our emotions contained, though in slightly different ways. Jasmine always deflected with humor, whereas I just bottled up whatever was bugging me as much as I possibly could. The only person who usually heard about my unfiltered feelings was Celeste. Until recently, anyway.

I exhaled a breath. *Might as well be honest with someone.*

"One," I said, not meeting Jasmine's eyes. I settled for staring at the shadow of the table and the umbrella above us fluttering softly in the breeze. "A hunter in the woods who shot Celeste. I don't even know what his name was. Never found out."

Jasmine nodded. "Mine were a white supremacist couple who attacked my brother and me back in LA."

"Sounds like they deserved it," I muttered.

Jasmine shrugged. "I…yeah, I don't know. Didn't ever make me feel better. My brother had to see me do that, and I'm not sure he's ever looked at me the same way."

My expression softened. "How did you deal with it? After, I mean?"

Jasmine pressed her lips together and rubbed the back of her neck. "I…I guess I just really threw myself into other things when I got home. Once they let ghouls out of house arrest post-SynFlesh and school started up, I joined a bunch of clubs, volunteered to be captain of the softball team, and took all the hardest classes I could. I figured that if I always had something going on, then I wouldn't ever be alone with my thoughts long enough to dwell on it too much."

"And now you're going to Yale to become a doctor," I offered. "And you were our valedictorian. Not a lot of people could manage that even if they weren't ghouls."

"I was just lucky whoever was on the admissions board at Yale appreciated my essay about wanting to start a clinic specifically focused on treating ghouls," Jasmine scoffed. "Regardless, when did you suddenly turn into the touchy-feely type?"

"I'm just saying." I settled back into my seat, eyes wandering up to the sun shining through the patio umbrella. "If you have to pick a coping mechanism, being a massive overachiever seems like a pretty good one."

"Pfft. Thanks." Jasmine sipped her drink. "What about you? I never heard much about what it was like for you after the Hollowing. I mean, I know that you came back to school a little later than everyone else, but…"

I nodded. "I got put in one of those facilities for underage ghouls whose parents didn't feel safe having them at home. I didn't get out until October—three and a half months after everything went down."

Jasmine's eyes rose. "Damn. I mean, I know your parents are…"

"Assholes?" I offered.

Jasmine exhaled a laugh through her nose. "Well, yeah. They basically just let you do what you want most of the time, right?"

"Pretty much, yeah." I tucked my hair behind my ears, tilting back and staring up at the cloudless sky. Out here in the desert, the sky went on forever. "It's been like that since I moved back in with them after the Hollowing. They've never treated me the same."

Jasmine's forehead wrinkled, but she didn't say anything. For a second, I wondered if she'd push, but she didn't.

Somehow, that was what made me decide to add, "I already felt like a monster, but they're the ones that made me believe I actually am one."

Jasmine's eyebrows shot up. "Zoey, you're not—"

"Three days after I got home, I realized that my mom was carrying a pistol around." As soon as the words were out of my mouth, it was like a floodgate had suddenly opened inside me. The back of my throat tightened and my eyes began to shine. "A fucking *gun*. One of those little ones that can fit in a purse. She tried to hide it from me, but the first time she watched me eat, I saw her holding it behind her back just in case I went feral. I think she keeps it under her pillow now."

A single tear slid free. "And they…just try to avoid me now. I don't think my mom has said more than ten words to me since I got home. They find excuses to be gone when I'm in the house and give me money once a month so I can do my own grocery shopping. That's all they ever give me—money. And my dad talks to me, but he never looks at me when he does it. He certainly hasn't, I dunno, *hugged me* o-or—"

I cut off as a sob shuddered out of me. Jasmine stood from her chair and came to my side, wrapping her arms around me. She hugged me tightly as I tried to catch my breath, apologizing between sobs.

Jasmine squeezed me once more before slowly easing back. "How the hell people sleep at night knowing they're screwing over their family I'll never understand."

"Sorry," I muttered, finally managing to swallow a breath. "This is a stupid thing to be crying about right now with everything else on our plates. This whole Kaiden situation has sort of... brought it back."

"Hey, come on. Be a little easier on yourself." Jasmine took her seat back, but reached out and clasped my hand across the table. "That *sucks*. Family shouldn't treat you like that. But you know what?"

My wet eyes rose to meet hers.

"You've got us," Jasmine said. She gestured to herself and back at the cabin. "Me, Celeste, and Val. We've had each other's backs forever, right? And nothing is going to change that. Especially not what happened last night."

I sniffled, nodding softly. "Yeah. You're right. Thanks, Jaz."

"Of course." She patted my hand. "I love you, Zo."

I bit back a smile.

"Love you too."

ten

The Slice, Reader Submission ***4190
Status: Pending

Dear Abby,

I've been following your advice column for years now. In fact, my mom used to get bored of reading me picture books when I was little, so instead we'd sit together and read your column. And we still read it over breakfast most days. We always love the ones with relationship advice, which I guess is kind of funny because we're both chronically single.

   The thing is, I'm Hollow. I just worry that no one will ever be able to look at me and see anything but a monster, no matter how nice I am. I try really, really hard to prove to people that I'm a good person because I'm so scared that they won't be able to look past it. I find myself keeping it a secret from people I've just met because I'm worried about being judged. It's not

that I'm ashamed or anything, I just hate feeling like
I have to justify my existence to everyone all the time.

I guess what I'm saying is: do you think there are
actually people out there who could love someone like
me unconditionally?

—*CF, Aspen Flats, CA*

Editor's note: This one might be a nice addition for the Hollowing anniversary issue, Abby. Say whatever you need to make them feel good. Corporate wants us to come across as pro-ghoul, at least during their anniversary month. Feel free to toss it otherwise.

*A*fter my chat with Jasmine, I still felt like I needed to clear my head. Celeste had gone back to sleep, and Val was still out, so I grabbed my backpack and decided to take a walk around the cabins. The hope was that being alone for a bit would relieve some of the anxiety that had made a home beneath my rib cage like a nesting bird.

It was a hot day, and people were everywhere, chatting as they made their way to their next events across the valley—not a care in the world. I wandered away from the festival grounds, walking along the edge of the dirt road toward the back of the valley, which was nothing but a field of boulders and dry brush. Patches of cacti dotted the dirt along with a few remaining wildflowers that stayed close to the rocks—yellow desert marigolds and tiny purple Mojave asters that had mostly faded away with the turn of the seasons.

I puttered over to the field of boulders, dodging Joshua trees and cactus patches. For the first time in a while, everything felt…quiet.

Until the soft sound of a guitar and singing blew past my ear on the breeze.

The dirt crunched under my feet as I drifted in the direction of the sound. Soon, I stepped around a boulder to find a familiar figure seated atop a large rock, strumming a guitar in his lap as he softly hummed. His red hair looked like copper fire in the sunlight, freckles bold like dark constellations on his nose.

It was Cole. And before I could dive out of view, he turned and pinned me in place with his gaze. I froze like a deer spotted by a cougar, my heart thrumming. How was I supposed to face the bandmate of someone I ate less than twenty-four hours ago? He was going to sense something was off—he'd know I was hiding something, he'd—

A huge smile bloomed across his face.

"Hey!" he called, letting his guitar rest on his leg as he waved. "Zoey! What are you doing here?"

No point in running now.

"Hey, Cole." I raked my hair out of my face and smiled sheepishly. "Sorry, I didn't mean to interrupt or anything—I was just taking a walk. Trying to clear my head."

"Great minds think alike, I guess." He patted the spot beside him on the rock. "I was getting kind of lonely out here anyway. Come, sit."

I had to stop myself from wincing. "I don't want to bother you—it sounded like you were busy."

"What, doing this?" He strummed the guitar so it let out a few discordant notes as he snickered to himself. "I'm just disturbing the wildlife at this point."

"I guess that's one way to ward off the rattlesnakes."

Cole laughed at that but didn't stop looking at me expectantly. Not having any better excuse to leave, I exhaled a breath and went to the rock, pulling myself up to sit beside him. He flashed me a winning smile, the breeze ruffling his hair.

My heart skipped a beat. *Shit, he's so cute. Why did Val have to murder his friend, of all people?*

"It was nice talking to you at the party last night," Cole started. He bumped his bent knee against mine. He had thick red hair up his shins that tickled my skin where we touched, and immediately my heart rate began to quicken. "Were your friends okay? You left in kind of a rush."

Sweat pricked on my forehead. At least I could blame it on the desert heat. "Um—yeah. Val just…got her period. Really bad. Like, just so much blood all over everything. Cannot overstate the sheer volume of it—"

Jesus Christ, Zoey, shut up, shut up, shut up—

To his credit, Cole just laughed. "Oh, bummer. I'm guessing she's all right now?"

I swallowed my mortification. "Yep. Crisis averted. She, uh, didn't want Eli to see."

"Fair enough. I feel like he's the kind of guy who'd be weird about it."

"And you're not?" I guessed.

Cole shrugged. "I had an older sister. She used to try and freak me out by throwing unused tampons at me. Had to get over my menstrual discomfort pretty quickly."

The noise I made lay somewhere between a cackle and an inelegant snort. "She sounds fun."

"Oh, she was. You guys probably would have gotten along."

Was. Would have.

My face softened. This was the problem getting to know people in a post-Hollowing world—as much as we had all tried to move on, the scars were still there. There was no escaping the fact that there wasn't a single person on earth who hadn't been impacted by it in some regard. Even the luckiest people who made it through without losing family or friends still knew someone who had.

And there was no rule book on how to deal with collective grief.

So gently, I asked, "Did…you lose her?"

Cole's smile faded a bit as he nodded. "Oh, um. Yeah. She died during the Hollowing." He shook his head. "Sorry, that's such a downer thing to bring up."

"No! Sorry, I shouldn't have asked."

He shrugged. "It's cool. I know I'm not exactly special in that regard."

A beat of silence passed between us. I almost asked what happened to her, but the last thing I wanted to do was make Cole relive something traumatic. I'd heard of people who had to kill their own feral family members to defend themselves. There was a reason everyone wanted to move on from the Hollowing so badly— staying stuck in a nightmare like that was simply too painful.

"Were you close?" I finally asked.

That seemed to help bring some of the light back into Cole's face. "Yeah. She was one of my best friends. After my dad died when we were kids and my mom remarried, we pretty much relied on each other all the time."

I nodded softly. "Sounds like she was a really lovely person."

Cole closed his eyes, then reopened them to look at the sky.

Softly, his fingers tapped against his guitar. "She's the whole reason I'm here."

"Yeah?"

Cole nodded. "She introduced me to Eli. They were dating at the time, and she knew I wanted to start a band, so it felt like the natural thing to do. Granted, when I envisioned my future band, I was singing *and* playing guitar, but Eli insisted he had to do vocals."

I scoffed. "From what I just heard, your voice is way better than Eli's."

"Thank you!" Cole said, throwing up his hands. "This is what I'm saying! I mean, come on, I write most of our songs anyway and somehow he still gets the credit. And maybe more people would take us seriously if Eli didn't sound like every single pop punk asshole who dates girls way younger than him and thinks he's a feminist because he wears nail polish."

I sputtered a laugh. "Or if he didn't look like a Tim Burton character with a nicotine addiction."

Cole lost it at that, throwing his head back and laughing while he clutched his guitar with one hand and steadied himself against the rock with the other. He gently bumped his shoulder against mine, and I giggled, turning to meet his eyes, only to find his face much closer than I was expecting. His lips were still curled in a warm smile, the skin beside his eyes crinkled. For a flashing second, his gaze went to my lips, then paused there.

Then, at the same moment, we both looked away from each other, my cheeks burning. Cole let out a little cough while I pulled my knees tightly against myself.

Am I imagining it, or did it seem like he was about to kiss me for a second?

"Sorry," Cole quickly said, slicking a hand back through his hair. "Spending all my time with the band makes it feel like I can't exactly vent about this sort of thing with anyone else. It's…nice to get it off my chest."

"Listen, when your solo career winds up being infinitely more successful than anything with Eli's name attached, I'll be the first to say I told you so."

Cole sputtered a laugh. "Thanks, I think?"

"You're welcome." I straightened up, slowly beginning to rise from the rock. "Anyway, I should probably get going. Gotta…meet some people. For stuff."

"Sounds riveting," Cole chuckled.

I nodded. "Very. But…I'll see you around?"

"Yeah. See you around, Z."

And as I left, I couldn't help but wonder if maybe there was something to the way my heart had begun to do cartwheels in my chest.

That night, as the sun began to sink beneath the rock walls surrounding De Luz Valley, Celeste, Jasmine, Val, and I each gathered our things as we prepared to execute our separate plans.

Celeste and I shoved flashlights into our backpacks and climbed into the Mini. We'd agreed to wait until it was dark to go explore the abandoned research site, just to be sure that we were less likely to run into anyone else who might be visiting the facility on a whim. Jasmine waved goodbye to us from the cabin window while Val did her makeup—the two of them were planning to try and crash another party that was happening at the pavilion so they could ask the bartender if they knew anything about the powder we found. For all of our sakes, I really hoped they could pull it off.

It took Celeste and me half an hour to get to the old research facility. We'd left our phones at home to avoid tipping off Patricia, instead following a hand-drawn map I'd made. The facility was down a sketchy dirt road that we had to open a gate to get to—Celeste nearly broke her ankle navigating the cattle grate under it in heeled ankle boots. She mouthed a curse as she flung the gate open.

As she climbed back into the car, I asked, "Really? Heels for breaking into a burned-out building?"

"They're the only closed-toe shoes I packed," Celeste grumbled. She pulled her hair back into a high ponytail, a few pieces escaping and hanging around her square chin. "Somehow I didn't think I'd be breaking into an abandoned building when I was packing for a *music festival.*"

"All right, all right. Point taken."

Gravel crunched under the tires as I pulled up to the looming, boxy structure. It was positioned at the top of a hill so it overlooked the surrounding desert. Joshua trees grew on either side of it, some of them charred and brittle. While most of the walls were still intact, the front one was crumbling, blackened and eroding. What must have once been a cement path leading to the front door was now cracked and sprouting small green plants.

Celeste and I climbed out of the car, swinging our backpacks over our shoulders. Celeste narrowed her eyes and said, "Do you see that?"

I followed her finger to a patch of still-rooted tumbleweed growing in a thorny clump. Beside it, however, were two thick lines in the dirt.

"Tire tracks," I said. "They look pretty fresh too."

"Maybe it's a little less abandoned than advertised," Celeste whispered under her breath. She clicked on her flashlight. "Come on."

The two of us followed the cracked path up to what was once a glass door. The fire had blown the glass out, and one of the doors hung at a strange angle, its hinge partially melted. Scorch marks marred what was once a stucco finish on the facade.

I reached out and tried the more intact door. It rattled but didn't budge—upon closer inspection, I discovered that the two sides of it were chained together. Pressing my lips together, I reached out a Doc Martens–clad foot and kicked off a few jagged bits of glass that were still hanging on to the doorframe.

"Careful," Celeste whispered.

"Don't worry," I said, knocking off another piece that fell to the floor inside and shattered. "I, for one, packed decent shoes."

Celeste rolled her eyes while I ducked through the bottom part of the door, careful to avoid touching the sides where there might still be shards of glass I missed. Celeste winced while she struggled to bend herself through the narrow space. I held out a hand and she took it, pulling herself back up to her full height.

As she dusted off her jeans, I shone my light on the darkened space. The inside walls were crumbling, only the skeletons of support beams still standing. Ash stained the tiled floor leading up to what must have been a front desk at some point.

I stepped over the broken glass on the floor and tiptoed to the desk. Most of it had been turned to charcoal, but a few of the metal drawers still pulled out as I tugged on them. I angled my flashlight up to look through them, but found only ash, office supplies, and Post-it Notes scribbled with reminders for whoever used to work there.

"Nothing here," I reported.

Celeste pointed through a burnt-out section of wall. "I see some desks this way. Maybe we should try those?"

I closed the drawers. "Good call."

The area behind the entrance was what must have, at one point, been an office space for a couple of people. It was a long hallway framed by decaying support beams, with six offices, three door-ways on each side of the hall. A few of the nameplates were still on the doors while others had been completely burned away. I stepped over a pile of rubble to go into the first office on the right while Celeste took the one opposite to it.

"Hey, Zoey?" Celeste asked as she opened a filing cabinet that was toppled over on its side and appeared to be somewhat melted to the floor. "I know this is probably a, ah, bad time to bring this up, but my brain is terrible and I just….shit, I'm sorry. Are you mad at me?"

I paused, furrowing my brows. Celeste had always been a chronic overthinker, which was partially because she had Generalized Anxiety Disorder and partially because she cared way more about keeping other people happy than I did. That said, it had been a long time since she'd asked me anything like that.

"What? No—why would I be mad?"

Celeste picked up a file from the cabinet and thumbed through it before tossing it over her shoulder, mouthing the world *useless*. "I mean—I dunno. We used to talk to each other about everything. Now it seems like you can't even look at me."

Shit, she noticed?

Of course she'd noticed. If someone randomly stopped being able to look me in the eye when we spoke, I'd think that I'd done something wrong too.

But what was I supposed to say? *Sorry about that, it's because I realized I'm in love with you, and now every time I look at you it feels like my heart is too big for my chest and my entire body feels like I've been sitting in a sauna for a week straight.*

"I'm sorry," I said before I could think of anything else. "It's not on purpose, I swear. You didn't do anything wrong." *Except that you had the gall to be extremely hot and kind and talented and kiss me at goddamn Cleo Jacobsen's graduation party.*

"Then what's up?"

For a brief second, part of me wondered if I should tell her. Maybe, just maybe, she felt the same way I did. That future I daydreamed about of the two of us in our little apartment wasn't so far-fetched. Maybe we could make it work.

Or I could completely ruin our friendship in one fell swoop.

"I guess I'm just…" I swallowed thickly. "I've got a lot going on. It's…hard for me to talk about."

Celeste closed the filing cabinet she was looking through and pursed her lips. For a moment, I wondered if she'd push anymore.

Instead, a beat passed, and we were both silent.

"I understand. You don't have to tell me," she finally said, not looking at me.

My heart dropped into my stomach. *Nice job, Zoey. Now she really thinks you're mad.*

Clearing her throat, Celeste held up a small object. "A-Anyway, dunno how useful this might be, but I found a USB drive in the back of that cabinet with a bunch of boring financial reports."

"It's probably more financial reports," I said, grateful for the change in subject. "Or porn."

Celeste slid it into her pocket. "Let's hope it's porn; statistical analysis gives me heartburn."

I snorted.

It took us each another twenty minutes to search through the remaining offices, finding little of note. The only light came from our flashlights and holes in the ceiling that revealed the nearly full moon.

"Not seeing anything else," Celeste announced as she joined me in the back corner office. She crossed her bare arms over her chest, shivering. "Maybe we should head out."

I nodded, straightening up from where'd I'd been bent over a desk, digging through its drawers. "Yeah—seems like a bust. Hopefully Val and Jasmine had more luck."

Celeste opened her mouth to add something, but the sound of crunching glass made us freeze.

It was coming from out in the hall. Celeste caught my wrist and yanked me down with her as she ducked behind the desk. I stumbled and fell back into her. She managed to hold on to me so I didn't crash into the floor, her eyes wide and bright in the darkness. This close, I felt her heart beating against her breastbone. The hair on the back of my neck stood on end.

From the gap under the desk, I caught a glimpse of movement in the hallway. Broken glass cracked and ground into the floor under heavy footsteps. Celeste and I both held our breath, Celeste's fingernails digging into my skin.

Something exhaled a wet, heavy breath outside the door.

Celeste and I tensed. I could feel her shaking.

But thankfully, whatever it was didn't seem to notice us. Slowly, the sound of footsteps turned back down the hall, growing quieter and quieter until the only sound was Celeste and I trying to catch our breath.

"The fuck was that?" I whispered.

"Must have been some kind of animal," Celeste breathed. Her hold on me loosened before she grabbed onto the desk and peered over the edge. She clicked on her flashlight, shining it into the hall. She flicked it left and right and said, "I think it's gone."

"I sure as shit hope so—that thing sounded huge," I exhaled.

Celeste nodded. She'd gone ghost-pale, big blue eyes rounded. Straightening up, she reached a hand out to me on the ground.

"Let's get the hell out of here," she whispered.

With a nod, I grabbed her hand and she hoisted me up. I went to pull my hand away, but after a moment, I realized Celeste wasn't letting go. Her fingers tightened around mine as she held the flashlight out in front of her, hurrying us down the hall.

We all but sprinted to the car, eyes scanning every shadow as we went, expecting it to jump out at us. As soon as we made it to the Mini, we slammed the doors closed and locked them. In record time, I'd turned the car on and slammed my foot on the gas, throwing up a cloud of dust in our wake.

"Seriously, what was that?" I said, swerving to avoid a bump in the road. The headlights bobbed, yellow beams carving through the darkness. We were the only car out this late, and even the highway at the end of the dirt road was shrouded in black.

"Coyote?" Celeste guessed.

"*Coyote,*" I repeated, hands white-knuckling the wheel. I tore my eyes away from them just long enough to lock onto Celeste and start to say, "Fucker must have been the size of a cow—"

"Zoey!" Celeste shrieked. "Look out!"

My head whipped back to the road just in time to see a shape standing in the center of it, eyes pointed directly at us.

I slammed on the brakes, and the Mini screeched to a halt. The figure was probably seven feet tall and humanoid, with unnaturally long, gangly limbs. Its clothes were ragged and torn, blotchy rust-colored stains covering the front of what was once a band T-shirt. It had long, greasy brown hair that hung partway over a skeletal face, the skin hanging loose over the bones. Where the lips should have been was nothing but ragged, red flesh and gnashing, jagged teeth behind it.

Its neck hung sideways like it had been snapped. Hollow eyes stared at us, milky white and unblinking, surrounded by black veins. Oily black tears leaked from the corners, staining its sallow cheeks. Clawed hands hung at its sides, fingers twitching like spider's legs.

Distantly, I wondered where the sound of screaming was coming from until I realized it was me.

I smashed my foot down on the gas as hard as I could. The engine roared, and Celeste braced herself against the sides of the car, shrieking. The figure leapt out of the way just as I swerved around it. Its screech, keening and pained, was audible even through the closed windows. It landed in the dirt just as I went around it on the other side of the road, still screaming at the top of my lungs.

"It's getting up!" Celeste cried, angling her body to look out the back window. "Zoey, faster!"

I didn't need to be told twice—I hit the gas as hard as I could.

The tires sprayed gravel behind us. I caught a flash in the rearview mirror of the creature covering its face with a clawed hand and shrieking.

"Go, go, go!" Celeste shouted.

I hit the highway pavement seconds later. The tires screeched across it as I threw the wheel to the left, the Mini whipping around and skidding sideways. For a second, the tires spun wildly before they finally managed to grip the road enough to launch us forward.

Without the bumps of the dirt road to slow us down, the Mini hit ninety within a minute. Celeste stayed turned toward the back window, breath short and eyes wide.

"Is it following us?" I asked, heart racing.

"I don't think so," Celeste said.

"Should I slow down?"

"No." She held onto the grab handle above her window for dear life. "Absolutely not."

I nodded, shifting the Mini into sport mode.

We sped the rest of the way back to De Luz Valley with the engine roaring beneath us.

eleven

DESERT BLOOM MUSIC FESTIVAL
SECURITY INCIDENT REPORT FORM

Date/Time of Incident: Thursday, June 23, approximately 11:30 p.m.
Location: Near Rabbitbrush Plaza

Description of Incident: I was on my break smoking a cigarette outside of Rabbitbrush Plaza when a very distressed young person (white, female-presenting, blond) ran up to me crying hysterically. It took her a few moments to compose herself enough to inform me that she had seen a figure dragging an unconscious body away from the party she was attending. I followed her to where she had allegedly last seen the victim, but there was no evidence of any sort of struggle, nor were there any other witnesses. When I pressed her for details on the figure, she informed me that it had appeared to be a particularly tall, slender Hollow person. It was at this point that I realized she was likely playing a practical joke. I reprimanded her for taking me from my post and gave her my card if she wanted to contact security further. I suspect this is yet another in what is turning into a slew of false reports about strange sightings across the festival.

Witness(es): The attendee, Jessica Whitten

Who was Notified: Police__ Fire Department__ Medical__ Admin__ Other__ Nobody X

Additional Comments/Follow-up Requests: Add these to the files with previous reports ("Alleged Kidnapping near Mallow Campground," "Attendee Reported Figure Outside Lodging Window," "Blood Found in Women's Bathroom") and forward them to Gary for review. If these continue, we'll need to inform PR.

Form Completed by: Thomas McClain

*I*t took us half the time to get back to Desert Bloom with me absolutely gunning it, still convinced that at any moment the creature was going to appear behind us. But it didn't, thank god, and we were able to make it back to the cabin without incident.

Celeste and I locked every door and window, pulling the shades shut. My heart refused to slow down, images of the figure fresh in the front of my brain. Val and Jasmine were still out, so we went into their room briefly to lock the windows before heading to the living room, where we finally sat down and caught our breath.

I was the one who finally broke the silence. "That was completely batshit."

"God, I can't even wrap my head around it." Celeste stood up, going to the fridge. "What the hell was that thing?"

"Beats me." I exhaled, sliding my hands back through my hair and holding it in place. "I wonder if anyone online has ever heard of something like that. I'll have to do some research—"

"At least catch your breath first," Celeste chided. She rubbled her temples with her forefingers. "Jesus, I need a drink. You want one?"

I nearly let out an actual, honest-to-god whimper at the sound of that. "More than anything, yes."

With an empathetic nod, Celeste opened the fridge, eyes scanning the contents. She grabbed the pitcher of lemonade Jasmine had made earlier.

She winced, teeth clenching. "Sh—*ouch*."

That's when I noticed the wound on her shoulder. It was a long slice that cut through her cream-colored crop top, leaving the edge ragged and stained. Her skin was smeared with blood, beginning to dry dark brown where the cut wasn't still bleeding.

"Celeste," I gasped, pointing. "You're hurt."

Celeste glanced over her shoulder at me, brows furrowed. She followed my finger to her shoulder and whispered, "Oh. Damn it, I really liked this shirt."

I stood up and went to the kitchen, taking the lemonade pitcher out of her hand and setting it on the counter. Before she could protest, I pulled her toward me and muttered, "Let me look at it."

"I must have cut myself on the glass when we left," Celeste said. "I was so freaked out I didn't even notice."

"We should clean this. Let me grab the first aid kit from my car—it has some disinfectant and Steri-Strips we can use."

Celeste started to say, "It really doesn't hurt—"

"Maybe, but it will once the adrenaline rush stops." I squared my shoulders. "You focus on drinks, I'll focus on first aid."

Celeste sighed but didn't argue. I quickly grabbed my keys and went outside, popping the Mini's trunk and digging out the massive first-aid kit that my dad had bought me to go along with the car—his clumsy attempt at indicating he cared about my safety. I quickly scanned left and right to make sure nothing had followed us and was lurking in the dark, then went back inside.

Celeste met me with a pink lemonade vodka in each hand. She held one out to me. "For you, Dr. Huxley."

I took it. "Too bad Jasmine isn't here—she'd probably have a much better bedside manner. Come on, you sit on the floor and I'll go on the couch."

Celeste nodded. I followed her to the living room, where she plopped down on the soft pink rug. I slid onto the couch behind her, my knees on either side of her shoulders. She reached back and peeled off her shirt, exposing the white, lacy bralette underneath. She had constellations of freckles spattered along her shoulder blades. In another situation, I would have loved to kiss each mark one by one.

My face immediately burned red.

Celeste glanced over her shoulder to say something, then frowned as she saw my expression. "Why are you looking at me like that? Is it really bad?"

I averted my eyes. My face was so hot it was practically steaming. Without thinking, I blurted out, "That bralette is hideous."

Celeste's mouth fell open and she choked out a laugh. "Oh, I'm so sorry. I didn't realize you were a member of the bralette police. Should I take that off too, Officer?"

My heart nearly punched out of my chest. My horrible brain began to shriek, *shirtlessCelesteshirtlessCelesteshirtlessCeleste*—

"Shut the hell up," I whispered, horrified when it nearly came out as a whine.

Celeste scoffed, the skin around her eyes wrinkling as she smiled. "Okay, weirdo."

She turned to face front again and I dug my fingernails into my bare thighs. *Snap out of it, Zoey.*

I refocused on the first aid kit, popping the latches and pulling out some disinfectant wipes and Steri-Strips. I set them down beside me, took a big swig of my vodka lemonade, and leaned forward to examine the wound.

"You know what I can't stop thinking about?" Celeste asked after a moment of quiet.

"Hm?"

"That thing…kind of looked like a ghoul." Celeste bit her lip. "I mean, I've never seen one of us quite like that, but with the teeth and the claws…"

"Yeah, but none of us have ever looked *that* messed up." I unwrapped a disinfectant wipe and carefully traced the cut—it was about six inches long, a clean slice that was still wet with blood. Beginning to dab around it, I added, "Even when we were starving in the woods, we never chewed our own lips off."

Celeste shivered. "I guess you're right. I just can't stop seeing its face… It looked like maybe it had been a girl once. What if she was just a regular ghoul and—I dunno, got sick or something?"

"What, with Fucked Up Monster Disease?"

She threw her hands up. "I'm just saying! This could be something really, really bad! What if there's a new strain of the Hollow virus that turns people into something worse?"

"Hey, come on—let's not get too ahead of ourselves. Speculating is only going to freak us out more." She winced as I brushed the cut with the disinfectant wipe, and I added, "Sorry, this part is gonna suck."

I got a second disinfectant wipe and rubbed it over the cut now that it was less obscured by blood. Celeste took a sharp, hissing breath through her teeth while I whispered, "Almost done, I swear."

"This is what I get for going along with your schemes," Celeste groaned.

I patched up the cut quickly, applying the Steri-Strips to it to help keep it closed and stabilize it. Celeste winced but didn't complain, her jaw tight as I applied the last of the strips.

When I finished, I said, "You're good. Just get better at ducking in the future."

"If you were my height, you'd understand why it's a little harder for me," she said. She squeezed her eyes shut for a moment as she adjusted her arm. Then, she took a big swig of her drink and added, "God, is it bad if we get drunk? Between Kaiden and whatever the hell that thing was, I would really like it if my brain were less on fire."

I reached around Celeste's side where I was straddling her and clinked the bottom of my glass against hers. "Cheers. I'll drink to that."

Over the course of the next hour, we both drained our first vodka lemonades, and Celeste made us each two more. Celeste sprawled out on the carpet and I slowly found myself melting off the couch to sit beside her. She left her shirt off, saying she wanted to let the wound dry out a bit so she didn't get blood on any other clothing. I had no complaints, especially after my second drink, when I suddenly found it a lot easier to look at her, no longer embarrassed by letting my eyes linger.

Ever since the kiss, it was like every day I noticed something else that I liked about Celeste. The way that she closed her eyes and ducked her head when she laughed, the way she always made a point to smile at my jokes even when no one else did. Little things I took for granted before but now made my face turn red and my palms sweat.

"I was supposed to livestream tonight," Celeste said, lying on her side and looking at me from across the rug. Her eyeliner had smudged into the pink shadow on her lids. When she angled her head, the highlighter on her cheekbones shined. "Can you imagine? Trying to just casually do a fun little festival makeup look for an audience right now? There's no way."

"Maybe it would be nice," I offered. "At least then you wouldn't have to be thinking about all of this shit."

Celeste snorted. "Please. You of all people should know that my brain has never once let me *not* think about the things that make me anxious."

I lowered myself onto my back and studied Celeste, chin still propped on her elbow. The vodka had turned her cheeks and the tip of her nose pink to match her hair, the way it always did when she got tipsy. There were bruise-like shadows under her eyes, dark enough that they showed through the layers of concealer she'd tried to use to hide them.

I pressed my lips together. "Is there anything I can do to help take your mind off it?"

I wasn't sure, but it almost seemed like her eyes flickered to my lips. Quickly, she glanced down at her nails, biting the inside of her cheek.

"I don't think so. All this stuff with Kaiden brought up a lot of feelings from Camp Everwood. I thought I'd worked through that but, maybe I was just kidding myself."

"Devin, you mean?" I asked gently.

Celeste nodded, still not looking at me. "I've always felt like I lost part of myself when I killed him. Like, before that I was just a kid who never broke the rules or hurt anyone's feelings if I could help it. But afterward, I didn't know how to reconcile who I was with what I'd done."

"It wasn't your fault," I reminded her.

Celeste exhaled a sigh. "That's what everyone says, right? That feral ghouls don't have the same reasoning as people? But if that's true, doesn't that just make all of us ticking time bombs? Doesn't Devin's death prove that—and the hunter's, and now Kaiden's?"

"Cel—"

So softly I could barely hear, she whispered, "Wouldn't it just be better if I was...gone?"

My eyes widened as the weight of what she'd said sank in. She went silent, her eyes shining faintly. She squeezed them shut, quickly wiping a tear away.

I reached out and grabbed her hand, squeezing it firmly.

Celeste met my eyes.

"No," I said, shaking my head. "No, it wouldn't be. And maybe this is a selfish fucking reason to say so, but *I need you*, Celeste. I always have and I—god, I think I always will."

Celeste blinked, two more tears snaking down her cheeks. Her eyes, ringed with red, were so wide that I could tell I'd caught her off guard. Her hand in mine was warm, her grip loose while she gazed down at me, coral-pink lips parted just slightly.

Slowly, she leaned forward, and my heart all but exploded.

But before she could close the distance between us, the lock on the front door clicked.

I threw myself back just as the door flew open. I went ramrod straight while Jasmine's voice rang out, "We are in *business*, ladies!"

Celeste pulled back, cheeks burning. Val shut the door, and she and Jasmine came into the living room as Jasmine started to say, "You are not gonna believe…"

She paused, eyes darting between us. We were both flushed and tense on opposite sides of the rug, pointedly looking away from each other.

Jasmine bit back a laugh. "Are we interrupting something?"

Celeste cleared her throat, running a hand back into her hair. "N-No, just"—she held up her half-finished lemonade—"polishing off the vodka."

"Without a shirt on?" Val pressed, raising an eyebrow.

Celeste angled her shoulder so they could see the cut on her back. "I didn't want to get blood on anything else."

Jasmine and Val's eyes widened.

I cleared my throat.

"We should get each other up to speed."

twelve

Two weeks into the Hollowing, the cracks in Valeria's foundation finally grew large enough to make her crumble.

The hunger had grown to such a violent crescendo that it had consumed every one of her thoughts. Lying in bed, she swore she could hear heartbeats through the walls. Her mother and father down the hall, her older brother across from her, her little brother one door down. And her abuela, who had finally started to recover, her heartbeat a gentle thump, thump, thump that was slowly beginning to strengthen.

Val's mind drifted to the image of her grandmother curled in bed, barely strong enough to stand. She wouldn't be able to fight back. Val could press a hand over her mouth, light enough not to wake her, then go for her throat—

Something poked into Val's lip. Her eyes flew open and she winced as a strange new pain tinged hot in her jaw. She opened her mouth, wincing as something pushed free from her gums, jagged and sharp. A tiny whimper escaped her throat and she bent in against herself, fingers clawing into her hair. As her they sunk in, though, something thorn-sharp dug into her scalp.

Her heart had begun to race, pounding in her ears. It wasn't enough to drown out the sound of breathing coming from every surrounding room. It was like every member of her family was breathing down her neck at once, the scent of their flesh redolent in the air. Her mouth began to water. She could tear into each of them, one after another, snapping each rib like a twig and carving out their thundering hearts. She imagined the way it would feel to sink her teeth into the still-warm muscle, blood staining her lips and tongue and dripping off her chin like juice from a ripened fruit.

Her eyes flew open. The edge of her vision was tinged with red.

Get out.

In one fluid motion, Val managed to throw open the window beside her bed, punching the screen out of place. She was lucky it was already loose from sneaking out for parties so many times—it fell to the ground with little more than a faint thump. She swung herself through it and hit the ground running, legs pumping as she willed herself farther and farther away from the sound of her family's hearts.

The streets of Aspen Flats were dead silent. Typically, summer meant there'd still be people out even in the middle of the night—mostly teenagers hanging out with their friends, their parents not bothering to set a curfew in such a humdrum small town. Val was typically one of them, sitting in the back of someone's car while they blasted music and went on joyrides through the sleepy streets, pushing the horsepower on their used Toyotas to the limit. Just a few weeks ago, she'd gotten dropped off in front of her house and climbed in the window as quietly as she could while her friends drove off going ninety.

She hadn't heard from most of them since the Hollowing.

Val came to a halt about half a mile from her parents' house. She'd reached the last street before Aspen Flats turned into desert, scraggly and empty save for a few patches of cholla, plus some crunchy, dry grasses. The mountains loomed in the distance, shadowy giants in the night.

While Val struggled to catch her breath, hands on her thighs, she tasted something sweet in the air.

Instantly, her face snapped up. The scent was a bit more pungent than what she'd smelled at home, but it was unmistakable:

Flesh.

It was coming from a culvert on the side of a hill. During the rainy season, a small creek typically flowed through it, but it had long since dried up in the sweltering summer heat. All that remained of it was a wash full of discarded beer bottles, some animal bones, and twigs and debris stuck on rocks that had once been underwater. The scars of water flow still marred the wash, carving curved stripes into the soft dirt.

Val picked her way around the broken glass and rocks, her mouth watering as the scent of meat grew stronger and stronger. The culvert was maybe six feet around, large enough for Val to enter without having to duck. The corrugated metal was cold under her bare toes, and each step echoed faintly as she padded inside.

It was dark—much too dark for a regular person to see inside. But Val's eyes adjusted quickly, roving side to side in search of the scent. She descended deeper and deeper, the darkness swallowing her whole. She opened her mouth to inhale, and saliva dripped off her jagged teeth.

At last, deep within the earth, Val found the source.

It was the corpse of an older man, maybe her father's age. His eyes stared sightlessly ahead, body rigid and ice cold. His throat had been slashed, blood staining his front like a grotesque scarf. There was a chunk taken out of the side of his face, leaving the teeth exposed where the cheek had been torn away. His entrails had also been exposed, large chunks of flesh missing from his abdomen.

Val's clawed fingers twitched for a moment. The tiny bit of humanity left in the back of her mind whispered, God, forgive me.

She threw herself onto the corpse, sank her fangs into his mangled throat, and tore.

The sounds of her feasting echoed through the culvert, drowning out every last one of her thoughts. The emptiness that had slowly drained away her humanity over the course of the last week began to dissipate. She slashed and tore at the corpse, cold blood soaking her fingers.

She was so distracted that she didn't notice the sound of footsteps entering the culvert behind her.

Val slowly began to catch her breath, gingerly licking her fingers clean. Her fangs had started to recede back into her gums. She braced herself over the body while everything came back to her. She barely remembered how she'd gotten there.

The faint sound of dirt scraping between boots and metal made her freeze.

Val's heart shot into her throat. She threw herself back from the body, claws skittering on the corrugated metal. A figure loomed a few feet away, shoulders thick and muscled. He was so big he had to hunch to fit inside.

The sound of his breath was wet and heavy. "That's mine."

Val instantly recognized him. Henry Kline, the Aspen Flats High star quarterback. He was white, brown-haired, and built like a brick wall, a good foot and a half taller than Val. She'd stood on the sidelines of football games for years cheering for him with the rest of her squad.

But that was before he was hovering over her, teeth sharpened and clawed hands tensed for attack.

Val's eyes darted to the body. She'd eaten all but the bones of his left arm and a decent part of his throat and shoulder. She hurriedly swiped her arm across her bloodstained mouth, as if that would hide the evidence of what she'd done.

"I'm sorry," Val choked out. "I was just leaving—"

Henry shook his head. He was shivering, eyes so wide they seemed to tremble, the whites flickering like twin ghostly lights in his skull. His fingers curled in and out of fists, claws sinking into his palms.

Val blinked. Was he...scared?

Henry's voice trembled. "You're going to tell everyone I killed that guy."

Val shook her head. "No, Henry, I wouldn't—I won't—"

"You can't leave," Henry said, taking a step closer. "No one can know. No one."

Without another word, he dove at her. Val shrieked, the sound ricocheting off the metal walls. She scrambled out of the way just as Henry landed hard beside the body where she'd been. His face twisted around, teeth bared. He swung his claws at her, missing her face by a millimeter.

Val pulled herself up, but before she could get to her feet, Henry's hand was around her ankle. She screamed as he yanked her back. The ground fell out from under her, and she slammed hard into the metal floor. She bit hard into her tongue, and her teeth rattled in her skull. The taste of blood flooded her mouth.

She clawed at the culvert's ridges, trying to get a hold, but Henry yanked her toward him with too much force. Val managed to wrap her fingers around the neck of a broken bottle. Before she could throw it, though, Henry grabbed the back of her shirt. He grunted, lifted her up, and threw her against the culvert wall with a sharp metallic bang. Red starbursts bloomed across Val's vision, and she gasped, blood sputtering from between her lips. She halted with her back against the culvert wall, head slumped as Henry descended on her.

Before she could even begin to move, his hands were around her throat.

"I'm sorry," Henry said through his teeth, a lock of curly brown hair falling into his fever-bright eyes. "You shouldn't have come here. You shouldn't—"

He didn't get the next word out, because just then, Val stabbed the jagged bottle directly into his stomach.

Hot blood drenched Val's hand, dripping down the bottle as she shoved it deeper into Henry's gut. Henry froze, his hands loosening around Val's throat as he stared down at the bottle, unblinking. Her knuckles were white around the neck as she twisted it free from his gut and a fresh burst of blood rained down on the corrugated metal floor.

Tears streaked Val's face. Her entire body shivered, breath gasping and shaking as she stared at the bottle. A gurgling sound snapped her attention to Henry's face.

He choked on a mouthful of blood before coughing it out, droplets spraying across Val's cheeks. He tensed for a moment before the light left his eyes.

His body slumped sideways, hitting the floor with a bang.

"Shit," Val whispered. Her throat still burned where Henry's hands had wrapped around it. She couldn't stop shaking, the feeling of blood sticky and coppery and everywhere. She covered her mouth with her hand, smearing more of it on her face. "Shit, shit, shit."

She staggered, barely managing to stand. The bodies of two men were at her feet, and she was soaked in their blood. It was beginning to pool, staining her bare toes.

She sprinted away as fast as she could, leaving them in darkness.

Jasmine and Val had been plenty successful in their own right.

"Getting into the party was super easy," Val said once the four of us were all seated in the living room. Celeste and I had switched to sipping waters while the others regaled us with details of their night.

Val added, "We just snuck around the back of the pavilion where we got out this morning—they totally left it unlocked."

"The bartender working tonight's party was different from the one who made the Groupies," Jasmine explained. "But she knew the guy from last night. He was attending the party as a guest, so she introduced us."

"He was pretty drunk," Val giggled, "so we didn't get much out of him. But he said we can talk to him tomorrow at a show he's playing."

"A show?" I raised my eyebrows. "The bartender is in a band?"

Jasmine explained, "It's an unofficial show. He said it's gonna be _underground_."

"The show is tomorrow morning," Val added.

Celeste bit back a laugh. "Who organizes a concert before noon? Who _goes_ to a concert before noon?"

"I got the sense the space was booked out the rest of the day," Jasmine explained. "It seemed like this guy and his friends aren't exactly...professional."

"Ooh, listening to an amateur rock band at 10 a.m.," I said with mock enthusiasm. "Best way to start the day."

"Do you want to find out who drugged Val or not?" Jasmine pointed out.

"She's right," Val said softly. "This could really help us."

I nodded to myself. The vodka that had made me feel so brave and bubbly before was suddenly threatening to reverse course. If I didn't go to bed soon, I was going to be sick.

"Fair enough." I stood up. "I, uh, need to lay down."

Celeste's expression softened. "Go ahead. I'll tell Jaz and Val about the research facility."

I nodded and wished everyone good night and shuffled off to the bathroom to throw up before bed.

By some miracle, my body and brain were so exhausted from the day that I managed to fall asleep minutes after my head hit the pillow.

When I woke up a few hours later, the room was still dark, but Celeste had climbed into bed beside me and fallen asleep with her face buried in the pillow. I winced as a headache throbbed at the front of my skull and a twisting pain radiated low in my belly.

I felt something wet between my legs and audibly groaned.

Voice muffled, Celeste asked, "You okay?"

"I think I got my period," I mumbled. I shoved tangled hair out of my eyes and rolled over, wincing. The inside of my mouth was bone dry, and nausea rocked my stomach. "Hey, you in the market for a uterus? It's all yours if you want it."

"Because you make it sound so appealing," Celeste chuckled. She met my eyes in the low dark and quarter smiled. "I think that's one part of girlhood I'm okay skipping, thanks."

Moaning, I rolled out of bed, grumbling a curse in Celeste's direction before I dragged myself to my bag to rummage through for a tampon. Celeste, meanwhile, rolled back over, seeming to fall back asleep immediately.

Once I found one, I rubbed my bleary eyes and made my way to the bathroom. The hardwood floor was cold on my bare toes as I padded forward, yawning. I gently closed the door behind me as I stepped into the living room, keeping my footsteps as quiet as possible.

To my surprise, there was a light on in the kitchen. It was coming from the fridge door, which was open, illuminating the figure standing in front of it. As I rubbed my eyes into focus, I realized it was Val.

To my surprise, though, she was in her ghoul form. Her teeth were sharpened and claws sunk deep into a piece of SynFlesh. Last night had been the first time I'd actually seen her eat since the Hollowing, so I couldn't help but make a small *oh* sound as she came into view.

Her eyes snapped up to me, and for a brief second, they looked totally blank. There were shadows beneath them, and her face was stained with synthetic blood. As she stared at me, she didn't even blink.

"Val?" I asked. "You, uh. You okay?"

The sound of my voice finally seemed to snap her back into focus. She blinked, squeezing her eyes shut before wincing. She shook her head, lowering the piece of SynFlesh she'd been eating from her mouth.

"Sorry. I didn't think anyone would be awake."

"Uh—don't worry about it. I was just using the bathroom. Carry on."

I shot her one last quick look before heading to the bathroom, locking the door behind me.

When I finished up, I came back into the kitchen only to find that Val was gone, the fridge closed and everything in order. I took a step toward my and Celeste's bedroom, but paused as my gaze caught on something. The lid of the kitchen trash can wasn't closed all the way.

I tiptoed to the trash, pressing down on the lid to try and make it close. Still, it popped right back open. Must have been overflowing.

Weird, I thought. *We've barely been here for two days. What—?*

I answered my own question as I lifted the lid and an empty SynFlesh package fell to the floor. To my surprise, the entire trash can was filled with them. There had to be fifteen empty plastic containers, all licked clean and unceremoniously shoved inside.

My eyes darted back to Val and Jasmine's bedroom door, which Val had closed behind her. My stomach twisted.

Something wasn't right.

The next morning, I awoke to the sound of Celeste's fingers tapping away at her laptop keyboard.

Soft sunlight warmed the walls, the air still holding a bit of its nighttime desert chill. I was wrapped tightly in most of the comforter, face barely peeking out. Craning my neck back, I glanced at the clock on the bedside table—it was just after 7 a.m.

"How are you awake this early?" I grumbled, letting my head fall back against the pillow.

"Hello to you too," Celeste said. I wrinkled my nose and narrowed my eyes at her and she added, "What? I'm a morning person."

"I don't understand how your brain works sometimes." I leaned in closer to the laptop screen. "Whatcha looking at?"

She pointed to a USB drive plugged into the side of the laptop and said, "This is the one I found in the back of that drawer at the research facility. I'm not sure who it belonged to, but there are… profiles." Celeste turned the laptop toward me. "Look at this."

Celeste clicked on the PDF in the folder. Before I could make a quip about whether or not Celeste had, in fact, found secret saucy pics, it opened up. For a moment, I squinted at it, unsure of what I was seeing. Celeste turned the brightness up on the laptop, and slowly it became more visible.

The page was split into two parts: a small section of text and a large photo. The picture showed a humanoid creature pressing itself to the wall of a makeshift cell. Its face was sickly pale, with the black veins of a ghoul, but there was something just a bit more…off about it. For one thing, it looked far too big to be a regular ghoul, as its body looked strangely elongated and bony, the vertebrae in the spine sticking out and the legs bent at a strange angle. Its rib cage was wide and barrel-like, and its face was gaunt, lips chewed to a bloody pulp. It stared directly into the camera, the rings around its irises blindingly red.

Beside it, the text read:

Anthropophagus ***001
Days Since Menthexus Exposure: 72
Status: Alive
Location: Facility B

"I looked up *anthropophagus* this morning," Celeste explained as I continued to gawk at the photo. "It's based on a word that means *human-eater* in Greek."

"Oh my god," I breathed. "That—that's what we saw last night."

Celeste nodded. "Or it's something similar, at least. Look at the hair—this one is different."

I squinted. She was right—the creature last night had long hair. This one had close-cropped black hair and an aquiline nose.

"There are two of them?" I breathed.

"More than that." Celeste scrolled down the PDF, revealing six more pages, each with a photo of a similar creature. Celeste explained, "There's seven, at least, with pictures saved here. And look closer at this one."

Celeste paused on one page featuring a slightly more human-looking creature, this one with long brown hair and a band T-shirt on. She had the teeth and claws of a ghoul, but was bonier, with slightly longer limbs. Instantly, I recognized her. While she had looked much worse last night, it was definitely the same person.

The text beneath her picture read:

> Anthropophagus ***006
> Days Since Menthexus Exposure: 4
> Status: Escaped (see log 801 for incident
> report)
> Location: Unknown

"I checked to see the last time this file was updated, and it was right before the fire burned down the facility we visited," Celeste explained. "Which was around a year ago."

I gaped at her. "If who we saw last night was the same person in this photo, then she's been out in the desert for almost a year?

How could someone survive that? Not to mention avoiding being spotted."

"Think about it, Z." Celeste opened a new tab on her browser and pulled up a map of De Luz Valley and the surrounding area. She moved her finger in a circle around it and added, "The closest town is almost fifty miles away, and there's barely any reason to drive out here. It seems like she'd have a pretty easy time staying hidden."

"That doesn't explain how she didn't starve to death," I pointed out.

Celeste nodded to herself. "Right. And animal meat would just make her sick, so…"

Celeste stopped when she saw me freeze. She raised her eyebrows.

"That bone we found," I breathed, eyes wide. "On the first day. It had ghoul bile on it, right? What if that was something an anthropophagus killed out of desperation and left bile on because it made them sick?"

"But that would mean…" Celeste straightened up. "Desert Bloom would be the biggest gathering of humans in this area since the Hollowing. That's basically a buffet for the anthropophagi."

"And if Menthexus is what made her into that…" I gulped. "Then the creature we saw last night might not be the only one."

Celeste chewed her lower lip. "But Val doesn't look like that, and if we're right about what the weird substance at the bar was, she's been exposed to Menthexus twice. So maybe we're missing something."

I paused, throat tightening. Thoughts of last night in the kitchen all came back to me at once—specifically, the blank look in Val's eyes as she stared at me over her fistful of SynFlesh. I couldn't help but think of how similar the expression had looked to the one the creature—the anthropophagus—had worn as it stood in the middle of the road outside the research facility.

Celeste tilted her head softly to the side. "You okay?"

I pulled myself up, gesturing to the kitchen. "I need to show you something."

Celeste raised her eyebrows but didn't say anything. The two of us slid out of bed, and Celeste followed me out into the kitchen, pulling a silk robe around herself as she did. It didn't look like anyone was up yet, the only evidence that anyone had recently used the kitchen being our empty lemonade glasses in the sink.

"I don't want to jump to conclusions," I said, going to the trash can. I gestured to it as I stepped on the pedal to open the top and added, "But this is—"

I cut off as I glanced down only to find the trash was empty.

I blinked. "Wait, there was—"

At that moment, the door to Jasmine and Val's bedroom opened. I hopped back from the trash only to whip my head around and find Jasmine in the doorway, still wearing the silk bonnet she usually slept in. She had her phone in hand and ground her teeth, jaw clenched.

"Oh—hey. Morning, Jasmine," Celeste said, smiling sunnily and waving.

"You all right?" I asked.

Jasmine shook her head, wrapping her arms around herself.

"Val's missing."

thirteen

The night I got home from the facility for young Hollow people started out on a quiet note.

My father was the one to pick me up. Once he was done signing the paperwork, we loaded into his Toyota without saying a word. I buckled into the passenger seat while he fiddled with the radio. He wrinkled his forehead as he twisted the knob left and right until he finally found NPR.

"They had an interesting interview with a Hollow person on here the other day," he said as he backed out of the parking spot. "She's a speechwriter for the president. Said that SynFlesh has really changed the game for her. She's able to sleep in the same bed as her human husband again and everything."

"Oh." I swallowed thickly, staring at my sneakers. "That's, um, cool."

That was the last conversation we exchanged the rest of the car ride to Aspen Flats. I leaned my head against the window, watching the desert pass by, the mountains nothing but shadows in the distance. It was the most I'd seen of the outside world in weeks.

When we pulled up to the house, all of the lights were on. My parents and I lived in a fairly sizable farmhouse, with two floors and enough

*space that both of my parents had their own offices, plus a guest room.
When Dad and I stepped over the threshold, the dining room table was
set with one plate and one set of silverware.*

*Mom bolted up from the living room couch at the sound of the door
opening. She was a bird-boned woman, slight and somewhat gaunt
with blond hair and blue eyes. She smiled at me, but it didn't crease her
crow's feet.*

*"Mom!" I shouted. I grinned and ran toward her, holding my arms
out. "I missed you so—"*

Before I could reach her, though, she sidestepped, face pale.

My words died in my throat.

*"W-Welcome home, Zoey," she said, wrapping her arms around
herself. She folded and refolded her hands in front of her. "You're
looking...well."*

*I sputtered a laugh. "Uh, thanks? I mean, I haven't really seen the
sun in three months, but I haven't turned into a cave fish quite yet."*

*She didn't laugh. Instead, she cleared her throat and said, "Are you,
ah, hungry, dear?"*

*"Oh." I crossed my arms, rubbing the upper part of one with my open
palm. "Uh—sure. I could eat."*

*My parents exchanged a look. Mom's eyes were rounded and
huge, while Dad just squared his shoulders. I wondered how many
conversations they'd had about this moment since they found out I'd
become a ghoul.*

*I swallowed thickly. "You two don't need to stay here to keep me
company while I eat. I know it's, um, sort of uncomfortable. I can
handle it myself."*

"Are you sur—?" Dad started to ask.

Mom cut him off. "Great! Well, there's plenty of SynFlesh in the fridge. It's all in the drawer on the left. Help yourself. I'm actually going to run to the store and get more."

"Kathleen—" Dad started to say.

But she didn't respond. She just grabbed the keys to her BMW that sat on the side table in the entryway. Without another word, she slipped out the front door, all but slamming it behind her.

Dad cleared his throat. "Well, you go ahead and help yourself, kid. I've actually got a project I've been working on in the garage, so you just shout if you need anything, okay?"

"Dad, come on." I felt my shoulders sink as he refused to meet my gaze. "You know I'm not going to hurt you, right? I'm still your daughter."

"Of course, Zoey." He cracked his neck, hooking a thumb toward the fridge. "Anyway, I'll leave you to it. Go ahead and drop your bags off in your room when you get a chance—we haven't moved anything. Since your other phone was, ah, damaged while you were at Camp Everwood, I bought you a new one. It's plugged in and charging on your nightstand."

He left before I could get another word out.

For a moment, I just stood there in the living room. The house still smelled the same—like lavender-vanilla candles and the faint scent of my dad's cologne. And my parents—nothing about them had changed on the surface. It was exactly the same as it had been back in May when I left for camp.

So why did I feel like a total stranger?

It's just the readjustment period. *I reminded myself, hanging my head and heading for my bedroom to drop off my suitcase.* They'll come around.

I found my bedroom door ajar. I shoved it the rest of the way open with my shoulder. As I did, something heavy clacked against the door.

I wrinkled my brow, glancing up at where the sound was coming from. It was a chain lock.

Affixed to the outside of the door.

I froze. Gently, I lifted the chain, feeling its weight against my palm. It was thick—sturdy enough that it would be almost impossible to break without some kind of tool.

Numbly, I let the chain slip through my fingers, where it clacked against the door a few times before coming to a stop. My entire body felt cold as I stepped inside, dropping my bag on the floor.

I sat down on my bed, picking up the phone. It still had all the factory settings in place, the contact list empty. As I stared into the bright light of the screen, I felt something wet on my cheek.

It took me a moment to realize I'd started to cry.

Sniffling, I typed in one of the only phone numbers I knew by heart.

After two rings, Celeste picked up. "Hello?"

"Hi." My voice cracked as I said it. "I, um, I'm home. Do you think… maybe you and Wendy could come pick me up?"

"Zoey? Oh my god!" Celeste's voice moved away from the receiver as she shouted, "Mom, it's Zoey! She's finally home!" Back into the phone, she added, "Literally of course, we'll be there in a few minutes. Holy shit, dude, I've missed you so much."

I hiccuped on a sob. "I've missed you too. God, I've missed you."

Even if I'd become a stranger in my parents' house, Celeste's voice felt like home.

After tearing through the cabin for a few minutes in search of Val, we all came to the same conclusion: she was gone, and she hadn't told any of us where she was going.

"I texted her four times already," Jasmine said under her breath as she thumbed through her phone. "It says they've been delivered but she hasn't responded."

"Hold on," Celeste said, pulling out her own phone. "Val shared her location with me a few weeks ago when I was trying to find her at graduation—she might not have stopped."

Jasmine and I quickly huddled together on either side of Celeste as she pulled up her text thread with Val. She clicked to the location sharing tab and, lo and behold, a little blue dot appeared on the map of the surrounding area.

Celeste pointed. "There. She's not too far—looks like the other side of the valley where more cabins are."

"The hell is she doing there?" Jasmine muttered.

The color drained from my face as I remembered last night with the packages of SynFlesh. If the Menthexus had made her hungry enough to eat all that, was it possible things had gotten even worse? An image of the creature from last night with Val's wavy hair bloomed in my mind's eye. If my and Celeste's theory was correct, that meant that any human in the area was in danger.

"We need to go," I said, frantically looking between Jasmine and Celeste. "*Now*."

Jasmine raised an eyebrow. "Zo, she might just be going for a walk—"

I shook my head. "Listen, I'll explain on the way. Just get some shoes on and meet me out front."

Luckily, Jasmine and Celeste didn't bother arguing with me. Within minutes we headed out the door, frantically following the path Celeste's phone drew out for us. The night chill still clung to the morning air, and the sky was dotted with cottony clouds for the first time since we'd arrived. I wrapped my arms around myself, goosebumps speckling my arms and legs.

As we walked, I told Jasmine and Celeste about what I'd seen last night in the kitchen, concluding, "What if it's getting worse? What if the Menthexus made it so she can't control her hunger and—"

"Uh, Zoey?" Celeste cut in as we rounded the corner to the last row of cabins at the edge of the festival grounds. "I think we found her."

My heart skipped a beat as my mind conjured images of torn flesh, a pool of blood—

But definitely not what I actually saw, which was Val curled up on a lounge chair in Eli McKinley's arms.

"The hell?" Jasmine breathed.

The two of them were on the back porch of the nearest cabin, Val with her head on Eli's chest and Eli rubbing her back. A striped blanket was draped over them, dragging on the hardwood deck. They were both gazing at the fading ripples of pink in the sky, the last remnants of sunrise left in the brightening morning. Val's eyes fluttered open and closed like she was fighting not to fall asleep, half her face hidden by the blanket.

Eli looked up, then, and his gaze fell on us. His small smile evaporated.

"Babe, what's—?"

Val opened her eyes. At the sight of us, her mouth pulled into a tight frown. She mouthed something that looked like a curse.

Jasmine, Celeste, and I exchanged a look. Celeste offered, "Morning?"

"Did you invite them?" Eli asked.

"No," Val said pointedly, eyebrows furrowing. She sat up, the blanket sliding off her and pooling on the chair. She had a cute white eyelet dress on and wore her hair in a fishtail braid. "What are you doing here?"

"You were missing," I managed, cheeks flaring pink.

Celeste added, "We were worried something might have happened."

"I've been texting you for an hour." Jasmine put her hands on her hips as she narrowed her eyes. "I mean, damn, at least leave a note. How were we supposed to know you were okay if you just vanished without a trace?"

Val pushed her mane of shiny brown hair out of her eyes and frowning tightly. "What are you, my mom? I was going to come back."

"Yo, come on, it's okay," Eli said, holding up his hands. He disentangled himself from Val, and added, "I get it—females worry about this kinda thing. Why don't we all sit down and I can make everyone some coffee? Simmer down a little now that we know everything's cool."

It was good Celeste was there to respond, because I was actively withholding a gag. *If you're going to be a misogynist, at least call us girls so it sounds less like we're a group of animals you spotted on a fucking safari.*

Celeste said, "Um—sure. Coffee sounds nice."

Val opened her mouth like she was going to say something, but after a moment, she just exhaled a breath through her nose and nodded.

"Sure. Coffee it is."

fourteen

HollowLife Employee Chat Transcript, 6/24

Patricia Hannigan: *Girl, you're not going to believe this shit.*

Ginger Poleski: *Let me guess, Rupert making an ass of himself again?*

Patricia Hannigan: *YES!! He FORGOT our ANNIVERSARY >:((((*

Ginger Poleski: *OMG.*

Ginger Poleski: *Are you serious? Patty, oh my god. Dump him!!*

Patricia Hannigan: *I KNEW he was going to forget. He doesn't care about anything but his job. And here I am barely even checking on my ghouls because I'm trying to make him this goddamn casserole I found on one of those great mommy blogs I told you about, and he doesn't give a rat's ass!*

Ginger Poleski: *Ugh, I'm sorry Patty. Your ghouls are all at Desert Bloom, right? Hillary from Precinct 10 in Los Angeles has six at Desert Bloom, and she says they've been all over the place. Three of them went off the grid for almost twelve hours two days ago.*

Patricia Hannigan: *Wait, seriously? Mine went off the grid too. Said they were watching the sunrise.*

Ginger Poleski: *Really?? Yeah, Hillary mentioned another rep for a town in Nevada said hers missed two SynFlesh check-ins in a row. Do you think we should flag for concern?*

Patricia Hannigan: *Hmmm, maybe. Let's start another chat with the other reps with Desert Bloom ghouls and see what they have to say.*

Ginger Poleski: *Good call. Although, I know Marianne from Dana Point has one and she's SO annoying. Remember when she kept sending pictures of her crusty little poodle to the chat RIGHT after Lily sent the pictures of her new baby? SO rude.*

Patricia Hannigan: *OMG, I totally forgot about that. Everyone but Marianne, then.*

Ginger Poleski: *On it.*

Ginger Poleski: *God, I hope this isn't something big. The last thing I want to do is fill out the paperwork for a feral murder. It takes FOREVER.*

Patricia Hannigan: *Preach, sister.*

END CHAT

"For the record," Val grumbled into her mug, "I'm *fine*."

I pressed my lips into a thin line. Val, Jasmine, Celeste and I sat at a table on No Flash Photography's back deck while Eli was inside brewing us a second pot of coffee. Raj and Cole were both still asleep, and the five of us had quickly polished off the first pot that Eli had brought out. He'd jumped at the chance to stop making awkward small talk with us and brew another.

"You're cuddling with the bandmate of a boy we ate less than forty-eight hours ago," I pointed out. "That doesn't strike me as *fine*."

Val elected to ignore that statement. "If you're jealous, just say so."

My face flared red. "The *hell* is that supposed to—?"

Luckily, Celeste cut in before I could fly off the handle. "I think what Zoey is trying to say is that this whole situation has brought up a lot of stuff from the past so we're all a little more…on edge than usual. And we just want to make sure that you're okay since we've all been where you are."

For a flashing second, Val's face softened, but she cast her gaze out toward the desert as she bit her lip. "I really don't want to talk about this right now, all right? Can't we just enjoy some coffee and not worry about it for half an hour?"

Jasmine all but laughed in her face. "Val, baby, it isn't like you dented someone's bumper. If Eli and the other No Flash Photography guys find out that Kaiden isn't just off messing around with some girl, you're going to be one of the first people they wonder about."

Val grimaced. She gripped her coffee tightly, staring inside— she'd barely had more than a few sips of it. For a moment, I thought I saw the shine of tears in her eyes.

But then, she heaved a sigh and squared her shoulders. "Can we please just drop this?"

Celeste and I exchanged a look. Jasmine, meanwhile, went uncharacteristically silent.

Val's face fell at the sight of Jasmine's reaction, but she didn't say anything.

"Look, there's something you don't know," I said, keeping my voice hushed, just in case Eli returned sooner than expected. I leaned across the glass table toward Val and added, "Celeste and I found a

USB drive at the research facility last night, and this morning we found evidence on it that ghouls exposed to Menthexus—the drug that probably made you go feral—turn into something way, way worse. And now that you've been exposed twice, I just think—"

The back door to the cabin slid open and Eli came out holding a pot of coffee in his hand. My mouth snapped closed, biting off the last of what I'd been saying.

"Coffee's ready," Eli said. "Brought some company too."

Raj and Cole followed him outside, Cole yawning and stretching. Raj was dressed in monochrome streetwear that was probably more expensive than anything I owned, while Cole still had on plaid pajama pants with a hoodie thrown over top. The side of Cole's red hair stuck up where he must have slept on it.

Despite myself, my cheeks warmed faintly.

"This is a nice surprise," Cole said, plopping down in the seat next to me. He flashed me a toothy grin. "Hope the coffee's not too gross. Eli always manages to screw it up somehow."

"It's from a machine, how could I mess it up?" Eli shot back.

"By making it so strong it's undrinkable," Raj chuckled, pointing to the pot in Eli's hand. "Looks like sludge, mate."

"I actually prefer my coffee strong," Val chimed in, all smiles once again. It was like the last conversation hadn't even happened—really, like nothing had happened at all. I felt my skin grow cold as she giggled and added, "I'm sure it's great, babe—don't listen to him."

Under the table, I pulled my phone out and texted Celeste, Are we in the fucking Twilight Zone right now?

Her phone buzzed, and when she glanced at the screen, she caught my eye for just a moment and shrugged.

Eli passed the coffee around. Raj asked us if we'd like to have some breakfast with them, to which I coolly lied that we'd already eaten but appreciated the offer. Celeste caught my eye more than once, and I got the feeling she was thinking the same thing as me:

Even with Kaiden's body deep in that mine shaft, we were on thin ice.

"You know, we should probably get going," I said after a few more minutes of Val and the boys making small talk. "We're going to a show this morning and we should probably get ready for that."

"A show?" Cole asked, face brightening. I couldn't help but notice how large his green eyes were. He had a somewhat impish face, with a slightly upturned nose and a sharp chin. "In the morning? I thought today's lineup didn't start until after noon."

"I wouldn't exactly call it part of the lineup," Jasmine snickered.

"It's a friend of ours," Celeste lied, keeping her smile pleasant and casual. *God she's good at that.* "Just a little underground thing. We were going to meet up with him after and chat. It's really not a big thing."

Obviously, she was leaving out the part that we were trying to interview him to find out if he'd seen who slipped Menthexus into the lava salt rim mix at the party the other night, but even just mentioning it casually felt like it could be saying too much.

"New talent, huh?" Eli pushed his chair back so he could kick his feet up and put them on the table. He was barefoot, and I withheld a gag as his pinky toe got dangerously close to touching the rim of Val's coffee mug. "Might be kinda fun."

"Uh." *How do I put this lightly without straight up telling them not to come?* "That wasn't—er, you probably don't want to go. These guys aren't exactly professionals."

"So? We've got nothing better to do." Eli glanced at Cole and Raj. "What do you guys think?"

"Shouldn't someone stay here in case Kaiden gets back?" Cole asked.

Immediately, Val, Celeste, Jasmine, and I tensed.

Eli, however, just waved his hand. "You guys know Kaiden. He'll get back when he gets back. He does this all the time at home when he gets with a girl. Remember that time he didn't text us for two weeks when he was with Monique?"

Cole muttered something under this breath, rolling his eyes. "I guess. It just feels a little weird with all the rumors going around."

"Rumors?" I started to ask. "What do you m—?"

Val cleared her throat, turning everyone's attention to her. "You guys should come! It'll be fun."

I set my wide-eyed gaze on her, raising my eyebrows.

Val's smile didn't crack.

Raj shrugged. "Sure. Why not?"

"That's the spirit." Eli pointed at Cole. "You in?"

He bit his lip briefly. For a second, his eyes darted to me before quickly shifting away. "I…sure."

"Great." Eli beamed. He tightened his grip on Val's shoulders. "Looking forward to it."

Before I came to Desert Bloom, I'd looked up the venue in detail—yet another of my attempts to quell my own nervousness by learning as much as I could about it. Specifically, I was interested in knowing how the organizers intended to keep thousands of attendees alive in the middle of the desert since there were no towns within a fifty-mile radius. It turned out that the venue had started out as a retreat center for the sort of spiritual weirdos who went to the desert to do nude yoga and avoid soap as much as possible. The cabins had been built for attendees, along with a number of large yurt-like structures for additional housing and group events.

The "show" the bartender's band the Waterheads—was playing wound up being in one of the yurts. It was an octagonal structure, and they were able to roll up the walls so the morning air blew through. It was sort of like the hippy version of a basement concert, which would have been cool if the band in question didn't suck monumental amounts of ass.

"Do you think anyone else is coming?" Celeste asked, leaning in close to my ear. Thus far, the only people in the yurt were my friends, No Flash Photography, and two other girls who appeared to be the band members' partners. They were seated behind a flimsy-looking merch table where they'd set up a game of checkers that seemed to be taking up most of their focus. Which meant it was just the seven of us staring up at the three white boys that made up the Waterheads.

"I'd like to dedicate this next one to Celeste Seasons here in the front," said the bartender from the party, who it turned out not only sang but also played one of music's more underrated instruments: the humble kazoo. He pointed at Celeste in the front row, who turned pink at the sound of her username. "You taught my little sister how to do her eyebrows, and she's gonna lose her shit when she finds out you came to our show!"

Celeste gave a faltering smile. "You're, um, welcome?"

The bartender—Tony, Jasmine had reminded me of his name—then leaned into the microphone and started to whisper lyrics, almost like a misguided attempt at ASMR, while the guys behind him jammed on the drums and guitar respectively.

Jasmine full-body shivered, then rolled some pieces of a tissue between her fingers before stuffing them in her ears. Behind her, Raj and Cole stood staring at the stage with horror in their eyes.

Val smiled. "I dunno, I think it's nice to see a little bit of the underground scene."

"Frankly, this should have stayed underground. Like, maybe six feet under," I said, mostly to Cole, who'd snuck a pleading glance at me. He stifled a laugh and bumped his shoulder against mine. My skin warmed and prickled faintly where he'd touched me.

On stage, Tony blew his kazoo in a long note and concluded, "All right, we've got one more for you folks before we need to get ready for our side hustles! I call this one 'Pink-Haired Girl.'"

"Is he making this up on the spot?" I whispered.

"My therapist will be hearing about it regardless," Celeste said through her teeth.

The Waterheads launched into a more traditional folk number, and they were almost in sync enough for it to be palatable. Partway through, Val, who was dancing like it was the best song she'd ever heard, said, "I like this! They're kinda like The Mountain Goats!"

Cole's forehead wrinkled. "If by that you mean this sounds like the best approximation of what literal goats playing music would sound like, then yes."

But Val just laughed. She and Eli swayed together, Eli holding Val from behind and gently kissing the top of her head. For what it was worth, Val looked…genuinely happy.

I hated to admit it, but it left a horrible, sour taste in my mouth.

The Waterheads finished their set a few minutes later, Tony winking at Celeste as he blew one more note on the kazoo. The other band members bowed, and Val and Eli burst into applause. Everyone else hesitantly clapped in response, trying not to wince.

"We'll be doing a meet and greet behind the yurt if anyone would like anything signed!" Tony called, pointing to a folding table set up in the corner with a few CDs atop it. The girls playing checkers didn't even look up from their game as he spoke. "Our EP is available for sale! Thanks for coming!"

"I think that's our cue," Celeste said, nodding toward the exit. "Should we head back?"

"You don't want to get an EP?" I asked with mock sincerity. "I mean, he wrote a whole song about you *just now*."

Celeste spoke through her teeth as she faked a smile. "I'd rather let a raccoon chew off my toes."

"This shouldn't take too long," Val promised Eli. "I'll text you when we're finished?"

"Totally," Eli said. He leaned down and kissed Val's cheek. "Don't take too long."

It was all Celeste, Jasmine, and I could do not to roll our eyes.

Ten minutes later, the bartender, Tony, finally joined us behind the yurt. There was an awning in the back with a small seating area—enough for us to sit at a table, the four of us on one side and Tony on the other so it almost looked like he was walking into a job interview.

He sat down just as Celeste was pulling her hair into a bun, fanning the back of her neck. The heat was already climbing—the forecast had projected it was going to be in the low nineties by noon. I dabbed at my forehead with the back of my hand while Val flapped the front of her dress to fan off her torso.

"Should have met somewhere with AC, I guess," Tony said. He steepled his fingers. He wore a dress shirt with a formal vest, which he had largely sweated through, leaving long streaks down the sides of his torso and on his back.

Jasmine pointedly sucked ice water from the straw valve on her water bottle, shooting him a sideways look.

"Thanks for talking to us again, Tony," Val said, grinning so the apples of her cheeks stood out. "I really liked your performance."

"Yeah? Well, I meant what I said." His gaze locked on Celeste. "My sister is going to *freak* when she finds out I performed for *the* Celeste Seasons. We watch your videos together sometimes."

"Oh," Celeste managed a weak smile. "That's—that's great. I'm glad you enjoy them. Do you, um, do makeup?"

"Nah. I just like to appreciate a pretty girl sometimes." He winked.

Celeste kept smiling, but I could practically hear the sound of screaming behind her eyes.

"Anyway," Jasmine cut in, not even attempting to fake a pleasant tone. She was all business. She pulled out her phone and opened a picture of the drink menu from the other night, zooming in on the ingredients list for the Groupies. "What do you know about this drink? Specifically, the lava salt. Anything...odd mixed in?"

Suddenly, the relaxed look on Tony's face faded. A new bead of sweat trickled down his temple, and he swallowed, his Adam's apple bobbing. His eyes darted around as he cleared his throat, refusing to meet any of our eyes.

"Oh—it's, ah. It's just black salt. Nothing special about it."

"Any reason it would smell minty?" I pressed.

"Minty?" Tony blinked, forehead wrinkling. "Uh—no, not really. Listen, I really don't get why this is important. I mean, it's not like I saw anyone—" He cut off. "No, that came out wrong. Um—"

Beside me, Celeste rose up just enough to lean across the table, getting much closer to him. Tony's face pinkened while Celeste's gaze bore into him, her eyebrows bent upward and her lips tight.

"It sounds like you saw something, Tony."

His skin grew even redder, sweat stains spreading wide across his shirt. He pulled on his collar and opened his mouth to speak, only to let out a squeak.

"Tony," I added, a little softer. "Please, we really need to know. People might have gotten sick because of it, and we just need to know why."

"Look—it's not like I meant for anything to happen!" Tony burst. He raked his hand back through his hair, lower lip quivering. "Listen, working at a festival like this is hard! You're constantly trying to balance partying and working, and sometimes you think you're microdosing mushrooms and then it turns out to be a macrodose and then you're hallucinating on the job and—"

"Whoa, whoa, slow down." Jasmine held up her hands. "You were on shrooms at the party?"

Tony rubbed his sweaty face. "Yeah, okay? I didn't mean to get that high, but I was really freaking out. So when I walked up to the bar to set up for the event, I just assumed the person rummaging around was another employee or something. I asked if they were new, and they booked it. Normally, I would have reported something like that, but I was so fucked up I could barely make a drink, much less face my boss and submit an incident report—"

"Do you remember anything about what they looked like?" Celeste cut in, gaze sharp.

Tony shook his head, folding and unfolding his hands. "Not really—the drugs made their face all…bright and wiggly? All I know is that they were wearing a really big, baggy hoodie with a band logo on it. Girlfool? I think that was the name? The logo was cool—it was like a bunch of thorns growing out of a brain. I couldn't stop staring at it."

"Oh," Celeste said, eyes widening. "Was the hoodie pink tie-dye?"

The four of us all snapped to look at her as Tony said, "Oh—yeah, exactly. It was."

"Girlfool is one of my favorite bands," Celeste explained, twisting her hair around her fingers. "And they had exclusive merch for people who got VIP tickets to their last LA show. I tried to get tickets, but they were super expensive and sold out immediately."

"They're playing a show tonight, right?" I asked.

"Yeah—they are. At the main stage, I think." Under her breath, Celeste muttered, "God what I'd pay to see them close up."

"Are you going to tell my boss?" Tony asked, finally managing to look at us. "Because I seriously can't lose this job. If people find out someone might have gotten sick because of a drink I served them, I'm totally screwed."

"You'd deserve it if we did," Jasmine muttered.

"We're not going to say anything," I quickly cut in, shooting

Jasmine a look out of the corner of my eye. "You sure you don't know anything else about the person you saw? Maybe their hair color or something like that?"

Tony shook his head. "Sorry, that's all I've got. I mean, maybe you could go to the Girlfool concert and look for them. Makes sense that they'd wear that hoodie to the show if they're such a huge fan."

"Not sure how easy it is to pick people out in a crowd like that," Jasmine muttered, peering at her nails over the tops of her cat-eye sunglasses. "Kind of a needle in a haystack situation."

"Unless they're in the VIP section like at the LA show," I pointed out. "That would narrow it down a lot."

"That's great, but how would we get into the VIP section?" Jasmine asked.

"I hear the main stage VIP section allows plus-ones, for what it's worth." Tony suggested. Trying to smooth his ruffled hair back down, he told Celeste, "I'm surprised you don't get free access to that sort of thing. I'd let you in if I was in charge."

"You know what? This has been great, but we should probably get going," I said, standing up. Celeste practically sighed with relief next to me. "Great meeting you, Tony. Give the rest of the Waterheads our regards."

"Oh, ah—anytime. Thanks for not telling anyone about this," Tony said as the rest of us got up and started collecting our things. Tony leaned forward on his elbow as he gazed at Celeste. "Any chance you might mention the band when you make your Desert Bloom wrap-up video? We could really use the promo."

Celeste gave an awkward arm swing. "We'll see?"

He nodded. "Cool."

I grabbed her hand, waving to Tony, and saying, "'Kaythanksagainbye."

The four of us made our exit before he could add anything else.

fifteen

*I*n November, nearly five months after the Hollowing, Jasmine attended the first Aspen Flats High rager of the season.

Aspen Flats parties typically either amounted to tearing up someone's house while their parents were gone, or meeting in the abandoned warehouse at the edge of town. This particular party was in the warehouse, a dilapidated old building with holes in the roof, echoey prison-like walls, and a wide-open floor space that was perfect for setting up lights and turning into a makeshift dance floor.

The lights and music were already blaring by the time Jasmine arrived with all of the other softball girls. She had a bat in one hand that she tossed and caught as she walked—she'd promised some of the freshmen they could use it to smash old beer bottles out back, the kind of thrilling activity that small-town kids thrived on. Now that she was captain of the team, it was up to her to make sure everyone got along at least enough to work together, and bringing everyone to a party like this seemed like the perfect way to bond.

The warehouse was packed when the team arrived. Hyperpop remixes of popular songs blasted from a set of speakers someone had set up atop a mile of old scrap metal while lights flashed from where they hung from heavy metal hooks affixed to the ceiling. People from school, plus some from neighboring towns, crowded the dance floor, grinding to the music. Others had retreated to darker corners to make out, while still others hung around the coolers full of ice, sipping White Claws and Twisted Teas.

"Hey Jaz," the shortstop, a Black nonbinary person named River said, throwing an arm around her shoulder. "You wanna do some shots with the newbies?"

Jasmine shook her head. "I shouldn't. Don't want to set a bad example."

The catcher, a butch white girl named Gia, scoffed. "You gotta unclench one of these days, dude. Plus, think about it: the freshmen have never been to a party like this. Who better to help guide them through their first foray into high school parties than Captain Owusu herself?"

Jasmine bit her lip, rubbing the back of her neck. River and Gia had a point—maybe she did need to unwind a little bit. Lord knew she hadn't done that since...

She stiffened. The faces of the couple she'd killed to defend Isaiah burned in the forefront of her mind, two sets of blue eyes staring at her in terror as she sliced into their necks.

Jasmine steadied herself, trying to swallow the images down. "What the hell? Sure—get me something good."

It wasn't long before River was shoving a can into Jasmine's hand. And then another. And another. Before long, the ledge that Jasmine was leaning against was filled with empty cans, and the world around her had started to feel like a watercolor painting, blurred and colorful and soft around the edges.

She hadn't had a drop to drink since the Hollowing. At one point, she'd Googled whether or not ghouls could get drunk, and immediately every article warned that it was a bad idea to mix cravings for human *flesh with a substance that impaired judgment—which was to say, ghouls could definitely get drunk.*

A fact that Jasmine was now distinctly aware of.

"Whoa, Jaz," Gia said, lifting the beer she was drinking and using it to point across the warehouse. "Look. Is that Valeria Vega with Zoey Huxley and—?"

Jasmine winced as Gia finished that statement with Celeste Fairbanks's deadname. Jasmine smacked her shoulder, and Gia shot her a wounded look.

"At least have the decency to call her by her name," Jasmine snapped. She looked back across the floor, narrowing her eyes. *She's been so distracted by Gia's fumble that she hadn't actually taken the time to notice what she'd been pointing out.* "Jesus."

Indeed, there stood former head cheerleader Valeria Vega in all of her glory, hanging with none other than two of the most elusive art geeks at Aspen Flats High. They looked comically mismatched—Zoey in her all-black Hot Topic digs, Celeste in a plain crop top and jeans, and Valeria in high heels and a sparkling silver dress with a tear-shaped cutout over her collarbone. Valeria and Celeste seemed to be talking while Zoey glared at the dance floor, presumably thinking about weepy poetry or necromancy or whatever the hell it was girls who only wore black and combat boots were interested in.

"Since when are they friends?" the left outfielder, a white girl named Kara, asked.

"Since Valeria's friends dumped her for being a ghoul," River said. They pointed to a group of the cheer girls on the other side of the room. "Those girls. They basically iced her out of the squad by making a big show of acting scared every time she touched them."

Jasmine crossed her arms over her chest. Her team still didn't know she was also a ghoul—she'd been playing off her absence from their lunch period by lying she got one-on-one tutoring then. While she didn't think they'd act like that, she doubted the reception would be warm.

It certainly hadn't been for any of the other ghouls.

"Hold up," Gia said. "Is that Sydney dancing with Quentin?"

Jasmine followed Gia's pointed finger to the dance floor. Sydney, one of the freshman newbies, slowly backed away as a senior named Quentin reached out to put a hand on her.

"Oh, hell no," Jasmine said. She passed her Twisted Tea and bat to Kara. "Hold these. I'll be right back."

Jasmine shoved her way through the crowd. Sydney was a petite, Latina freshman girl with a dark pixie cut and rounded cheeks. Quentin was a senior, towering over her as he rubbed a hand up and down her arm. Sydney bit her lip, trying to step back, but he followed her.

"Hey," Jasmine snapped as she closed the space between herself and the pair of them. "Syd, the girls were just asking if you wanted to head outside and get some air."

"Ah, come on." Quentin met Jasmine's eyes, flashing her a sideways smile. "We're a little busy."

Quentin had an air about him that said he didn't care what anyone said—he hadn't been told no once in his life, and he wasn't about to hear it now. Something about his face and demeanor felt familiar, and it took a moment for Jasmine to recognize it.

Just like before, the skinhead guy she'd killed back in LA appeared in her mind's eye. His face burned so brightly it seemed to superimpose itself over Quentin's, the memory of the blood dripping down his throat coming back so strong Jasmine could nearly smell it. Her body went totally rigid as she thought of Isaiah's tear-filled eyes staring through her as the skinhead threatened to kill him.

"*Did you hear me?*" *Quentin asked. He grabbed Sydney's shoulder, squeezing it. She winced as he added, "We're busy."*

Jasmine's heartbeat started to race. There was Isaiah's face again as that man had swung his gun toward him. He'd smiled just like Quentin did now, no joy in it—it was more like when a feral dog pulled its lips back and bared its teeth. The ground under her felt like it was about to open up.

Jasmine lashed out with a clawed hand.

She stopped inches from his face. Her claws reflected the dance floor lights, shining where they hung within gouging distance of Quentin's eyes. He stood rigid, all signs of mirth gone from his expression.

Jasmine gasped for breath, her shoulders shaking. She felt eyes on her and glanced around to find that people had stopped to look, jaws agape. On the other side of the dance floor, Jasmine caught Valeria with a hand over her mouth while Celeste and Zoey just stared, wide-eyed.

Slowly, Jasmine pulled back. In the pause, Sydney slipped out of Quentin's grip and rushed from the floor. At the same time, Quentin's eyes bore into Jasmine's, a bead of sweat trickling from his forehead down the side of his jawbone.

Jasmine withdrew her hand, claws sinking back into her fingers. Her stomach churned as the red at the corners of her vision faded. She took a step back, head turning left and right to meet the eyes of everyone staring.

Without a word, she spun, shoving her way back toward the softball team. No one took their eyes off her as she went to Kara, grabbed her Twisted Tea and baseball bat from her hands, and made a beeline to the exit. She shoved her way through, bursting out into the cool night air.

There was no one outside. Heart still racing, Jasmine skirted the edge of the warehouse to the firepit behind the property. Luckily, no one was sitting at it when she arrived. The circle of charred stones sat cold, surrounded by rotting old patio furniture that may or may not have been stable enough to sit in. Jasmine decided to take her chances with one of the chairs, collapsing down into it. She kicked a few loose beer bottles and cans away, then leaned forward, hands wrapped around the grip of the bat. She pressed the end of it into her forehead, the back of her throat tight and tears threatening at the corners of her eyes.

Leave it to her to screw herself over the second she even marginally unclenched.

A sob rattled her chest. Tears slid down her cheeks into the dirt. She was so distracted she didn't notice the sound of footsteps approaching behind her.

"Jasmine?" a soft voice asked.

She straightened up, looking over her shoulder. Standing there was Valeria, hands folded in front of her. She offered a small smile—she had near-perfect teeth, painstakingly straightened and white.

"I saw you run out," she said. She came to Jasmine's side and gently lowered herself into the chair beside her. "And I just wanted to make sure you're okay."

Jasmine sniffed, wiping her eyes and not looking at Valeria. "I'm fine. Thanks for checking."

Valeria pursed her lips. She tapped her yellow-painted fingernails against the chair's metal armrest for a moment before she leaned a little closer to Jasmine.

She said, "You know, I get what it's like. Being a ghoul, I mean. As if turning into a monster isn't bad enough, no one will let you forget what you are even when you look like everyone else."

Jasmine glanced sideways to catch Valeria's eyes. She had soft features arranged around a sharp jawline, her eyes big and golden brown. There was no way anyone could look at her and see a monster if they didn't know she was a ghoul. Something about her smile made Jasmine feel like she could tell her anything.

"You're not a monster, Valeria. I don't think anyone could look at you and think that."

She blinked, eyebrows raising before she bit back a smile. "I guess you'd be surprised then. Thank you, though. It means a lot."

Jasmine nodded. "I heard about the cheer squad sort of…kicking you out. That's fucked up."

Valeria shrugged. "There was too much drama in cheer as it is. It's kind of nice to hang out with people who don't give a shit about staying skinny enough to be flyers."

Jasmine pantomimed a gag. "God, that sounds awful."

Valeria giggled. "It was! And I had to wake up at, like, five in the morning for practice. No thanks."

"You could always join the softball team," Jasmine offered. She used her bat to point to Valeria. "You look like you can run pretty fast."

Valeria scoffed. "Thanks. I'll pass, though. By the way, what exactly is the bat for?"

Jasmine straightened up. She twisted the bat around and pointed to the pile of beer cans and bottles near the firepit. "Some of the team and I like to come out here and break bottles. Nice way to work out your feelings."

"Oh. Cool." Valeria looked into Jasmine's eyes and smiled. "Think you could show me how to do it?"

Jasmine's heart fluttered. Everyone knew that Valeria was one of the prettiest girls at Aspen Flats High, and while she'd only ever dated boys, there was a rumor going around that she might be bi. Jasmine *didn't exactly want to get her hopes up, but she wouldn't say no to a chance to spend more time with her.*

Jasmine smirked. "Sure. Why the hell not?"

And for the next hour, Jasmine set up bottles atop a boulder and watched with pure delight in her eyes as Aspen Flats golden girl Valeria Vega shattered them into a thousand sparkling pieces with her bat.

And for a moment, she thought, maybe everything would be okay.

That night, as darkness fell over the festival grounds, everything came alive.

Across the festival grounds, lights blinked on all at once, like a neon carnival right outside our doorstep. The multicolored beams of spotlights lit up the main stage, where Girlfool would be playing in a few hours. The colors from the festival leaked in through the cabin windows, casting spinning shapes onto the tiled floor.

"No word from my manager about getting VIP passes to the Girlfool show," Celeste muttered as she refreshed her email for the tenth time. The two of us sat on the couch while Jasmine scrolled through her phone in the adjacent armchair. Val was in their room—she hadn't wanted to talk much once we got back from the Waterheads concert with No Flash Photography.

"It seems like they're pretty much reserved for other musicians and the press," Celeste continued, scrubbing her face with her hands. She hadn't put on makeup since she'd taken a shower after our conversation with Tony. "So who knows if the person who slipped Menthexus into the lava salt could even get VIP tickets. For all we know, they might not even be at the show."

"It's kind of our only lead," I reminded her. "We at least owe it to ourselves to try."

"You're right," Jasmine said, not looking up from her phone. "Especially because, uh, I think we might have another problem."

She stood up from the armchair and held her phone out between Celeste and me. We both leaned in to look at the screen only to find a TikTok playing on repeat.

There was a girl seated in front of a tapestry, wearing dark, heavy makeup. She said, "Everything I'm about to show you is actual footage from Desert Bloom that, in the last twenty-four hours, has been taken down off TikTok, Instagram, and Twitter. There is something going on at that festival, and someone is trying to cover it up."

The screen cut to shaky footage that appeared to be outside one of the attendee cabins. It was dark, and the only thing illuminating the scene was the light on the back porch and the moon's shine filtering through the clouds. Whoever was filming was doing it through a window, pointing the camera at the trash can on the left side of the cabin, below the deck.

A figure stood hunched over the garbage, barely more than a spindly shadow. Its hands dug through the can, sifting through food scraps. Thick blond hair hung over its face, obscuring it from view. Its shoulders were bony, protruding from its pale skin beneath a torn pink tank top.

"Hey!" the person filming shouted. "What the hell are you doing?"

The face jerked up, revealing a person with a gaunt face and jagged teeth. They were a ghoul, clearly, from the black veins around their eyes and the claws on their fingers wrapped around the sides of the trash can. But there was something more...animalistic about this one. They were so slim their bones were visible beneath their skin, and their back seemed to have extra vertebrae, making it longer and more bendable. Blackish liquid streamed from their eyes, and at first I thought it was just mascara tracks, but they weren't wearing makeup. Still, they weren't tall like the anthropophagus Celeste and I saw last night, nor were their lips chewed off.

This person looked to be somewhere in the middle.

With a shriek, they dropped the lid of the trashcan and took off running.

The screen flashed back to the girl from before. "People have been tweeting about similar sightings of strange ghouls around the festival for two days now. And the county police have received almost *twenty* missing persons reports, all of which Desert Bloom has done their best to shove under the rug. At what point is Desert Bloom going to admit something is going on? Follow for part two."

Jasmine clicked the screen off and raised her eyebrows.

"Oh," I breathed. "*Shit.*"

"Something tells me Val isn't the only one who got drugged," Jasmine said as she slid her phone back into her pocket.

Just then, the door to Jasmine and Val's room popped open and Val strolled out. She'd changed into short-shorts and a yellow crop top, her hair pulled back in a high ponytail. She'd already done her makeup, and her foundation was applied a fair amount thicker than usual.

My stomach tightened.

"Great news—Eli and the boys will be going to the Girlfool concert," she said, beaming and shimmying her shoulders. She held up her phone, which had her text conversation with Eli pulled up. "*And* they can get us into the VIP section as their plus-ones."

"Val, we gotta talk," Jasmine said, crossing her arms. "Seriously this time. Something bad is happening to ghouls who have been drugged."

Her shoulders instantly wilted. "Not this again."

"Look at yourself," I snapped, pointing to the dark shadows under her eyes. The corners of her mouth began to fall as I added, "We're trying to help you, Val. You just have to let us."

Val bit her lip. She folded her arms over her chest, nails digging into the skin. It took me a moment, but I realized that her nails looked too thick on her fingers, a layer of black nail polish doing little to hide the fact that they'd clearly been filed down.

"Did you clip your claws down to look like fingernails?" I exhaled.

Val's cheeks immediately flushed red. She jammed her hands into her pockets.

"Holy shit," Jasmine breathed. "You're turning into one of those things."

Val's forehead wrinkled. "What are you talking about?"

Before Jasmine could respond, Celeste clicked something on her laptop screen and turned it around for Val to see. Immediately, the faces of the anthropophagi all appeared at once, hollow and gaunt like the skin was too loose over their skulls.

"This," Celeste said. "Ghouls exposed to Menthexus. They're called anthropophagi."

All of us went dead silent as Val's skin paled and her eyes widened, the screen reflected in them. She reached up and gently touched her cheek where the anthropophagi had hollow divots, her honey-brown eyes blank.

"No," she whispered faintly. She shook her head. "That's ridiculous."

"Val—" I started.

She cut me off. "Look, I get that you're all worried about me—and really, it means a lot to know that you care—but you have to believe me when I say I'm okay. Sure, I haven't felt… exactly normal since the other night, but I'm also not some bony monster chewing my own lips off. And even if I was, what would you want me to do? Chain myself to a wall and lock all the doors?"

I exchanged a look with Celeste. I started to say, "I mean…"

Celeste cut in, "No, of course not. I think we just need to keep an eye on it, right? If you start to feel worse, we need to know. For your safety and everyone else's."

"And you should probably stop cuddling up with Eli," Jasmine added, examining her cuticles. "I'm not sure we can get away with hiding two bodies in one week."

Val opened her mouth but immediately closed it again. She exhaled through her nose, scrubbing her hand over her face. A beat of silence passed.

Then, she said, "Okay. Understood. I'll back off."

"Really?" I blurted out. When Celeste pointedly cleared her throat, I added, "I'm just saying—"

Val nodded. "Look, I get it. I don't want anyone to get hurt either. But that just means that we need to really be on it tonight, right? We have to try to find the person that Tony was describing."

I crossed my arms. "And if you start to feel off, you'll say so, right?"

"Right." Val pulled out her phone. "Okay, I'm going to tell Eli to put us down as their plus-ones. We good?"

Celeste, Jasmine, and I glanced at each other. Celeste

nodded softly while Jasmine pressed her lips together but didn't say anything.

"Yeah," I finally said. "We're good."

Dressed in our best concert outfits and decorated with Celeste's custom makeup, the four of us made our way to the festival grounds.

The night air felt electric. The minute we entered the main space between the stages, people began to flow forward from every direction. As we pressed into the crowd, we passed people with blacklight paint splattered on their faces and bare chests. They wore glow sticks around their necks and wrists and ankles. Despite the temperature dropping, clothes were in short supply. People of all genders walked around in bikinis and unitards, skin adorned with glitter and tattoos. Bodies bumped against us while people held their drinks aloft and cheered. The smell of weed and cigarettes clogged the air with musky sweetness, and the Ferris wheel stood like a spinning beacon guiding us deeper into the crowd.

By the time we made it to the main stage, my heart was racing—I couldn't help but glance toward Val every few seconds just to make sure that the sound of blood rushing through these strangers' veins hadn't overwhelmed her. But Val's expression never shifted, staying in a soft, airy smile that wrinkled the sides of her eyes.

"Val!" came a voice over the din. Eli appeared through the crowd, shirtless and smeared with blacklight paint. Cole and Raj were on either side of him, Raj in a mesh shirt with sparkling eye shadow framing his eyes. Cole had his red hair styled back from his face with pomade, looking infinitely less flashy than the other band members with a white T-shirt and ripped jeans.

Despite myself, something about his flushed face and toothy smile made my heart flutter. Not enough to distract from the palpable aura of electricity that had appeared in the small space between my arm and Celeste's, but it was something.

"Hey!" Val grabbed Eli's hand and went on her toes to kiss his cheek. "Thank you so much for letting us tag along!"

"'Course. This show's gonna be wild." Eli wrapped an arm around her shoulders and nodded toward the stage. "Follow me— I'll see if security will let us go around the crowd."

Eli led the way to a side entrance to the main stage, which was a large amphitheater near the back of the festival grounds. He and the other No Flash Photography boys had passes on lanyards around their necks marking them as VIPs, so when we reached the entrance, security quickly stepped aside to let us through a small gated pathway. After a brief exchange with some folks just past security, Eli passed out four more VIP badges for the rest of us, which we quickly draped around our necks.

"Through here," he said.

We took a sharp turn into the amphitheater, to two long rows of seating nestled between the typical rows of arena chairs. Instead of folding amphitheater seats, there were little oval-shaped white tables arranged in front of leather couches built into the back half-wall that divided the VIP section from regular seating. There were thin, rectangular lamps on each table to light the way, and black napkins already set out for drinks. Black hardwood had been installed in place of the usual concrete, giving it an added air of elegance. Waitstaff went from table to table taking orders from people dressed in the kind of name-brand, high-fashion outfits that would wind up in style influencers' Desert Bloom wrap-up videos when this was all over.

Eli sat down at one of the couches, and immediately pulled Val into his lap. The rest of us followed suit, and somehow I wound up squeezed between Celeste and Cole on one couch. At once, I felt the heat leach from their bare arms into mine, and my cheeks turned pink. My skin tingled with each brush of clothing or skin.

You do not have time for this right now, I reminded myself. *You can go back to being a disaster when people aren't being drugged and turned into monsters.*

"You good?" Cole whispered in my ear. His lips just barely grazed my skin, sending a shiver down my back. "You seem kinda tense."

That was a fair assessment—it was entirely possible that I would fold myself into a pretzel just to avoid being touched by two people I found ridiculously attractive if this continued. "Oh— I'm fine. Really."

Cole put a hand on my knee. "Maybe I can buy you a drink to help you feel better?"

I blinked, glancing up into Cole's green eyes. His eyebrows were just faintly bent, lips parted while he offered a small smile. A blush warmed my skin from my throat to my ears.

At my side, Celeste stood suddenly and said, "I'll be right back. Just gonna… mingle a bit."

"Celeste—" I started to say.

But she was already up, walking down the aisle in the opposite direction. Jasmine quickly stood as well, rushing to catch up.

Probably just checking to see if anyone has that hoodie she recognizes, I reminded myself. *It's not like she has any other reason to—*

"If you don't mind me asking," Cole said, rubbing the back of his neck, "are you and Celeste together?"

Immediately, my face turned red. I tried to swallow, but my throat had gone dry. I attempted to clear it, but wound up making a noise that sounded vaguely like a cat before it puked.

"No?" I finally managed. Cole raised an eyebrow and I added, "Er—no, we're not. Celeste is my best friend. W-Why do you ask?"

"Just wondering." Cole seemed to be withholding a laugh. When he smiled, dimples appeared on his cheeks. He brushed his shoulder against mine and added, "Don't want to step on anyone's toes, y'know."

I froze while my brain processed that statement. *Step on anyone's toes? Why would he—?*

Oh, holy shit.

He was flirting with me.

It wasn't like he was the first person to ever give it a shot, but the list was depressingly short. I hadn't been particularly popular back at school, which I usually blamed on being a ghoul, but probably had more to do with the fact that I'd spent years acting as Celeste's shadow and refusing to befriend most other people unless she pulled them into my orbit. People always assumed it was because I was shy, but really I just didn't care about trying to impress strangers.

Which meant this was something of a curveball.

Quickly, I drew up a mental pros and cons list.

Pro: Cole was very attractive, and there were no strings attached.

Con: It had been approximately two hours since I chewed Val out for getting distracted by a boy when chaos was brewing just beneath Desert Bloom's surface. I couldn't exactly justify doing the same thing.

Pro: Would probably get my mind off Celeste.

Con: Might piss Celeste off, considering the aforementioned chaos.

"Zoey?" Cole asked.

"Sorry." I shook my head, gently biting the edge of my lip. "You wouldn't be stepping on anyone's toes."

Cole smiled. His hand slid from his thigh over the fabric of my plaid skirt before resting on my knee. His touch made the baby hairs on the back of my neck stand up. The warmth of his touch spread through my skin like ink across paper.

"Good to know," he said with a wink.

A few moments later, the lights began to dim. Cheers surged through the crowd as a spotlight shone on the stage. The opener emerged to thunderous applause not long after, the lead guitarist hitting a riff that sliced through the buzzing crowd. While no one in the VIP selection stood, a number of people in the regular seats did, swaying to the beat.

Midway through the set, Jasmine and Celeste returned to their seats. Celeste leaned over to me and whispered, "No luck, but plenty of seats are still empty. They may not have arrived yet."

I nodded. "Let's keep an eye out."

The rest of the opening set was pleasant enough, though my racing thoughts didn't give me much of an opportunity to enjoy it. My attention split between scanning each new person who walked by to take a seat in the VIP section to Cole slowly stroking my knee and flashing me more little smiles that made my heart race. If someone had asked me a week ago if I was the type to enjoy casual flirting with near strangers, I would have resoundingly said no, but maybe that wasn't the case.

Focus, Z, I chided myself. *Not the time.*

The opener played their final song and walked off the stage to howling cheers. The lights brightened to give everyone a chance to shift around before Girlfool took the stage. My phone buzzed.

I took it out of my pocket to find that Jasmine, who was sitting on Celeste's other side, had sent a message to our group chat. Split up to see if we can find anyone with the hoodie elsewhere?

Celeste stared at the screen and texted back, I'll come with you. Val and Zoey, you okay keeping an eye on this section?

I leaned forward and flashed the two of them a thumbs-up.

Jasmine and Celeste took off, and I spent the rest of the break between bands chatting with Cole while trying to casually keep an eye out for anyone in pink. Cole didn't seem to notice, however, instead asking me questions about how I was enjoying the festival so far and who some of my favorite bands were. It was easy enough to keep up appearances—all I had to do was ask a question every now and again, and Cole didn't seem to suspect I wasn't listening.

Twenty minutes later, the back of the stage suddenly lit up and Girlfool stepped out, waving and grinning. The audience burst into wild applause, and everyone instantly jumped to their feet. The band members were all dressed in gem-encrusted clothes that glinted under the stage lights, refracting the rainbow glow around them like glass prisms.

"We are Girlfool, and you are in for a great fucking show!" the lead singer screamed as she took her spot in front of the mic. She pumped a fist in the air and cried, "Let me hear it!"

The crowd shrieked, arms flying up and waving in the air.

Girlfool launched into their set with a burst of yellow and pink light that shot across the audience. The back of the stage scintillated with a spinning fractal of light that made the stage look like a cosmic vortex.

I glanced to my side. Celeste and Jasmine still weren't back yet, and neither of them had texted. That probably wasn't a big deal, right? They were just being thorough and doing their best to sweep the entire venue. Probably.

I felt something brush my side and found Cole holding out his hand to me.

"Come here," he shouted over the music. "I wanna dance with you."

My stomach fluttered. Cole was a basically a stranger—some rando I literally met at a motel who played the guitar in a no-name band that only Val knew about.

But he wasn't my best friend. I would never have to worry about blurring the line between romance and friendship with him. I'd never have to worry that letting him know how I felt might drive him away. The complete opposite of Celeste.

Maybe I needed that.

I took his hand and let him pull me closer. My heartbeat picked up, and my skin prickled where it touched his. As the music continued to blast through the amphitheater, Cole's hands found their way to my hips and the two of us swayed together, dancing as the beat picked up. While I was a little tense at first, the more he touched me, the less I felt like I was breaking a rule by letting him get close to me, and the crowd around us melted away. A few times he spun me around, and I looked into his eyes, grinning.

His gaze darted to my lips, lingering there for a moment as he smiled to himself. My heart stalled in my chest.

You know what? Fuck it.

I reached up a hand and touched his cheek. He started to say something, but before he could, I went up onto my toes and kissed him.

The tension in Cole's shoulders immediately melted, a soft groan escaping his lips as he pulled me in tightly against him. His fingernails dug into the bare skin on my lower back above my skirt. His lips parted and his tongue slid into my mouth. I hadn't kissed anyone like this aside from Celeste at Cleo's party, always too afraid to get close to non-ghouls just in case I couldn't stay in control. He tasted like weed and cinnamon and—

Wait a minute.

I pulled away, eyes wide. He blinked, arms still wrapped tightly around me.

"You okay?"

My mind raced. How could I have missed it? But then—up until that moment, he'd always been with his bandmates. Eli and Raj had the faint sweet scent of blood and soft flesh beneath the skin—just like Kaiden had before Val killed him. But now, with Cole's body against mine, it was so obvious—he didn't smell like them.

In fact, he didn't smell like anything.

"You're a ghoul," I whispered.

His eyes widened. "I—"

Before he could finish, though, a voice behind him said, "Zoey?"

Standing in a pool of twisting yellow light behind Cole was Celeste, loose pink hair glowing like a halo around her head. Her coral-pink lips were faintly parted, all the color drained from her skin. Her lower lip quivered and her eyes shone, huge and round, her gaze shooting a painful pang through my chest.

She blinked and two fat tears rolled down her sparkling cheeks. *Wha...what?*

"Celeste?" I asked. I pulled away from Cole. "Are you okay? What—?"

She shook her head and wiped a hand across her cheek before turning toward the exit and taking off. Behind her, Jasmine met my eyes and frowned, shaking her head.

"Oh my god, Zo," Jasmine said. "Really?"

I blinked, jaw slackened. Quickly I turned to Cole and said, "Sorry, I—we'll talk about this later, okay? I have to go."

Cole said my name again, but I was already off. I shouldered past Jasmine and ran to the entrance to the VIP section, frantically searching for Celeste. I cursed under my breath.

Then, my eyes fell on a head of pink hair to my right, slowly weaving through the crowd toward the hallway where we'd entered. Her face was downturned and her eyes hidden behind a curtain of hair. In a weird way, it felt like seeing her when we were younger, when she was always disappearing into her too-big hoodies or her overgrown bangs.

"Celeste!" I called. "Wait up!"

I elbowed my way through the crowd, ignoring the shouts of protest. I kept running all the way to the exit, where the din of the show faded out just enough for me to hear my own thoughts again. *What the hell happened? Why would she run off like that? And—why was Jasmine acting like I should know?*

I came to a skidding halt outside the amphitheater. There were a few scattered people around, some smoking while others rushed toward the bathrooms. No Celeste, though.

Just as I was going to dig through my pocket to get my phone and call her, a sharp scream suddenly cut through the air.

Celeste's scream.

I spun in the direction it had come from and hit the ground running. A few other people turned at the same time, looking up from their phones and their conversations. Vendors selling light-up accessories glanced toward the desert, distracted from their transactions.

All at once, eyes fell on Celeste, who was standing in front of a large rabbitbrush bush at the edge of the festival pathway. A shadow lay at her feet, unmoving. As I sprinted closed, a gruesome scene came into view.

Sprawled out beneath the rabbitbrush, just out of sight to anyone walking through the festival, was the body of an anthropophagus. The limbs were unnaturally long and spindly, the bones protruding from the skin with no muscle or fat to cover it. I could count each rib jutting out from its torn T-shirt, the skin bruised all over in watercolor-like yellow and purple. Its face was hollowed out, skull-like and pale. Its lips had been chewed off, revealing pearly white, jagged teeth.

That wasn't the only part missing flesh, though. Bite marks covered the skin, each stained with smears of oily black liquid. Chunks of skin were missing, torn off with sharp teeth. The eyes had been gouged out, and claw marks marred the bloody sockets.

"Oh my god," I breathed.

A few other onlookers halted in their tracks, and soon a few more people had come up behind us, muttering, "What is that?" and "Is that a ghoul?" Before long, shouts rang out as people crowded around the body, snapping pictures with their phones.

Celeste looked back at me, her face gone completely white.

"Fuck."

sixteen

Cole Greenleaf
Today 10:22 p.m.

hey zoey
i just wanted to say please don't tell anyone about what you
said to me this evening at the concert
no one knows that about me
like the guys in the band do and my family and the HollowLife
people obviously but no one else

Today 11:15 p.m.

look our fans can't find out
our careers are barely getting off the ground and this could ruin it

Today 12:01 a.m.

please zoey
please

*D*esert Bloom security worked fast to clear the scene around the dead anthropophagus.

"Please do not exit the scene!" a man shouted to the crowd as other members of security began to put up yellow tape to make a perimeter around the body. "Security will be interviewing witnesses as soon as we finish closing off the area!"

"Come on," I told Celeste. "Let's get out of here before they notice."

Celeste nodded numbly, and the two of us quickly peeled off from the crowd. Luckily, there were so many people standing around the body and rushing past that they didn't notice us ducking away toward the other side of the festival grounds. Celeste kept checking over her shoulder like she expected someone to be following us. The whole way back to the cabin, we didn't say a word—there were too many people doing the same thing, and the last thing we needed was for it to get out that we knew about the anthropophagi.

When we did finally get back, we closed and locked the door behind us. Both of us were quiet as we sat down on the couch for a long while, the silence only stretching out wider and wider between us. While Celeste began to curl into herself, I stood back up, beginning to pace back and forth. Celeste didn't look at me, instead opting to lean forward, elbows on her thighs as she hung her head and stared at her clasped hands.

"There were bite marks on the body," I finally said. My mind was absolutely reeling, and I really only verbalized it for my own benefit. "And flesh missing and—fuck, are the anthropophagi *eating each other*?"

"I don't know, Zoey," Celeste muttered. As she hung her head, her hair fell like a curtain to hide her face, shutting her off from me. She exhaled through her nose. "What can we do if they are? We don't even know if there's a way to turn them back."

"We can't do *nothing*," I said, continuing to pace. I pressed my lips together, shaking my head. "Maybe the person who drugged Val has, I dunno, something that can counteract the Menthexus? Something that could stall the transformation or—"

"And how exactly do you expect to find them?" Celeste finally tilted her face up, her eyes were shining with tears. She wiped one away and, voice thick, she added, "We are so out of our depth here. Hiding bodies and trying to save people. We can't do this."

"We don't have a choice!" I threw my arms out. "Val is turning into one of them! What are you going to do, give up and let her run off into the desert with the rest of those things so they can cannibalize each other? No! There has to be something we're missing—"

The front door opened, cutting me off. Jasmine and Val stepped in from outside, Val leaning on Jasmine. Val was sniffling while Jasmine rubbed her shoulders.

"Val?" Celeste asked, standing from the couch. "You okay?"

When Val stepped into the light, the problem became clear immediately. The hollows under her eyes had grown much darker, and the veins on the sides had begun to turn black. Her normally warm, tan skin had grown waxen and sickly, the color drained from her cheeks. When she opened her mouth, I spotted two rows of jagged teeth.

"It's getting worse," was all she had to say.

"Oh, Val," Celeste breathed. "I'm so sorry."

While Val sniffled and hung her head, Jasmine said, "They

evacuated the concert not long after you left. Didn't say why. Just that everyone needed to go back to their lodgings and shelter-in-place until further notice. Val started feeling worse right as we were leaving, so we ran back here before anyone could see."

"No sign of the pink hoodie?" I guessed.

Jasmine pressed her lips together. "No. But there was something else."

She pulled her arm from Val's shoulders and came over to me, holding her phone up. On the screen was an Instagram Live shot by someone in the passenger seat of a car. They held the phone out the window to show a line of cars stopped on the road out of De Luz Valley. Their brake lights glowed red as horns went off, urging others forward.

A security guard in uniform walked down the line of cars, shouting, "The road is closed! Return to your lodging immediately and wait for further instructions! Do not try to force your way over the barricade!"

"Barricade?" I repeated, eyes widened.

Jasmine nodded. "They're shutting the road down. Whatever happened has them really freaking out."

"The body," Celeste breathed. She pressed her palms hard against her eyes. "*Fuck.* This is my fault. I-I could have hidden it or if I'd just kept my mouth shut—"

"Body?" Val asked. She'd already gone to the fridge and was taking out a package of SynFlesh. She was lisping—probably because of her fangs. "What body?"

Celeste and I quickly explained the situation with the anthro-pophagus, and how its corpse showed signs that it might have been killed by one of its kind. All the while, Val kept her back turned to us as she bit into the SynFlesh. I did my best not to stare, but it was hard not to—Val had never willingly eaten in front of us before.

Not to mention that we were getting dangerously close to running out of SynFlesh.

"Well," Jasmine said when we finished, crossing her arms and closing her eyes while she sighed. "Shit."

"Yeah. Not much we can really do," Celeste whispered.

We were all quiet for a beat. Jasmine pulled her purple braids over one shoulder and cleared her throat while Val got another package of SynFlesh from the fridge. I shifted my weight from one foot to the other. Celeste glanced at her phone, and I caught a flash of the time on the screen: 11:45. I would have checked my own, but it had died at the concert.

"Maybe we should sleep on it," I finally said. "If there's a shelter-in-place order and we don't have any leads, maybe the best thing we can do is just wait it out."

I tried not to look at Val as I said it, but I felt her eyes on me. Her expression fell.

"I think you should lock me in my room tonight," she whispered, barely loud enough for us to hear. Her hand tightened around the edge of the SynFlesh package. "If that anthropophagus was killed by another one of its kind…it might not be a good idea for me to be around you all. Being ghouls might not be enough to keep you safe from me."

"Val, no—" Jasmine started.

"She's right," I cut in. Celeste and Jasmine's eyebrows both shot up and I quickly added, "Look, we don't have a lot of options right now. If something happens, Val can just text us. Better safe than sorry, right?"

Jasmine slowly shrunk back as she hazarded a glance at Val,

who had taken to inhaling her second package of SynFlesh in a row. Jasmine bit her lip, then squeezed her eyes shut.

"Fine," she said. "I'll stay on the couch. But—you just shout if you need anything, okay? We're not going to let anything happen to you."

Val lowered her clawed hands from her mouth. Her lips were faintly stained red with synthetic blood. The bottom of her chin wrinkled and her eyes shone, but she nodded.

"We'll get through this," Celeste promised her, "one way or the other."

Val went quiet, staring at her reflection in the shiny surface of the metal faucet head.

"Yeah," she breathed. "I hope so."

That night, an unexpected thunderstorm passed over De Luz Valley. Lightning cut across the sky as rain drenched the parched earth, pattering against the roof as I struggled to fall asleep. I tossed and turned in bed, my body feeling like it had been charged with electricity. I couldn't stop thinking about Celeste's face right before she stormed out of the amphitheater.

I knew that, ultimately, that was the least of our problems, but I'd never seen her look at me like that before. The way her eyes had glinted with unshed tears and her shoulders had wilted like flowers in the desert sun. Like finding Cole with his hands on me was a knife directly between her shoulder blades.

"Celeste?" I whispered. She had her back to me, and she hadn't moved since we'd gone to bed. "You awake?"

She didn't respond. But based on the sound of her breathing, I got the sense she wasn't asleep.

"I'm sorry about tonight," I said. I closed my eyes, fingers tightening around the fold of the blanket over me. "I don't know what happened at the concert but…I never meant to hurt your feelings. If there's something I did, I want to know. You're my best friend and I don't ever want you to think you can't tell me something."

Silence.

After a long, painful beat, Celeste murmured, "Go to sleep, Zoey. It's not important."

I bit the inside of my cheek. If it wasn't important, why did I feel like my chest was collapsing in on itself every time I tried to breathe? Why did my heart keep punching against my ribs so hard it felt like they might crack every time I thought about it? Not to mention the way my stomach was twisting in knots, threatening to bring up the tiny amount of SynFlesh I'd managed to get down before bed.

"I'm sorry," I whispered.

Celeste didn't reply.

The next morning, Celeste and I woke up to our phones buzzing in tandem.

I lifted mine from the bedside table to see eight missed texts from Cole—in the chaos I'd almost totally forgotten about the revelation I'd had about him at the show—plus an alert that dominated the screen.

EMERGENCY ALERT

The CDC has issued a quarantine order for all Desert Bloom attendees, effective 6:01 a.m. National Guard is on location to provide assistance. Do not leave your lodging until further notice. Quarantine will be strictly enforced. For more information on this order, please visit: desert-bloom.ca.gov/quarantine.

I sat bolt upright in bed. "Shit."

I tapped the link and it opened to a CDC page that gave little explanation of the situation other than how to effectively quarantine. I quickly opened Twitter and went to the Desert Bloom tag to see what people were saying about it.

The very first one I found was a picture of the anthropophagus's body.

CDC quarantined Desert Bloom because of this, the person had tweeted. Is this some new kind of ghoul?

Another user had commented: Quarantine? Does that mean there's a new strain of the Hollow virus?

And another directly after that: Welcome to The Hollowing Part II, we're fucked.

The original tweet already had almost a thousand likes and it had only been posted ten minutes ago.

I tried to swallow, but my throat had gone dry. Of course they'd think it was a new strain of Hollow virus. For years, people had worried about a second Hollowing, this time one that impacted more people, or created a hunger that couldn't be satisfied by SynFlesh.

They had no idea that Menthexus was to blame.

I closed my phone and jabbed my finger into Celeste's cheek. "Wake up."

"Ow." She opened her eyes and pointedly glared at me. There were bags under her eyes, and she squinted at me like I was glowing brightly enough to blind her. She rubbed her forehead with the heel of her palm, wincing. "What?"

"Look at this," I said, ignoring her question. I unlocked my phone again and went to pull up the tweet. "Someone posted—"

But when the tweet reloaded, the image was gone, replaced with a message saying the tweet had been removed for violating community guidelines. I hurriedly refreshed the tag. *There has to at least be a screenshot or something—*

Nothing came up. Just the usual music festival tweets about people's outfits, images from concerts, rumors about upcoming setlists—nothing about the body. I kept scrolling, even going to the most recent tweets instead of the top ones, but all of a sudden, everything about the quarantine and the body were gone.

"What the hell?" I breathed. "It was just here!"

Celeste glanced at her phone, finally seeing the alert. "Whoa—what?"

"I just saw a picture of the anthropophagus on Twitter," I explained, refreshing the feed. After a few times, a screenshot of the image came up. "Oh, here! Someone reposted it."

But just as I tapped the tweet, I got the same message again. Removed for violating community guidelines.

"Someone's deleting the evidence," I breathed. "Like, as we speak. But—"

When I tried to refresh the feed, I got a new message.

No internet connection.

"What the hell?" I muttered. I turned to Celeste. "Did your cell service just go out?"

She unlocked her phone, and immediately her eyebrows shot up. "Um—yeah. It did."

I swallowed thickly. "Something is seriously wrong."

I slid out of bed, bare feet hitting the cool floor tiles. I held my phone aloft like I'd seen people do in old movies, looking for a connection. Nothing appeared. Grinding my teeth, I opened our bedroom door and paced into the living room.

Jasmine was already awake as well, sitting upright on the couch and staring at her phone. When I came out, her head snapped up and she held up her phone. "You seeing this shit?"

"That depends—did your service go out too?"

"Yeah!" Jasmine scrolled through the blank page. "So the road out is closed and they shut off cell service? What are they trying to do?"

My heart rate picked up. What *were* they trying to do? With the road out of the valley closed, we were hemmed in on all sides by the towering rock walls that were way too steep to climb safely. And with no cell phone reception, it wasn't like we could call for help.

We were trapped.

"Shit," I breathed, running a hand back through my hair. A cold sweat broke out on the back of my neck. I stuffed my phone into the pocket of my pajama pants and jogged to Val's door, banging on it with my fist. "Val! You awake? Something's happening!"

I didn't get a response. Lips curling into a frown, I knocked even louder. "Val, seriously! Wake up!"

Silence.

"She's a really light sleeper—that should have woken her up," Jasmine said, standing from the couch. She came to my side and knocked on the door as well, calling, "Val! Come on!"

Again, no response.

A cold feeling began to spread across my skin. My tongue felt tacky and dry in my mouth as I tried to summon my voice. I stared at the doorknob, which we'd pushed a chair against to block Val inside.

I reached for the chair, pushing it out of the way.

"Zoey—" Jasmine started.

"She might need help," I said, wrapping my fingers around the knob. "Stand back."

I swung open the door.

I took a sharp breath. My eyes darted around the room, scanning for the shape of Val under the covers, then in the corners. That's when I spotted the open window, the curtains fluttering softly in the breeze.

I swore colorfully and went inside.

Jasmine followed me. The two of us both went to the window, leaning out. There were footprints in the rain-damp earth outside.

"Guys?" Celeste asked behind us as she shuffled to the doorway from our shared room. "What's going on?"

I turned, meeting her gaze with shining eyes, nearly choking on the words.

"Val's gone."

seventeen

Listen, I'm well aware that the Hollow didn't choose to be what they are. As I've stated before, my own son is Hollow. But that doesn't mean that I subscribe to the idea that they should be walking among us. God chose to give them this obstacle to overcome in life, and that journey should be taken far from the rest of society—for everyone's safety. I propose the best solution to the ghoul problem is to give them their own niche societies—perhaps in less-populated areas where they can set up towns and self-govern. It may seem harsh, but separating them from us means we stay safe and they are no longer tortured by their inhuman urges. Everyone wins.

—Genevieve Niedermeyer, author of
The Ghoul Agenda: Keeping Your Family Safe in a
Backward America

*W*e have to follow her," I decided. "Maybe there's still a chance she's nearby."

"Z, what if she…?" Jasmine trailed off. She lowered her voice. "What if she's too far gone?"

"What if she's not?" I countered. I pointed outside. "What do you think the CDC and the National Guard are going to do if they find her? Politely escort her home?"

Jasmine went uncharacteristically quiet. Her eyes glazed over in the sort of distant stare that I knew well, the full-body shutdown that came whenever something triggered a memory of the Hollowing. That said, it wasn't usually Jasmine who shut down. She was always cracking a joke to defuse the tension, changing the subject before it could linger.

But she didn't this time.

"Jaz?" Celeste asked. She gently touched Jasmine's shoulder. "You okay?"

Jasmine swallowed, squeezing her eyes shut. "Yeah. I just remember what the National Guard did to ghouls in LA. They're not going to hesitate to…to…"

I nodded. "Right. So we find her before they can, okay?"

Jasmine and Celeste exchanged a look before they both nodded.

"Okay," Jasmine said, hooking her thumb toward the back door. "Let's go."

The three of us quickly put on shoes and clothes that were a little less noticeable than pajamas before slipping out the back door. A cold breeze blew through the valley, ruffling my hair while I skirted the edge of the cabin. Val's tracks led north toward the festival grounds. At the edge of the cabin, I poked my head out to peer around the road. Jasmine and Celeste followed me, pressing in close.

A truck filled with men in camo uniforms slowly drove by, tires crunching the gravel beneath. They wore N95 face masks that covered their noses and mouths, but their eyes darted back and forth, searching for movement from the cabins. Each of them had a sizable rifle strapped to their backs, black as crude oil.

"I guess that's what they meant about quarantine being enforced," I muttered.

"They really think this is about to be another Hollowing, don't they?" Celeste breathed.

I nodded. "Looks like it. Come on, let's follow those tracks. She was heading toward the festival grounds."

We waited for the truck to roll farther down the road before we darted to the next cabin, stopping to peer out at the road again once we got there. We did it once, twice, three times more before the tracks veered to the west, across the road.

My eyes widened. I pointed to the tracks, then up toward the opposite row of cabins where we'd been barely twenty-four hours ago. "I think I know where she's going."

Jasmine let out the most world-weary sigh I'd ever heard. "If she eats another goddamn member of No Flash Photography, I swear to god I'm throwing her down a mineshaft too."

Just then, another truck came down the road, and we quickly ducked back behind the cabin. We stood stock-still, hearts pounding. The truck was moving so slowly I could hear the men inside chatting, even with their voices muffled by the masks. I closed my eyes, silently praying they wouldn't stop.

Thankfully, they didn't.

"How are we supposed to get across the road?" Jasmine asked. "We'll be completely out in the open!"

"We need a distraction," I said, nodding to myself. My fingers tightened on the edge of the cabin, knuckles turning white. "Maybe one of us can try to talk to them while the others run across the road."

Celeste nodded. "I'll do it."

I jerked my face toward her. "Celeste—"

She held out a hand to stop me. "I haven't exactly curated a subtle aesthetic, Zoey. You and Jasmine have a way better chance of sneaking by than I do."

I pursed my lips, trying to think of an argument. Ultimately, though, I knew she was right—plus, if any of us could talk our way out of getting in trouble for breaking quarantine, it was Celeste. For all of mine and Jasmine's strengths, playing the role of a sweet, innocent lost girl wasn't one of them.

After a beat of silence, Jasmine put a hand on Celeste's shoulder. "You got this."

Celeste nodded to herself. "Right. I'll flag down the next patrol that goes by. As soon as they're all looking at me, run."

Jasmine and I exchanged a look. After a beat, we both wrapped our arms around Celeste, pulling her into a tight hug.

"We love you," Jasmine said.

"Don't get hurt," I muttered into her shoulder. "Seriously."

Celeste sputtered a laugh, hugging us both back. "I'll do my best. Run fast, all right?"

We didn't have to wait long for the next patrol to come—they seemed to be driving by every five minutes or so. As the truck started to roll by, Celeste jogged out from the other side of the cabin, waving her arms and calling, "Stop! Please, I need help!"

The truck ground to a stop. They were maybe twenty feet down the road. While the guards all turned their attention to Celeste, Jasmine and I nodded to each other.

We took off sprinting. Our arms pumped in tandem, heartbeat roaring in my ears. Jasmine was faster than me, but I managed to keep pace as we ran. We kicked up dust behind us, sneakers slamming into the dirt hard with each step. We swerved around patches of cacti and bare, thorny brush that clung tightly to the chapped earth. I gasped for breath, tasting copper in my mouth.

When we finally reached the other line of cabins, we all but dove behind the first one. We pressed ourselves to the edge of the back porch, chests heaving. Our breath was the only sound for a beat.

I waited to hear someone shouting after us, but it never came.

"Goddamn," Jasmine wheezed.

"Val is gonna owe us so much after this." I craned my neck up toward the back deck. It was empty aside from the table and chairs where we'd had coffee yesterday. Was it possible that she'd managed to stay human enough to find Eli again?

"I don't see her," I said.

"Maybe she's inside?" Jasmine guessed. "And hopefully not ripping Raj, Cole, and Eli's throats out?"

I nodded. "I'm gonna look in the windows. You stay here just in case."

Jasmine offered a thumbs-up while I straightened up. I crept silently around the edge of the back porch, climbing the stairs onto the faintly creaking wooden deck. I winced at the tiny groan that came from each step, like maybe the camo-clad men in their trucks could pick it out all the way from the other side of the road.

When I got to the back window, I cupped my hands around

111

the sides of my eyes to block out the light. Inside, the kitchen was empty, if very messy—it looked like the boys had just dropped their things wherever they happened to fall, not taking the time to put anything away. Empty beer cans and Gatorade bottles littered the surfaces along with dirty dishes with silverware still on top. I withheld a gag. *God, boys are so gross sometimes.*

I pulled back, going to the other window. This one looked into one of the bedrooms. Clothes were strewn about, mostly street-wear in shades of black and red. A person lay sleeping, dark hair messy and face pressed into the pillow. Based on the warm tone of his brown skin, it had to be Raj.

Just as I was about to step away to look elsewhere, the back door slid open.

I clapped a hand over my mouth to keep from screaming. Just then, a sleepy-looking Cole stepped out, squinting at me. He wrinkled his forehead. He had on boxer shorts and a pink hoodie.

My breath caught in my throat.

A tie-dye pink hoodie, the word GIRLFOOL printed across the chest.

The entire world ground to a halt around me.

No. There's no way.

"Zoey?" he asked. "What are you doing here? Isn't there a quarantine?"

"It's you," I breathed, eyes darting up to him. I took a step back, my mind reeling for an explanation of how it was possible. How could the nice boy who had chatted with me at the hotel pool and softly played his guitar by himself in the desert be the person who'd hurt my friend?

The boy had been kissing me so sweetly just a few hours ago.

Cole's eyebrows pressed together. "Were you expecting someone else?"

I couldn't process it. He was a ghoul. Sure, Eli and Kaiden and Raj had mentioned not being fans of ghouls, but Cole hadn't. He'd barely batted an eye when he talked about noticing my claws back at the motel. So why…?

"You're the one who's been drugging ghouls," I breathed. "Aren't you?"

Cole froze. The air between us seemed to crackle, suddenly charged with electricity that could spark a fire at any moment. His muscles went rigid as he stared at me, any trace of his usual lax attitude gone.

Softly, he asked, "What did you say?"

"You're the one who's been giving ghouls Menthexus." I said it as a fact, not a question. I took another step back, pointing to his hoodie. "The bartender—he saw you slipping it into the lava salt at the party the other night. How could you do something like that? For god's sake, you're a ghoul too! Do you not have any empathy at all? Or are you just some sick freak who gets off turning people into monsters?"

"Zoey," Cole said. All the softness had left his voice—in fact, there was no emotion at all. He took another step toward me, and I backed up. His hand went into the pocket of his hoodie. "Keep your voice down. We can talk this out."

I shook my head, feeling as my face turned redder and redder. "Do you have any idea what you've done? One of my best friends is out in the desert right now turning into an anthropophagus because of you! Not to mention—fuck, how many people are missing because of you? How many of those people are *dead*?"

Cole's face suddenly went blank. He didn't even blink as he stared me down, and it took me a second to realize why.

His eyes had begun to shine with tears.

"You wouldn't understand, Zoey," he breathed. "You have no idea what I've done. All this—this is how I finally make up for it."

"By hurting other ghouls?" I shook my head. "That's not repentance, Cole. I know what it's like to feel guilty for what happened during the Hollowing, but this isn't the way to honor the people we hurt back then. Whoever it is you hurt…they wouldn't want you to do this."

He tensed, jaw working. His skin had gone even paler than normal, and his shoulders shook.

"Cole—"

But before I could finish, his hand shot out from the pocket of his hoodie. An arc of sparkling dust hit the air, and the moment I inhaled, the scent of mint overwhelmed the inside of my nose. I choked, grabbing at my throat.

He took a step back, the Menthexus falling in a silver curtain before him.

"Sorry, Zoey," he said, reaching for the door handle. "But no one can know."

My stomach twisted. I fell to my knees as my fangs pushed through my gums of their own accord, claws sinking into the porch wood. I snarled as the grip of hunger clamped down on me, stealing away every rational thought.

The last thing I saw before the hunger overtook me was Cole's green eyes through the sliding glass door.

eighteen

Before the Hollowing, Galetown, California, had been a truly unremarkable place. It was home to a single stoplight, a Walgreens, and a lot of citizens who wore cowboy hats as a part of their everyday fashion. But after, it had earned a somewhat infamous distinction that finally set it apart from every other sleepy desert stopover: Galetown had the highest rate of Hollow people in the United States.

Which was how it earned its nickname: Ghoultown.

The Hollowing had started off similarly in Galetown as it had in every small town. Rumors flew, neighbors stopped talking to neighbors, and everyone stopped going outside. Cole remembered staring through the window before his stepfather, Hank, boarded it up.

"It's for everyone's safety," Hank told him. At sixteen, Cole had learned to deal with his stepfather, even though he still didn't like him. Hank Niedermeyer was the reason that Cole's mother, Genevieve, had recently started attending church nearly every day of the week. She'd always been religious, but being married to Hank meant that faith had stopped just being faith—it had turned into an obsession.

Suddenly, Genevieve was strict about everything that Cole and his older sister, Melanie, watched on TV, read about in books, and searched *online. When his mom had caught his sister looking up tips on how to get birth control, Genevieve had nearly kicked her out of the house. Cole probably wouldn't have cared that Melanie was searching for that sort of thing if it weren't for the fact that she was dating one Eli McKinley, the lead singer of Cole's newest musical project—who was also one of Cole's best friends. And he definitely didn't want to think about Eli sleeping with his sister.*

In a different timeline, though, Cole imagined that his mother would have at least been passively supportive of Melanie's romantic life. She used to be the kind of mom who always stood up for her kids even when she didn't agree with them. But that was before Cole's father died.

The Genevieve who was married to Hank Niedermeyer was a different story.

"Seems a little overkill," Cole muttered, crossing his arms. "What are the sick people going to do? Puke us to death?"

Hank put on a big smile—the one he always seemed to wear that didn't quite reach his eyes. He chuckled to himself, but there was no humor in it. "Watch yourself, son. You never know when He's listening."

Oh, right, *Cole thought.* Classic God.

Cole didn't say that out loud, though. In fact, he kept his mouth shut all through the initial week of the Hollowing, even when he started to feel sick. Every night, he picked at his food while he listened to Hank ranting about how God had chosen the Hollow to atone for their sins by becoming His warriors.

What an absolute crock of shit, *Cole had thought.*

But when week two rolled around, something changed. Cole couldn't keep food down anymore, and every time he looked in the mirror, his skin had grown even paler. The hunger grew, and before long, he found himself lying in bed so consumed by it that he couldn't sleep.

He climbed out of bed, his mind blank. Slowly, he shuffled out of his bedroom, the corners of his vision burning faintly red. His entire body felt numb as he his teeth elongated and his fingernails curled into claws. Each step he took became blurrier and blurrier until he looked up and found that he'd come to stand in his sister's cracked doorway.

Melanie sat on the floor of her room on a round pink carpet. She was eighteen, with a head of fiery red hair like her brother and their mother, plus the kind of smile that could warm up anyone she aimed it at. Being so close in age meant that most of the time, Melanie felt more like one of Cole's friends than his big sister. They'd always been close, but when their dad died and their mom stopped talking and coming out of her room most days, they'd always leaned on each other for support. And after Genevieve and Hank got married, she'd always let him tag along with her and her friends just so he had an excuse to get out of the house. He could always count on her to be there when he needed her.

At the moment, she was on her phone, FaceTiming with Eli. Melanie giggled as she watched him make a kissy face and wink at her.

"Stop," she said, shaking her head and grinning. "You're so embarrassing."

"Nah, you like it," he grinned. "Listen, as soon as Hank lets you out, I want to take you somewhere special. Make a nice night of it, you know? You deserve that."

Melanie laughed, sweeping a hand back through her long hair. It shone copper in the low light from the Christmas lights that she had permanently affixed around her bedroom windows. "Oh my god, Eli. Why are you like this?"

"Because I love you," he said. "And because—"

He cut off, though, as Cole stepped into frame.

"Mel?" Eli's eyes rounded. "Wait, do you see that?"

She blinked, tilting her head to the side. She chuckled, "See what? Is this another one of your stupid jokes?"

"No—" Eli hopped up from where he was sitting. "Mel, there's something behind you! Turn arou—"

He never got the words out, though, because the next moment Cole was on top of her, teeth sinking into the flesh where her neck met her shoulder. Melanie screamed, the phone flying from her grasp and hitting the floor, instantly shattering the screen on impact.

Blood burst from the bite into Cole's mouth, and the sweetness of it instantly made him bite down harder, tearing at her and shaking her like a rag doll. The flesh tore, stringy bits of it holding in place until Cole shook it free. Melanie's fingernails weakly clawed at Cole's neck as she fought to get him off her. She shrieked his name, voice choked with sobs.

Cole blacked out to the sound of Eli screaming for him to stop and Melanie going quiet in his arms.

When I came to, I was in bed back in the cabin.

I shot up with a gasp, looking around the room in a panic. It was just the same as when I'd left this morning, though Celeste wasn't beside me. For a moment, I wondered if the morning had just been a nightmare. I fumbled for my phone where I'd left it on the nightstand before we left and checked the time.

It was nearly six in the evening, and there was still no cell reception.

Under the covers, my stomach rumbled.

I pressed a hand to it, trying to remember what had happened.

I slowly slid out of bed and padded toward the door, rubbing my eyes. We'd been looking for Val, following her tracks until…

I stepped into the living room, and Celeste lifted her head from the journal she was writing in. The sunlight caught her face, illuminating the way her brow was wrinkled, Cupid's bow lips in a small frown. As soon as she saw me, though, her expression immediately brightened. She dropped the journal on the couch, jumped to her feet, and closed the distance between us in a few bounds, throwing her arms around me and pulling me into a tight embrace.

"Oh my god," she breathed. "You're awake!"

I weakly hugged her back. "I'm—yeah. I'm all right. What's going on? Last I remembered I was talking to Cole and then…" My eyes widened. "Shit—he drugged me, didn't he?"

Celeste pulled back, keeping her hands on my shoulders. She studied my face, mouth in a line. Then, she pulled me into another hug, squeezing me tightly.

Well, that's not a great sign.

"He did," Celeste whispered. She rested her chin atop my head, unwrapping one arm from around me so she could run it through my hair. "And if I ever see him again, I'm going to rip his arms off and hit him with them."

That almost would have made me smile if it weren't for the fact that my stomach was beginning to twist around itself like some feeble attempt at creating an organ-based balloon animal. "What happened? Did I…?"

Did I kill someone?

"No one died," Celeste quickly said. She pulled away enough to look at me. "Just…injured."

Celeste went on to describe the rest of the morning to me while holding me so tightly I thought I might crack a rib. After I'd inhaled the Menthexus, I'd made a break for the road, barreling toward the truck where Celeste had been trying to distract the guards. Jasmine had tried and failed to catch me before one of the guards pointed a gun at me. I'd avoided the first shot, managing to make it all the way across the open road before I dove on the man who'd fired at me.

"You took a chunk out of his arm," Celeste explained. "Which, honestly, might not be the worst thing in the world because...well, they shot you."

She pointed to my shoulder, and for the first time, I noticed the stained, torn edge of my tank top. Beneath it was a star-shaped scar, warm and pink. I gently touched it and winced—still tender.

Celeste let go of me and pulled back the fabric of her shirt to reveal her own gunshot scar. "I guess we match now."

I looked between our scars, feeling the back of my throat tightening. To have nothing but darkness where memories should have been felt like I'd somehow slipped into an alternate universe. My brain struggled to connect the dots between my last flicker of memory on the porch and now, creating an almost out-of-body sensation. I found myself wishing I could rewind and pick up where I'd left off just so it wouldn't feel like I'd accidentally hopped forward in time and left something behind.

"Then..." I trailed off, meeting Celeste's eyes. "How did we get back here?"

Her face fell. Softly, she said, "Come on."

She waved for me to follow and went to the kitchen window that looked out at the porch. As I came to stand beside her, I spotted two figures on either side of the porch stairs. Both were in camo uniforms, and both were armed with rifles.

"We're under house arrest," Celeste explained. "Guarded house arrest. They didn't have anywhere to put us, so instead we're trapped here until the CDC can figure out what's causing ghouls to turn into anthropophagi."

"But we know what's doing it," I argued. I threw my hand out toward the guards. "We have evidence, and a culprit!"

Celeste's shoulders fell, her gaze downturned. "I know. I tried to explain that, but they wouldn't listen to me. Jasmine did too, but they didn't believe us. They think we were just trying to talk our way out of house arrest."

"Where is Jasmine?"

"Bedroom. She wanted some time to be alone. It's not exactly a surprise but she's pretty upset and worried about Val."

My gaze fell. Of course she was. Val was still out there somewhere, probably getting worse and worse by the hour. Even if Cole *did* have something that could help her, and even if I could somehow convince him to give it to us, there was nothing I could do about it. Not with cell service down and armed guards waiting on our doorstep.

"We're kind of screwed, aren't we?"

Celeste flexed her eyebrows but nodded. "Unless you have some kind of bright idea on how we can fight off a bunch of armed guards…yeah, a little bit."

"I mean, give me a few days." I shrugged. "Cole drugged me, right? So I guess sooner than later, I'll be eight feet tall and have very sharp teeth. Might be able to take care of them then."

To Celeste's credit, she didn't shoot me the pitying look that basically anyone else would. Instead she shrugged and said,

"That's true. Plus, you'll finally get to be taller than me for once in our lives."

I sputtered a laugh as she added, "Sorry, that was terrible."

"No, I like it—you should deflect more often." I scraped a hand back through my hair to get it out of my face. "Listen, I feel like I should apologize. I shouldn't have said anything to Cole after I realized it was him. I was just so shocked it kind of…slipped out."

At the mention of his name, any light remaining in Celeste's eyes vanished. She averted her gaze, wrapping her arms around herself. "It's fine. You clearly liked him. It makes sense you'd want to trust him."

I paused. The image of her face from last night bubbled up again, with her wet eyes and quivering lower lip. Now, she looked tense, shoulders tight as shifted her weight from foot to foot.

You know what? I thought. *Fuck it. I'm going to turn into a monster in a few days. Might as well get this off my chest.*

"Celeste, what happened at the concert? What made you run away like that?"

She winced. "It's really nothing. We don't need to talk about it."

"We do, though." I reached out, grabbing her hand. Her gaze ever so briefly met mine and I added, "Look, we're not exactly in the best situation right now, are we? And unless some miracle happens in the next few days, it's only going to get worse. And I don't want this hanging over our heads. So just *tell me.*"

Celeste took a shaking breath. For a beat, she didn't speak—she just looked at me, eyes tracing the angles of my face before lingering on my lips. My heart began to race, and my stomach suddenly felt like it was about to drop into a black hole. *Shit, why did I ask? Oh god, this is bad—*

But then, with her eyes shining faintly, Celeste said, "Because…
seeing you with Cole made me realize that I can't sit here and pretend I want to be your friend anymore."

Every muscle in my body went rigid and cold at once.

"But—" I cut off, the corners of my eyes stinging with the threat
of tears. "I don't understand. Why—?"

"Because," Celeste breathed, "I'm in love with you, Zoey."

The world came to a screeching halt.

As soon as the words were out of Celeste's mouth, a blush shot
up from her throat to her ears, and she averted her gaze. Meanwhile,
I just stood there, jaw dropped and eyes staring at her unblinkingly.
The connections in my brain sparked and short-circuited as I tried
to process what I'd just heard.

"I have been for a long time," she added, blurting it out like
if she kept it in, the words would burn the inside of her mouth.
Turning even redder, she went on, "Maybe since I met you? I-I
mean, you've always been here for me, even when you didn't know
what you were doing, and that always meant so much to me, not to
mention the fact that you *literally* helped me hide a body—"

She didn't get the next words out, though, because I cut her off
with a kiss.

For a moment, Celeste froze. But as she realized what was happening, it was like her entire body melted into the kiss. Her lips
were warm and gentle, softer than they'd been when we kissed at
Cleo's party. Heat stained my skin pink from my cheeks down to
my chest, the space around my heart crackling like a sparkler. The
scent of her perfume overwhelmed my senses, the soft floral notes
of it wrapping around me at the same time her hand took hold
of my waist. Her other hand reached into my hair and tightened

while my fingers found the bare skin of her neck. She smiled against the kiss, and I had to stop because I was smiling too.

I pulled away an inch, bumping my nose softly into hers. "I never thought I'd hear you say that."

"I never thought…" Celeste opened her eyes, staring into mine. "Do you feel the same?"

"I mean, I definitely didn't just platonically stick my tongue down your throat."

Celeste rolled her eyes, but she was still grinning. "Can you just give me a straight answer for once?"

"Nope, nothing straight about this."

Celeste narrowed her eyes like she might actually throw me out the nearest window.

I quickly added, "Kidding. In all honesty? Yeah, I do. Ever since we kissed at Cleo's party I just knew something changed, but I didn't want to say anything in case you didn't feel the same way. I was scared it would ruin our friendship."

Celeste gently tilted her head to the side, wavy pink hair cascading down her shoulder. "Who said being in love would ruin a friendship? What better way to fall in love than to do it with the person you already care about the most in the world?"

My heartbeat fluttered in my chest. "But what if we break up one day?"

Celeste lifted her hand, covering mine. Our fingers twined together, hers long and thin and mine stubby like a child's. The warmth from the evening sunlight streaming through the windows couldn't hold a candle to the way her touch lit my every nerve ablaze.

"What if we don't?" Celeste countered.

I blinked, and tears rolled down my cheeks. I scooted closer to her, wrapping my arms around her and leaning my forehead against hers. Her eyelashes quivered against my cheek, her breath soft and warm against my skin.

"I'm probably not even going to be human in a few days," I reminded her. "Our odds aren't exactly great."

Celeste clasped my hand, gently placing it over her heart. "Then I guess that just gives us more of a reason to figure this out."

She leaned down and kissed me again, sending another flush of heat from my cheeks all the way to my toes. When she pulled away, my eyes fluttered open and I met her gaze, feeling like my heart was about to explode.

"Okay," I whispered. "I'm in."

nineteen

With the night, quiet fell over No Flash Photography's cabin. Cole sat in one of the armchairs while Raj and Eli stood at the kitchen bar, looking at a map of the area spread out across it. Their voices were low enough that Cole couldn't hear them.

After a moment, Eli folded up the map and stuffed it in his back pocket. He said something to Raj and then grabbed his backpack from where he'd left it in a chair at the kitchen bar.

"Are you leaving?" Cole asked, narrowing his eyes.

Eli and Raj exchanged a look. Eli cleared his throat and said, "Yeah. Figure it's probably best to get a move on before even more ghouls start turning. This place is about to be a bloodbath. We figured Facility B had the satellite phones—we can take the Jeep and call for help from there."

Cole stood. "I'll get my stuff."

Raj and Eli both froze. Raj raised his eyebrows at Eli, nodding toward Cole. Out of the four members of No Flash Photography, Raj was the least likely to start conflict, but the most likely to show it on his face when he wanted to.

"What?" Cole asked. He cocked his head to the side. "You just said

*we're going to Facility B, right? You need Hank's pass to get inside and
I have it in—"*

He cut off as Eli reached into his pocket and withdrew the
white key card.

"I think we're good," he said, tucking it back into his jeans.

Cole's lips parted. He wrinkled his brow. After a beat, he said,
"Guys, what's going on?"

"You're not coming," Eli finally said. He pulled the backpack over
his shoulders. "Sorry, man. We can't risk having a ghoul with us."

Cole wrinkled his nose. "What the hell is that supposed to mean?
I've done everything you asked me to! I–I got you into my stepdad's lab,
I grew the stupid seeds to make the Menthexus—hell, I even snuck into
all the bars and added it to the drinks just like you asked me to!"

"And you did great," Eli said. His voice was completely even as he
stared directly into Cole's eyes. "Melanie would have appreciated it."

Cole flinched at the sound of his dead sister's name. He crossed his
arms over his chest, averting his eyes.

"Don't bring her into this," Cole muttered.

"That's why you agreed to do it, though," Eli pointed out. His eyebrows flexed, mouth twitching toward a scowl. "To honor your sister's
memory. And this how you can keep doing it—let us get out of here
before shit really hits the fan. She wouldn't want us getting caught
up in this."

"We were supposed to do this together," Cole shot back. He threw his
arms out at the two of them. "You're just going to abandon me? After
everything I've done?"

When neither of them spoke, Cole looked at Raj. "You're seriously
okay with this?"

Raj was silent beside Eli, his gaze turned pointedly toward the window. So quiet Cole could barely hear him, he said, "It was always going to be like this, mate. You're a ghoul. We can't trust you to not turn on us."

"Bullshit," Cole spat. He took a step toward Eli. "Give me that key card—"

Eli stumbled back, snatching something out of his pocket and holding it out. It caught the lamplight, glittering silver in a small vial.

Menthexus.

"You wouldn't," Cole snarled.

Eli set his jaw. His eyes darted to Raj for a moment before he gave the other boy a nod.

"Would I use it on Cole Greenleaf? Never." Eli said. "But on the monster that killed my girlfriend? Different story."

In one fluid motion, Eli slammed the vial on the ground. As it shattered on impact, a burst of silvery power shot into the air. Cole tried to hold his breath, but it was too late.

His stomach clenched, and he fell to his knees, choking.

"That's more like it," Eli muttered. "At least now you'll look like what you are." He nodded to Raj. "Come on. Let's get out of here."

They left Cole writhing on the floor, snarling their names as the humanity drained from his body.

That night, I awoke to the sound of gunfire.

I stirred from where I'd fallen asleep on the couch. With nothing else to do, Celeste, Jasmine, and I had sat around playing board games for a couple hours just to pass the time and try to get our minds off everything. It didn't work, but I did win at Yahtzee twice.

Celeste had fallen asleep in the middle of a Monopoly game, and Jasmine hadn't been far behind.

So when the unmistakable sound of gunpowder igniting came, I hopped to my feet. Screaming came next, high pitched and strangled. I reached over and shook Celeste awake before hopping up to run to the front windows. I threw the curtains open while Celeste made a sleepy groaning sound behind me and Jasmine whispered a curse.

Outside was a brutal scene.

Two bodies lay in the road, throats torn out and blood pooling in the dirt beneath them. Two huge, spindly figures stood hunched over them, bones jutting out from beneath the skin. They sliced their claws through the corpses' chests and pulled back with dripping flesh in their hands, immediately shoving it in their mouths, which unhinged to accommodate.

Two National Guardsmen—the ones who had been watching our cabin, I guessed—fired a spray of bullets. The monsters didn't even pause their feasting. As soon as the bullets shot through the skin, it stitched closed instantly, the bullets falling lamely to the ground. Instead, the creatures just tilted their heads back, letting out a horrible keening sound before digging back into their kills.

"Holy shit," I breathed.

I pivoted to tell the others, but just then, something tapped on the glass of the back door.

Through the sliding glass, a slim, tall figure lurked in the darkness. For a moment, my heart squeezed in my chest.

Val?

"The hell is happening?" Jasmine muttered as I sprinted to the back door. "Zoey? What—?"

I threw the sliding door open. Maybe Val had somehow held back the Menthexus's effects, maybe—

But standing there, ragged and covered in blood, wasn't Val.

It was Cole.

I started, "The fu—?"

"Um. Hey?" Cole cleared his throat and forced a smile, though it came off droopy at the edges. "Long time no see."

"What are you doing here?" I demanded. I threw a finger out toward the bloody scene in front of the cabin. "Dunno if you noticed, but there's a whole Sam Raimi film happening out front!"

"I needed something to distract the soldiers," Cole said quickly. When my eyebrows shot up, he quickly added, "Look, I'm just begging for you to listen to me for a minute, okay? I think we might be the only people who can help each other."

"What in the world is that supposed to mean, and why the hell would I believe you?"

"Look, I'm sorry." Cole put his foot in the door to stop me from slamming it on him. Which was a good idea, because I was, in fact, about to do just that. "I panicked this morning and didn't know what to do, so I made a terrible mistake."

"I bit a guy's arm off because of you, dickweed," I snapped. "And now I'm going to turn into a weird gangly monster, so you know what? I don't really want to talk to you."

"Is that Cole?" Celeste asked. She hopped up from the couch, hair sticking to the side of her face where she'd fallen asleep on it. Her eyebrows slanted inward. "Little bastard—"

"Look, I know!" Cole held up his hands before I could further my attempts to shut him out of our cabin. "You have absolutely no reason to trust me, but just listen for a second, okay? I can get you out of De Luz Valley *and* get you an antidote to the Menthexus—you just have to give me a minute to explain."

I paused, breath hitching in my throat.

"There's an antidote?"

Cole nodded. "Hank Niedermeyer—the scientist who created Menthexus—was my stepfather. He had a change of heart after ghouls started turning into anthropophagi. He was the whistleblower who alerted the media that Blackwell Pharmaceuticals was doing the unethical human testing. He managed to craft an antidote, but the company fired him and banned him from returning after they found out that he was the whistleblower. He never got to use it—but we still can."

I paused, studying his face. A lock of red hair hung in his eyes, and there was a bleeding wound on his cheek. Upon closer inspection, it looked almost like a bullet graze. In fact, based on the holes in his shirt, it appeared he'd been shot not once, not twice, but *three* separate times. That said, none of the wounds were currently bleeding despite the fabric of his T-shirt being spattered with it.

"Please," he urged. "If we don't help each other, we're both out of options. Because it turns out Eli screwed me over, and now I've been exposed to Menthexus too. So...I guess you could say we have a common interest."

I hated to admit it, but he wasn't wrong.

Finally, I crossed my arms and nodded.

"Fine. But we don't have a lot of time—whatever made the guards run off isn't going to distract them for long."

"*What?*" Behind me, Celeste made a choked sound in the back of her throat. "Zoey, this is the guy who drugged you *and* Val! Why would you—?"

"Because we don't have much of a choice, do we?" I gestured outside. "And this may be our only opening so—talk fast."

"We need your car," Cole said, pointing to the Mini. "And we need to go before the guards deal with the anthropophagi."

Jasmine's eyes widened. "How many are there?"

"Total? No idea. The new ones turn at slightly different rates depending on age, gender—stuff like that. But I saw at least three on the way here. They smelled blood from the guards I knocked out and attacked."

All of our eyes widened in horror.

Cole cleared his throat. "Right, sorry. Look—there's another road out of De Luz. I can explain in the car."

I looked over my shoulder at Celeste and Jasmine. Jasmine's eyebrows edged toward her hairline while Celeste was stock-still and slack-jawed. Okay, so not a lot of help coming from them.

But it was true what I'd said: we literally didn't have anything else to go on.

"All right," I finally said. I pointed a finger between Cole's eyes. "I'm going to get my keys, but if you put even a *toe* out of place, I will rip every fang out of your mouth one by one, understand?"

He gulped.

"Understood."

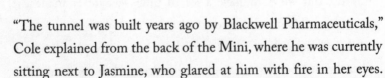

"The tunnel was built years ago by Blackwell Pharmaceuticals," Cole explained from the back of the Mini, where he was currently sitting next to Jasmine, who glared at him with fire in her eyes. It was good we'd convinced her not to bring her bat, because she absolutely would have knocked Cole's head off his shoulders if given a chance. "They used De Luz Valley as their meeting place before going off the grid to Facility B. No one outside the company knew it existed."

"That's why the CDC and the National Guard don't know about this road?" I guessed. Not shockingly, the Mini wasn't doing great off-roading. Each bump jostled us in our seats, and it was slow going. The only upside was that there was somewhat of a path worn in the dirt, so I didn't have to worry about driving over a patch of cacti and ruining my tires. My headlights, however, were moving so much it was hard to keep straight where that path actually was. It was lucky the soldiers had been so busy with the anthropophagi that we were able to drive away without them giving chase. We definitely wouldn't have won against one of their hefty trucks.

"How do you know so much about Blackwell Pharmaceuticals?" Jasmine asked, crossing her arms.

"My stepfather, Hank, was the lead scientist on the Menthexus program—the one who originally created the drug," Cole explained. He held on tightly to the safety bar in the back. He'd begun to turn a bit green, and it occurred to me that I might need to add *puked all over my car* to his list of crimes if we didn't make it to steadier ground soon.

He went on, "Hank died of a heart attack a year or so after the Hollowing, but he left his research notes on his computer at our house. It was easy for me to look through everything and find maps and coordinates to the two facilities Blackwell Pharmaceuticals were operating out of here."

"Did those notes also teach you how to make Menthexus?" Celeste asked, her eyes spearing through him in the rearview mirror.

Cole nodded, biting his lip. "Yeah. Hank kept a few of the modified spearmint seeds at home, so I planted them and worked from there. It's surprisingly easy to make."

"Oh, great," Jasmine muttered. "At least we don't have to worry about running out of that anytime soon. Never know when you might need to ruin a ghoul's life."

Cole winced. "I deserve that."

Outside, the rock wall grew closer and closer, and with it, an arched hole in the rock, concealed behind two sizable juniper trees. There was a gate out front, but it looked like someone had already opened it.

"Raj and Eli came through here," Cole explained. "We're probably an hour or so behind them. They're headed to Facility B to get satellite phones."

"They're in on this too?" Celeste said.

Cole nodded. "Kaiden was the one who originally came up with it, but they're all in on it. Eli sort of became the de facto leader, if only because Kaiden's less of a *plans* guy and more of a *I don't care how but I want to see ghouls dead* guy."

All of us shivered at the sound of Kaiden's name.

"You all okay?" Cole asked.

"Long story," I muttered. "So the plan—what was it exactly? To randomly drug ghouls at a music festival so they murdered innocent people? What's the rationale there anyway? Just for fun, or…?"

Cole hung his head, silent for a moment. He reached up and gently touched one of the bullet wounds in his arm, which was already most of the way closed. He flinched, hissing faintly under his breath.

"We wanted to use the Menthexus to cause as big of an incident as possible," Cole explained. The tunnel was pitch dark, so the only light in the Mini came from the glowing red ring around the center console. His freckled skin looked sickly.

He went on, "The goal was to do something that would damage the reputation of ghouls enough that they'd be permanently sent to specialized facilities away from the rest of society. As soon as I told them about my stepdad's research, we knew that's how we could do it."

"Why the hell would you agree to that?" Jasmine pushed. "I mean, you're a ghoul, right? You really wanna be trapped in a jail cell for the rest of your life?"

"Of course not." Cole looked out the window as the darkness rushed past. "But...I owe it to Eli. Some stuff happened during the Hollowing that I regret, and helping him with this felt like the only way I could atone."

"Did you know about the anthropophagi when you made that plan?" Celeste grumbled under her breath. "Or was that just an added bonus?"

Cole rubbed the back of his neck, shoulders tense. We were nearing the midway point of the tunnel now, the moonlight on the other end barely visible. He breathed out a sigh through his nose, then shook his head.

"All I knew was that Menthexus turned ghouls feral," he explained. "But a few weeks before the festival, Eli, Raj, Kaiden, and I went to Facility B to use its tech to make as much Menthexus as we could. And when we got there..."

"Facility B," Celeste repeated. She turned toward me, eyes widened. "Zoey, that's where the logs we found at the burned-out lab mentioned they were doing the human testing."

"Oh, shit. But…" I threw a look over my shoulder at Cole for just a fraction of a second before looking back at the road. "How…?"

Cole swallowed grimly. "When the project got shut down, they just…left the anthropophagi and locked the facility down. They didn't want anyone to know what they'd created.

"So when we got there, we found most of them right where the Blackwell team left them. A few of the cells were broken, so some of them may have escaped, but the others were still inside. Somehow, they've just been in a weird state of stasis. As soon as we went inside and they smelled us, they beat themselves bloody throwing themselves against the walls of their cells trying to get to us."

We all went quiet. The engine roared beneath us as I pushed the Mini to go faster, my fingers tightening around the wheel. All I could think of was those poor people, parents and siblings and children, volunteering to test a drug that could keep their families safe only to become monsters that refused to die.

And about Val, who was out there somewhere turning into the same thing.

"You said something about an antidote though, right?" Celeste said, barely raising her voice above a whisper. "Can we reverse it?"

Cole nodded. "Assuming the antidote is still where Hank said he left it before the shutdown. There should be a ton of it at Facility B, but getting to it is another story, and we're running out of time before even more ghouls at Desert Bloom turn completely."

I narrowed my eyes at the road. "Then I guess we'd better hurry."

I slammed my foot down on the gas.

twenty

Dale Verge
@DaVergen

Trapped in my cabin @DesertBloom and I legit think I'm gonna starve to death here. This shit cannot be for real.
At least Fyre Fest had salad ffs.

–Excerpt from BuzzFeed's 29 Tweets That Show WTF Is Happening at Desert Bloom.

Facility B took another fifteen minutes to get to, and each second felt like it was sliding through my fingers like smoke. The moon crested high in the sky, lighting the path as the Mini cut through the night. The others braced themselves as I revved the engine as hard as it would go.

"There," Cole said, pointing ahead. "That's it."

From the outside, Facility B looked unassuming. It was white, with few windows and a slanted roof that gave it the look of more recent architecture. The back of it, however, was a large dome with a glass roof that seemed to plunge into the earth, giving an almost alien look to the whole thing. The outside had a small, paved walkway that was overgrown, much like the one Celeste and I had seen at the burnt lab. Scraggly brush framed it on either side, yucca and Joshua trees scattered around the perimeter. Light streamed from what few windows there were, but they were high up enough it was impossible to see anything through them.

A black Jeep sat parked outside. At the sight of it, Cole scowled.

"The only way to get in is to use an employee key card," Cole explained as I pulled the Mini to a stop in front of the building. "And Eli stole mine."

"There's no way I'm climbing in through one of those tiny windows," Jasmine muttered.

"What's your plan then?" I popped my door open and stepped out, everyone else following my lead. I spun on Cole once we were outside and added, "Wait for Eli and Raj to come out?"

Cole turned his gaze up toward the facility, scrunching his nose as he thought. After a second, he pulled a brief frown before saying, "There's…one other option."

Jasmine, Celeste, and I raised our eyebrows.

"All the locks in the facility are on the same power grid," he explained. "If I cut the reserve power, everything unlocks."

"Great." I gestured toward him. "So let's cut the power. Clock's ticking, buddy."

"Right, but—" Cole cut off, wincing. "You saw pictures of this place, right? Including the anthropophagi in cages?"

I nodded. "Yeah?"

"Well… Cutting the power will free them too."

Jasmine started to mutter under her breath, "This fucking guy—"

"Fine," I cut in. Celeste and Jasmine both jerked their heads around to look at me. I added, "What choice do we have?"

"Zoey, he may well be lying," Celeste whispered, leaning in close so only Jasmine and I would hear. "We have no reason to believe he's actually got any sort of antidote in there, and if there actually are anthropophagi inside, those things will eat anything they can get their teeth in, us included."

"She's right," Jasmine agreed. "We have absolutely no idea what's behind those doors. This could easily be a trap."

I nodded. I couldn't exactly argue that Cole was deserving of our trust—he certainly hadn't done anything to earn it. But he had gotten us here, and just making it to Facility B was the biggest and best lead we had.

"Look, I don't trust him either. But this is our best shot at helping Val," I said. I held a hand out to both of them, and after a moment, they each took one. I squeezed both. "We just have to watch each other's backs. We get in, we figure out if he's telling the truth about an antidote, and we find Val ASAP."

"Fine. But if any anthropophagi attack us," Jasmine whispered, "I'm tripping him and running for it."

"Ditto," Celeste said.

"Hey, um." Cole cleared his throat. "So are we doing this, or…?"

"Agreed—definitely in favor of tripping him and leaving him for dead." I squeezed my friends' hands again. "For Val."

"For Val," they both agreed, squeezing back.

I turned to Cole, switching to a normal volume. "All right, Cole. Lead the way."

The backup generator that had been powering Facility B since its shutdown was in a small fenced-in area at the side of the building. While Cole hopped over the fence, I grabbed the two flashlights I had in the Mini and gave them to my friends. Just as Celeste was taking hers, there was a brief flicker of light from the facility windows.

Then, the whole place went dark.

Jasmine wandered forward to get a better look at the entrance. I took a step to do the same, but Celeste caught my wrist before I could.

"Wait," she said, gently meeting my eyes. I stopped and she reached out, pulling me into a tight hug. Into my hair, she whispered, "Promise me something."

"Something specific, or…?"

"Don't be a martyr." Celeste pulled back, keeping her arms around me but staring into my eyes. "I know you, and I know how much you're willing to sacrifice for other people. Just this once, please think of yourself. For me."

I nodded gently. "Promise."

The next moment, Celeste leaned in and pressed a hard kiss to my lips. Whereas our first two kisses had been soft, this one was rushed, desperate and scared and hopeful. I gently cupped her cheek and kissed back, pressing onto my tiptoes to reach.

Celeste drew back, then pulled me into another hug. "Thank you."

"Um, hello?"

We turned to find Jasmine staring at us wide-eyed. "Did I miss something? I thought y'all were still pining!"

"Pining?" I repeated.

Jasmine scoffed. "You're not subtle."

Celeste and I exchanged a look, both turning pink. I crossed my arms over my chest while Celeste rubbed the back of her neck sheepishly, coughing out a little laugh.

"All right," Cole's voice came. He approached, wiping dust off on his jeans, adding, "Power's off. We're good to head in."

"Took long enough." Jasmine gestured to the door. "Lead the way."

Cole nodded. As we approached the door, he said, "Just keep in mind—anthropophagi don't have great vision, but they can hear really well. We need to keep our voices down once we're inside."

"You heard him," Jasmine muttered to Celeste and I. "Suck face quietly."

"What?" Cole said.

"What?" Jasmine repeated. "None of your business."

I withheld a snort as Cole rolled his eyes and lit the flashlight on his phone. I did the same while Jasmine and Celeste turned on the big flashlights.

Cole pulled open the front door and waited for everyone to step inside before he let it swing closed behind us. Immediately, the darkness enveloped us.

The entryway was similar in layout to the burned-out lab, starting with the front desk area. Overturned potted plants littered the ground, their contents long dead. Two sets of footprints were visible in the dirt, leading deeper into the facility.

Cole pointed to them. "Eli and Raj."

"Let's hope they get eaten," Jasmine whispered.

We pushed deeper into the room, following Cole toward a door to the back area. He carefully shouldered it open, revealing a long hallway. Waving us forward, we tiptoed in.

I shone my flashlight at the doors as I walked, the faint tap of our footsteps the only sound to keep our frantic breathing company. Most doors were closed, but one near the end was just faintly ajar. Cole held a finger to his lips before going to it, gently pushing it open.

Someone—some*thing*—screamed.

I jolted back, throwing my hands out for my friends. It took me a second to realize the sound was coming from somewhere below us. It had that specific keening, animalistic quality that I'd become far too familiar with recently.

In response, another scream, slightly farther away, echoed up through the floor. My heart raced and sweat wetted the back of my neck.

"They're out," Cole whispered. He nodded into the room. "This might help us, though."

We followed after him into the side room, lights illuminating what appeared to be an equipment closet. A lot of it was lab equipment—goggles, gloves, the usual—but hanging on the wall were a number of long, black batons. Cole reached up and grabbed one before passing it to me.

"Stun baton," he explained. "For the anthropophagi. Press the button on the end, and it'll produce a few thousand volts of electricity."

I took it in my free hand, feeling its weight against my palm. "Cool."

He handed two more out to the girls before taking one for himself. He slipped it into his belt loop and gestured for us to follow.

The hall took a sharp turn, and we came upon a shiny silver elevator door and an emergency staircase beside it.

Another screech, this time much closer, rang out.

I cursed. "Is it on this floor?"

Cole shook his head, pointing to the elevator. In the silence, I could just barely make out the sound of something sharp scraping against metal.

"I think it's climbing up the elevator shaft," Cole whispered.

"No *thank you*," Jasmine said, eyes rounded into twin moons. "Man, screw this place—"

Just as she said it, the elevator door let out a metallic screech. It opened a tiny sliver.

And from the darkness inside, a long, inhuman hand reached out, claws gripping the edge of the door.

"Go!" Cole shouted. "Stairs, now!"

We didn't need to be told twice. Celeste, Jasmine, and I took off sprinting for the door. Meanwhile, Cole ignited the end of his stun baton. He jerked it, hard, into the anthropophagus's hand, shooting blue bolts of electricity into its ashen skin.

The creature shrieked and recoiled into the elevator shaft. Cole's shoes squeaked on the floor as he pivoted, sprinting after us.

Once he pushed through the door, we slammed it closed. I spotted a dead bolt lock on the side and threw it into place. Something on the other side slammed into the door with a snarl.

"Come on, come on!" Cole cried. "Follow me!"

The four of us bounded down the stairs three steps at a time, descending into inky darkness. Behind us, the dead bolt rattled as the creature on the other side slammed against it once, twice, three times in a row. It shrilled, and I had to throw my hands over my ears to block out the sound.

Despite my better judgment, I threw a glance over my shoulder. The door at the top of the stairs had a small, rectangular window at the top. For a moment, I caught a sliver of the anthropophagus's face staring through, even gaunter and more skeletal than the one I'd seen outside the other lab. This must have been one of the ones in stasis, just waiting for its chance to feed again.

It opened its mouth and snarled once more before it vanished from the window.

The banging stopped.

"It's not following," I told the others.

"It'll try to find another path around," Cole said. "We should keep moving."

"Let the record show," Celeste whispered under her breath, gripping the fabric over her heart, "I hate this."

We descended the rest of the way down the stairs, flashlights held low.

At the bottom, we found ourselves in a lab. Towering machines sat next to workstations covered in loose papers and pipettes. A microscope lay overturned on the floor in front of us, its glass slide shattered into a thousand pieces that reflected back the light from my phone. Papers were scattered across the floor, some shredded where claws had torn through. I sidestepped to avoid the microscope, letting my flashlight rove over the walls.

Up against the wall on the left side were five ajar doors, each with a small window at the top. There was a small slot near the bottom with a sliding mechanism to open and close it. As I shone my light on it, a myriad of white claw marks became visible around it.

My breath caught in my throat.

"Those were empty when we first got here," Cole explained, his flashlight beam joining mine to illuminate the cells. "All the anthropophagi were kept in cells on the next floor down."

"Any chance some of the antidote you mentioned would be in here?" Celeste asked. She wandered up to a metal cabinet and popped the door open. Inside appeared to be a number of bottles, each with a different chemical label. She squinted as she gave the labels a once over.

Cole shook his head. "It's down in Hank's old office, which was in the basement. He was trying to test it on the anthropophagi to see if it would work on them."

"Hm." Celeste narrowed her eyes. "That sounds like an awfully convenient way to get us to go to the spooky basement full of cannibal monsters."

Cole blinked. "What are you saying?"

"Nothing." Celeste crossed her arms. "Just that I think you're full of—"

Just then another shout exploded from a door to our far right. This time, though, it sounded much more human.

Unlike the shriek that came immediately after it.

"Hide!" Cole cried.

I took a gasping breath. Celeste's hand caught my wrist and she yanked me with her to the closest hiding spot—which just happened to be one of the cells. We stumbled through the half-open door, Jasmine and Cole right behind us. We landed in a crouched position out of sight. I clapped a hand over my mouth.

The metal door swung open.

Raj stumbled through. His normally coiffed pompadour was wild and unkempt, his cheeks drained of warmth. He spun and slammed the door closed behind him, quickly followed by banging from the other side. He pressed his back against the door, gritting his teeth as the creature on the other side flung itself against it. The door rattled, Raj's fingers clamped as tight as possible around the handle.

We sat frozen, completely paralyzed. Softly as I could, I pressed my hand to the ground to hold me steady. However, as I did, I felt something crack under my weight.

Shattered into pieces beneath my splayed fingers was a human jawbone. The bone was pearly white in the low light. A few loose teeth were scattered on the floor around it. Each one was pointed like a canine, perfect for tearing.

Despite myself, I screamed.

Raj was so startled by the sound that he lost his grip on the door for half a second—which was just enough time for the creature on the other side to burst through.

Raj hit the ground with a shout. From the open door leapt another anthropophagus, this one short-haired and even larger than the first one we'd seen. It opened its mouth to cry out, spittle flicking from its jagged fangs. Raj scrambled backward, trying to crawl out of its way. He grabbed a hot plate that had been knocked to the floor and lanced it at the creature. It wasn't fazed—instead, it leapt on him, pinning his arms down. It snarled in his face, cords of spittle flicking onto his cheeks.

For a moment, the image of Kaiden's body resurfaced from my memories. His lightless eye sockets pointed toward the stars, teeth peeking through his shredded cheek. Then the hunter, with nothing left but his feet in his boots, and Devin Han, bathing in his own blood.

Not again.

I can't watch another person die.

I jumped to my feet, igniting the end of my stun baton. Cole and the girls jerked around in time to see me burst from the cell door. I waved my baton in the air, electric blue light bouncing off the walls.

"Hey!" I shouted. "Over here!"

"Zoey, no!" Celeste cried.

At the sight of the baton, the anthropophagus drew back, a growl rumbling in its throat. It occurred to me that it had definitely seen one before—and probably been shocked more times than I could count.

Raj used the distraction to free himself from its grasp, scrambling backward and pressing himself to one of the metal worktables.

Meanwhile, the anthropophagus took a step sideways, its back arched as it crawled on all fours like an animal. Its claws clicked against the linoleum floor with each step. Black bile drip, drip, dripped from its mouth, spattering onto the floor.

"Back up," I told it, taking a step forward. I waved the baton in front of me, hoping it couldn't tell how hard I was fighting not to shake with terror. "Or I'll put this in your eye."

The anthropophagus opened its mouth wide, jaw elastic. With no lips to hold it back, its rows and rows of jagged teeth were on full display, its lower jaw hanging at an angle like it was broken. Its eyes were almost entirely white, clouded over and dry in its unblinking sockets.

It took a step back toward the hallway.

"Good," I said. "Keep go—"

Without warning, the creature reeled back before launching itself into the air.

Its body slammed into mine. I hit the ground so hard it knocked the wind out of me, red bursts scattering across my vision. Its teeth snapped in my face. I barely had time to wedge the stun baton between its jaws, using all my strength to hold it back. Bile and saliva dripped from its mouth onto my face, dappling my cheeks with black spatters. The muscles in my arms strained to hold its weight back.

A shape appeared at my side and jammed their baton into the monster's side. It shrieked as electricity jumped across its skin, the smell of burnt skin rising from its skeletal ribs. It hopped back with a snarl as another baton crackled to life on my left.

Jasmine and Celeste flanked me on either side. While I gasped for breath, they descended on the anthropophagus, batons sparking. They drove it back with each step, even as it snapped at the air between them and snarled. Celeste jerked her baton toward it so it recoiled with a wince back into the hallway.

Jasmine took the opening to slam the door shut and twist the lock into place.

With a final screech, the anthropophagus fled down the hall.

For a beat, we all just stood trying to catch our breath. Raj slowly peeked out from around the edge of the workstation, tears in his eyes.

"Thank you," he said to me, voice nearly cracking as he said it. He cleared his throat. "That was, ah. Pretty ballsy."

"You're welcome," I managed between wheezes.

"What are you doing here, anyway?" he asked. "How did you even find this place?"

"I showed them," Cole's voice came from the cell. He stepped out and lit his flashlight, shining it in Raj's face. His gold septum piercing winked as he squeezed his eyes closed, flinching away from the light. "Where's Eli?"

"Cole?" Raj cracked an eye open. "You're…"

"Here? Alive? Yeah, no thanks to you." Cole cleared his throat. "We came for the Menthexus antidote. You'd be wise to get out before another anthropophagus shows up."

Raj shook his head, "You shouldn't go down there. Once we got the satellite phones to call for help, Eli decided he wanted to torch the place—starting with your stepfather's office. He wants to get rid of the antidote so there's no way to turn back anyone at Desert Bloom."

"Wait, as in set it on fire?" My jaw dropped. "But—if he's in the basement, how will he get out?"

"There's an emergency exit down there," Cole explained, narrowing his eyes. "I would have suggested we try to get in that way, but it's padlocked, and the key is in Hank's office."

"He told me to come up here and look for flammable chemicals we could use to start a fire," Raj explained, pointing to the cabinet that Celeste had been looking at before. "Then the power went off. I tried to hide, but…"

"You were gonna help him?" I accused, eyebrows shooting up. I'd managed to catch my breath enough to stand, so I used the opportunity to get up and loom over Raj where he was still sitting on the floor. "What the hell is wrong with you? Without that antidote, everyone you drugged at Desert Bloom is doomed to stay a monster for the rest of their lives!"

"They're ghouls," Raj shot back. "They were monsters to begin with. We just made it more obvious to the untrained eye."

"We should have let that thing eat you," Jasmine grumbled, rolling her eyes.

Before she could continue, I cut in, "Listen, while we're all clearly having a lot of fun here, we're on kind of a tight deadline, so I say we should get a move on. Save the theatrics about how evil and monstrous ghouls are for when we have Val back."

Celeste and Jasmine began to nod just as Raj said, "You're looking for Val?"

We froze. Slowly, I held the baton out in his direction.

His eyes widened.

I held my finger against the button at the end but didn't press it. "You know something, don't you? Where is she?"

He held up his hands. "Whoa, okay, back up. Yeah, I know where she is—she attacked our Jeep on the way over here. Didn't realize she was a ghoul until she tried to rip our throats out. Clearly she hadn't eaten recently, because Eli was able to knock her out and put her in the back without much effort."

"Did he hurt her?" Jasmine demanded. She stormed forward, coming to stand beside me, her fingers twitching toward the button on her baton.

Raj shrunk back. "I-I dunno! Look, all I know is that she was still breathing and he took her down to the basement to put her with the rest of the anthropophagi. No idea if she's still down there, but she was before the power went off."

"Come on," I said, nodding to the sign at the far end of the room that indicated the next staircase down. "Let's go see if he's telling the truth."

"Wait!" Raj frantically looked between the four of us. "You can't just leave me here!"

"What goes around comes around, asshole," Cole muttered under his breath. He waved us forward. "Let's move."

Celeste, Jasmine, and I exchanged glances before nodding and following him toward the basement.

If you're down there, Val, I thought to myself. *We're coming for you.*

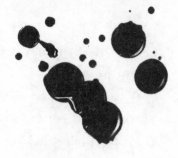

twenty-one

What do you owe a friend
When your heart is still beating
And they've reached the end?
Skin turned to dust, I'll lay you to sleep
Baby, I promise, I'll bury you deep.

—*"Monster" by No Flash Photography*

The basement of Facility B was silent as a tomb.

After leaving Raj in the lab, we'd found the next set of stairs down. Descending the steps, the anthropophagi's screams began to sound more distant—it seemed at least two had made it to the first floor, in addition to the one still on the second. I had no idea how many were left in the basement, but I prayed that maybe they'd all dispersed.

We found ourselves in a long hallway at the bottom of the stairs. At the end was a large, two-door entryway with warning signs on each side: ENTER WITH CAUTION. SPECIAL

CLEARANCE REQUIRED. LIVE SPECIMENS. On either side were three doors, a few of which were ajar.

"Where's your stepdad's office?" I whispered to Cole.

"Through there," he explained, pointing to the door with all the warnings. "He kept a sort of...personal lab down here. He didn't work well with others, but he got results, so they let him set up this nightmare."

"That's where the anthropophagi were kept?" Celeste guessed.

Cole nodded. "With any luck, they'll have taken care of Eli for us. Better yet, maybe even attacked each other. They don't seem averse to cannibalism if the need arises."

"Our friend might be in there," I snapped. "Have a heart."

"Oh—right, sorry." Cole waved us onward. "Follow me."

The four of us crept down the hall trying to keep as quiet as possible. My heartbeat rang in my ears, and the hairs on my arms stood on end. Every nerve in my body seemed to crackle at once, electric and waiting for something, anything, to touch me so I could zap it. I gripped the stun baton so tightly my knuckles blanched. Every tiny breath and shuffle around me set my teeth on edge.

On either side of me, Jasmine and Celeste seemed to be feeling the same, judging only by the way they kept their flashlights low and their batons at the ready.

At the end of the hall, Cole gripped the handle. With a click, the door opened, letting out a high-pitched squeak that nearly made my heart vault out of my chest.

For beat, we stood in perfect, still silence.

Nothing happened.

Cole gestured for us to follow. Silently, we tiptoed forward.

What I realized the moment we entered was that we'd made it

to the back of the building where the massive dome rose up from the earth. From the inside of it, I could see the chalky glow of the moon directly above us in the sky. Its light illuminated what had once been a huge underground greenhouse, tables lined up and covered in dead plants.

"Hey." Jasmine tapped my shoulder. "Look over there."

Along the sides of the walls were cells made of what appeared to be plastic, completely clear so we could see inside. The doors, made of white bars, all hung ajar.

Except one.

"Val!" Jasmine cried.

She broke off in a run, and Celeste and I followed after her, dodging around tables. The moonlight was bright enough that it was easy to pick out Val's unconscious form. As we got closer, though, my stomach clenched.

While we were clearly looking at Val, her body had changed. Her formerly short legs were long and willowy, her kneecaps visible beneath dull, lifeless skin. The yellow dress she had on was torn, revealing a stretch of her rib cage, each bone jutting out from beneath. Her face had gone gaunt, and while she still had her lips, her features had turned startlingly skeletal. Black veins pulsed beside her eyes, and her elongated fingers were each tipped with a wicked black talon.

Still, she was breathing.

Which meant we could still save her.

"You shouldn't have come here."

We spun around, flashlight beams joining to illuminate Eli, who stood with a stun baton of his own in hand near one of the greenhouse tables. His skin was slick with sweat, and a lock of black hair fell in his eyes. He had a long, bleeding cut on his jawline, and claw marks down the side of his left arm, slicing through his tattoo sleeve and leaking blood down his forearm and onto the floor drip by drip.

My stomach snarled and red stains began to push inward from the corners of my vision. I drew back, wincing. God, I was starving.

"There you are," Cole growled. His teeth lengthened into fangs. "You left me for *dead* after everything I've done for you!"

Eli coughed on a laugh, then held a finger to his lips. Quietly, he said, "I'd keep my voice down if I were you."

With his free hand, he pointed up. My entire body stiffened as I followed his finger up to the towering walls that lead to the domed roof. There, twenty feet up and hanging by their claws, were two anthropophagi. One was big, masculine-presenting, and maybe nine feet tall with scraggly black hair and jaundiced-looking skin. The other was a foot or so shorter, with a shaved head and wrinkled skin like it must have a couple decades older. Their cloudy eyes stared directly at us. The younger one ran a long black tongue over where its lips used to be, hissing faintly.

My heart shot into my throat and I choked.

"Doesn't take much to provoke them," Eli said, keeping his voice low. He lazily waved his baton in their direction. "I kept them back with this, but who knows how long that'll last."

"Cut the shit," I growled. "Where's the Menthexus antidote?"

"Hank's office is that way," Cole said, pointing to the other side of the room where another door hung ajar. "It'll be in little vials in a fridge next to his work desk. There should be syringes we can use to inject it in there as well."

Eli shook his head. "No—no, let's slow down a little. No one is using that stuff. Not while I'm here."

"You really hate ghouls that much?" Celeste asked, wrinkling her forehead. "That you'd condemn people like your bandmate and the girl you've been flirting with for days to being trapped as monsters for the rest of their lives?"

"They already are monsters," Eli said. He pointed his baton at Cole. "Did he tell you what he did? During the Hollowing?"

"Eli—" Cole started.

"He murdered his own sister!"

The anthropophagi growled above us, one of them jumping sideways and landing a little lower on the wall. Black bile leaked from its mouth, and I could smell the rotten stink of it from where I stood. We all stood paralyzed for a moment as it tilted its head back and forth, staring.

It didn't make another move.

"Don't talk about Melanie," Cole growled through his teeth after a beat, careful to keep his voice low.

"You'd love to forget that, wouldn't you?" Eli spat. To me, Jasmine, and Celeste he added, "Cole here tore his own sister to pieces in the middle of a FaceTime call with me. I got to watch him eat my girlfriend in real time and there was *nothing* I could do."

His voice caught as he said it, and he cut off, hanging his head. He reached his uninjured arm up, hand fisted as he rubbed his shining eyes. He added, voice shaking, "I can't wait to see you suffer half as much as she did—to finally get what you deserve. It's what Melanie would want."

"You get my sister's name out of your goddamn mouth—!"

Up above, the anthropophagi screamed. I was barely able to dive out of the way in time for them to drop down onto the floor, their bones and joints cracking as they straightened up and snarled at us. The girls and I stumbled back, arms out in front of each other, while Cole and Eli cursed, trying to duck out of the way.

The younger creature straightened up to its full height and wailed. A black tongue lolled out of its mouth as it dove onto Cole, knocking him back into the metal table with a bang. Eli screamed, and the older one slashed its claws across his face. The skin tore like wet tissue paper, blood bubbling up from inside and dyeing his left cheek crimson.

"Come on!" I told the girls. "We have to get to the office!"

They nodded and the three of us sprinted toward the door on the other side of the dome. We vaulted over the greenhouse tables, breath ragged between our teeth as we ducked and weaved through the maze of dead plants and equipment. Behind us, Eli screamed louder and louder, his voice echoing off the walls in a sharp cacophony. The stun batons surged, and blue flashes of electricity lighting up the room.

Halfway to the office, something huge tackled me from behind.

I yelped as I hit the floor, baton flying out of my hand. My chin hit linoleum and my teeth sliced through my tongue, the taste of blood sharp and metallic. Jagged claws dug into my back, piercing through skin and muscle. Hot pain shot up my spine, and I cried out as they sunk deeper, tearing through nerves and sinew.

"Zoey!" Celeste cried, skidding to a halt and spinning around. She held her stun baton up and lit it, only to go pale as it illuminated the creature's face.

"No," Jasmine choked. "*Val.*"

I craned my neck backward to find Val's skeletal face glaring down at me, her honey-brown eyes clouded over with white and her features sharp and elongated. Her mouth stretched from ear to ear like a Glasgow smile, two sets of broken glass teeth winking back at me from her bile-stained lips.

She tilted her head back and let out a wailing scream.

Well, I thought. *Nice knowing you guys.*

Just then, Jasmine jabbed her baton into Val's side, sending a shock through her. Val screamed, her voice suddenly more human, more familiar, like our friend and not a monster. She jumped back, whimpering.

Celeste grabbed me under the armpits and hauled me up while Jasmine waved her baton in the air, driving Val back a few feet. I finally got my feet under me just as Val let out another cry and lashed out at Jasmine. She barely had time to duck, and a claw snagged her shoulder. It tore, blood pouring down her side.

I unsheathed my sharpened teeth and claws in one motion. This was my opening.

I took a running jump and crashed into Val's back. She roared as I wrapped my arms around her neck and my legs around her torso. She flailed, trying to shake me off, but I had too tight of a hold on her.

"Valeria!" I shouted in her ear. "Come on, it's us! You have to remember!"

With another ground-shaking scream, Val reached back and grabbed ahold of my shirt. I yelped as she yanked me free. My claws tore at her skin on the way off, too shallow to rupture anything too important.

Val launched me into the air. I screamed, flailing as I came to a crashing halt, body slamming hard against a metal table. I felt something in my chest crack. Hot agony shot through my nerve endings with each tiny breath. I moaned, unable to move as I came to a stop in a pile of dead plant matter and dirt.

I shakily lifted my eyes. The world seemed to move in slow motion as Val came bounding toward me. Spittle flicked from her teeth and her claws were held aloft, stained red.

A figure stepped between us just in time, jabbing her baton directly into Val's chest.

Val's body convulsed before hitting the ground, twitching.

Celeste turned to me, baton lighting her face in pale blue light. She had a fine spray of blood on her left cheek, and a red mark around her eye that was definitely a few hours from bruising black. Her veins stood out black around her eyes, and her teeth and nails were sharpened, deadly points. It had been a long time since I'd seen her fully in her ghoul form, and something about it made my already thrumming heart beat faster.

"You okay?" she asked.

I shook my head. "I—rib, broken. I think."

At the same time, Val faintly lifted her head, moaning. She blinked, and for a moment, I thought I saw the cloudiness across her eyes clear.

"Val," I choked, wincing as another burst of hot pain jolted through my rib cage. "Please—we're your friends. We don't want to hurt you."

"We can help you," Celeste added softly. "You just have to let us."

"You're not a monster, Val," Jasmine added. She lowered her stun baton and took a step closer to her, expression soft. "You remember when I told you that, way back at that warehouse party in Aspen Flats? I never stopped believing it."

Val was quiet aside from the shuddering sound of her breath.

Slowly, she began to rise up again, and the three of us all drew back, tense.

Then, from across the room, one of the other anthropophagi wailed. Val took a step back and paused.

She turned and bounded off toward the sound.

The three of us all let out the breaths that we were holding at once. Celeste held a hand out for me and helped me to my feet as I winced at the jagged pain in my ribs. She took my arm and pulled it over her shoulder so I could lean on her.

"Come on," she said, nodding to the office. "While they're distracted."

The three of us limped as fast as we could, wincing with each scream and shriek behind us. Jasmine kept looking over her shoulder while I gritted my teeth, trying to brace myself for the pain that came with each step. Celeste gently offered words of encouragement, steady against me.

When we finally made it to the office, we closed the door behind us with a click. Only Jasmine held up her flashlight—Celeste must have dropped hers. The office was large, maybe double the size of what I'd expected, and looked to be a mix of metal workstations from the lab upstairs and a traditional office workstation with a heavy wooden desk and a computer. On the desk were dusty papers and framed family photos—one showed a man who must have been Hank Niedermeyer posing with two red-haired children. Cole and sister, I assumed.

"Cole said it'll be in a fridge next to his work desk," I said.

"Got it," Jasmine said. She pointed to a black cube beside the metal workstation and then knelt down to pop the door open. She shined her light into it, illuminating rows and rows of small glass vials with handwritten labels. A box of syringes was shoved in the door.

"We should hurry," Celeste said. "If they need to be refrigerated, they might not stay good for long."

Jasmine nodded. She swung her backpack around and started loading it with vials and a few ice packs that were in the little freezer box at the top of the mini fridge. Meanwhile, Celeste let go of me and knelt down to snag one and pry a needle from the box. She jabbed the needle through the vial's lid, drawing liquid inside.

"What are you doing?" I asked, leaning weakly against the wooden desk.

"Saving you from turning into one of those things," Celeste said. She turned around, syringe ready in hand. "Give me your arm."

"Do you know how to use that?"

Celeste shrugged. "There was a weird few months where my insurance was threatening to only cover my estrogen if I took it via injection, so I got a lot of pamphlets on how to do it. Granted, I have no idea how much of this you need, but we'll start small and add more if it's not working."

"Guess I don't have much of a choice." I held out my arm. "Go to town."

I barely felt the needle as Celeste sank it into my arm, pressing the syringe plunger down. The liquid felt cold going in, and I winced faintly.

"Done." She tossed the syringe in a wastebasket nearby.

"Hey," Jasmine said, pulling her backpack over her shoulder. She unpeeled something from the inside of the mini fridge, holding it up in the light. It was a key, a piece of tape still stuck to the side of it. "Do you think this goes to the emergency ex—?"

Before she could finish, though, something banged against the door. We all whipped around just in time for the door to fly open and a body to fall inside.

Covered in blood and laying on the ground was Eli, his face riddled with slashes and his clothes in tatters. He crawled over the threshold, dragging his leg behind him. It was mangled, the bone exposed beneath where a chunk had been bitten out. He moaned, reaching out for us with a shaking hand.

"Please," he begged. "She's going to—"

Just as fast as he'd appeared, a clawed hand appeared from the darkness and yanked him backward by the ankle.

As fast as we could manage, we darted after him. In the doorway, Jasmine held up her light, revealing Val dragging Eli back, her mouth now stained with his blood. Eli's nails scraped against the dirty floor as he tried to grip onto something, but Val was too strong. She lifted his leg to her mouth, jaw cracking open to reveal rows and rows of teeth.

"Help me!" Eli bawled.

"Ooh," Jasmine said, holding up a syringe, "he does *not* deserve this."

She launched forward, flying at Val with a shout.

Val's face jerked away from Eli's leg. She growled, dropping him, and tried to move out of the way. Jasmine let her fingernails curl into claws, teeth extending. She dove at Val, sinking her claws into her shoulder to anchor herself.

Val let out a scream, trying to shake Jasmine off. But in a single fluid motion, Jasmine jabbed the needle into her arm and shoved the plunger down.

The tension left Val's face. Jasmine pulled her claws out and Val swayed, eyes fluttering. Eli's leg slipped out of her grasp, and she braced herself against the floor.

"Did it work?" I asked.

After a tense beat, Val looked up at me. Her eyes had unclouded, and slowly the color seemed to return to her cheeks.

"Zoey?" She turned to the others. "Celeste? Jaz? What's going on?"

Jasmine threw her arms around her. "Oh, thank god."

"We can explain later," I said. The pain in my ribs was enough that I felt like I was going to pass out soon if I didn't get some kind of relief. Not to mention the wetness on my back that I knew was the bleeding puncture wounds from Val's claws. "Gotta find the emergency exit. Get out of here."

"You fuckers aren't going anywhere," Eli spat from the ground. He lifted himself onto one arm, shaking as he glared at us, the whites of his eyes blistering as the bore into us.

I hadn't seen it until he lit it—a zippo lighter, burning orange and blue, shaking in his hand. He used the last of his strength to throw it onto one of the tables. There was a beat, and a crackle.

The dead plant matter burst into flames.

Fire ripped down the table, black smoke dispersing in the air. On the ground, Eli laughed as the flames began to grow taller. Across the room, the two anthropophagi wailed, jumping up onto the wall. They hissed, beginning to climb toward the glass roof.

"Over there!" Celeste cried, pointing to the back of the room, past where we'd first found Val. "The emergency exit!"

"I've got the key," Jasmine said. She reached out for Val. "Come on!"

Val and Jasmine took off running while I limped to catch up. Celeste halted, looking over her shoulder at me.

"I—I can't—" I wheezed, clutching my ribs. "It hurts, it—"

Without a word, she came to my side and lifted me into her arms.

"Not leaving you behind," she promised. "Not now, not ever."

She hit the ground running, holding me close.

The fire spread fast. With all the dry plants to fuel it, it shot down the metal tables, sparks jumping from one to another, lighting up the entire room in shades of orange. The heat was stifling, sweat pouring down my face where I pressed it against Celeste's shirt. The air was choked with smoke, and Celeste coughed as she trailed behind the others.

Just as we passed the last line of tables, a voice called out, "W- Wait, please!"

We paused. Laying in a pool of his own blood was Cole, one hand pressed tightly to his side to stanch the bleeding from a bite wound. His green eyes glittered in the firelight, skin sickly pale and dappled with blood.

"Please," he begged, holding out a hand. "I know I hurt you—I *know* that this is all my fault. But please, let me make it right. Take me with you."

The four of us exchanged glances. Val's limbs were beginning to shrink back to their regular size, and her cheeks had begun to fill in again. We all looked to her—after all, she was the one who had suffered the most because of him.

She nodded softly. "You owe us, you little bastard."

"You're lucky she's the nice one," Jasmine growled to Cole as she held out a hand for him. "I would have left you here."

Cole took her hand, and Jasmine pulled him to his feet.

She and Val took either side of him, supporting him as he limped forward.

"Thank you," he whispered, tears in his eyes. "Thank you. *Thank you.*"

With that, we ran for the emergency exit, the sound of the anthropophagi's screams fading out behind us.

epilogue

*I*t was good that we decided to save Cole, because he was the one they finally believed when we told the authorities the truth.

We'd driven back into the valley just to be stopped immediately by more National Guardsman who had finally contained the situation with the anthropophagi. When they'd opened the doors and found all of us bleeding inside, they'd called for backup to help.

As soon as they'd treated our injuries enough to stabilize us, the medics turned us over to the police, who kept us for hours. Even though my head was pounding, my body ached, and I desperately needed to get some sleep, it seemed like the cops had to ask me the same couple of questions over and over. *How did you find out about Blackwell Pharmaceuticals? How was Cole Greenleaf involved? What happened at the facility?*

When they finally let us out, Jasmine, Val, Celeste, and I all limped to the cabin in silence. It felt odd returning, watching Celeste type the code into the door like we were still just regular girls on our summer trip to Desert Bloom. We each took turns showering so we could go to bed without the stink of blood on us.

The cops had told us that they'd need to speak to us again in the future, but for now, we were free to go.

Cole hadn't been so lucky. But then again, with Raj and Eli still considered missing in the ruins of the Facility B blaze and Kaiden unaccounted for as well, he was the only one left to take the blame.

When I finally plugged my dead phone in at the cabin, I got a couple of texts from him. It turned out that cell reception had been turned on shortly after our conversation with the cops.

Cole Greenleaf
Today 5:22 a.m.

hey zoey
wanted to text since they're probably going to take my phone away soon. apparently the fbi has to get involved. probably not a huge surprise considering they sent in the cdc and the national guard because of me
i just wanted to say sorry again for all of this. a lot of people are dead or hurt, and it's my fault
i keep thinking about what my sister would want me to do. she wouldn't want me ruining ghoul's lives. i think the guilt was just too much for me to handle any other way, so i let eli tell me what to do when there's no way melanie would want that. she'd want me to come clean and try to make it right.
sorry again. you really are a cool girl. in another life, i would have liked to take you out sometime. although, it seems like celeste has that covered.
good luck, z.
thanks again. for everything.

"You okay?" Celeste asked as I looked up from my phone.

I nodded, wiping a tear away. "Yeah. Just got a little dust in my eye."

She put a hand on my shoulder and squeezed before heading to take her shower. Not long after, even with my thoughts swirling, I managed to lay down in bed and fall into a dreamless sleep.

The next day would have been the final day of Desert Bloom, had it not been for the quarantine. We awoke in the late morning to a text that the quarantine was lifted, and any Hollow people experiencing symptoms were to come to the medical tent for treatment—presumably, so that the CDC workers could use the vials Jasmine had turned over to them yesterday when we got back. With the barrier gone, the road out of the valley instantly clogged up, the line of cars seeming to stretch for miles. And with cell service back, messages had been pouring in for hours.

One, however, stood out to me more than the others.

Dad
Today 11:31 a.m.

Hi, Zoey. Your mother and I heard about the incident at Desert Bloom. The press release said that the impacts on Hollow individuals were caused by a substance, not a new strain of the virus, but your mother would be more comfortable if you stayed at the Fairbanks' house for a few days when you return, just to be sure. I'll send money to your account for groceries and gas in the meantime. —Dad

I read it over a few times, feeling my body go numb. Celeste, who was texting her mom on the other side of our shared bed, looked up. Her eyebrows pressed together.

I cleared my throat, trying to keep my tone even. "Hey, um… Would it be okay if I stayed with you and Wendy for a few days after this?"

Celeste's expression softened. Her eyes darted to my phone questioningly and I turned it around so she could see the message. She took the phone and read it over, gaze narrowing as she did. She blew out a breath through her nose and handed the phone back.

Then, without warning, she leaned across the bed and wrapped her arms around me.

"What—?" I started.

"Of course," she said into my hair. "You're always welcome where I am."

I hugged her back. It had been such a whirlwind the last few days with so many emotional gut punches that it felt weird this was the one that made me want to cry the most. Now that the quarantine was lifted and Cole was with the police, my brain was still struggling to process that now life was just going to continue as it had. Jasmine would go to Yale, Val to USC, and me to NYU. And in the meantime, I'd be going right back to my parents' house, with the lock on my door and the silent dinners alone.

I sniffled. "It's gonna be weird next year not having you around. Where am I supposed to go when I need someone to tell me it's gonna be okay in New York?"

"Well…" Celeste pulled back just enough to push my dark brown hair out of my eyes with her long fingers. "What if I went with you?"

I froze for a millisecond, my brain unable to process what she'd said. Then, I straightened up, eyes widened and a smile slowly forming across my face. I reached out a hand, putting it on her knee.

"Are you serious?"

She shrugged. "Why not? New York is a great town for what I want to do. There are artists everywhere. And plus," she cupped my cheek in her palm, "I think we'd make a nice little space together. We could get a place in Brooklyn, buy a bunch of plants at IKEA, frame some nice art prints, see what we can score on Craigslist. Stuff like that."

"Even if I can't make us any money for four years?" I asked.

Celeste bit back a laugh. "Are you asking to be my sugar baby?"

"*Stop*." I reached out and playfully shoved her shoulder. "I'm just saying. I don't want you to rush into a cross-country move because you feel bad for me."

"Can I be honest for a second?" Celeste straightened up, crossing her legs and facing me completely. She'd braided her hair before she went to sleep, and now a cloud of loose hairs glowed pink in the sunlight around her face. "I've felt so lost since I graduated. With everyone else going to school, I've just been… floating, I guess. With no idea where to go. LA, London—hell, maybe Milan or Berlin—but there was nothing drawing me to any of those places. Maybe what I need isn't a place to draw me somewhere."

"But what about Aspen Flats?" I asked softly, my cheeks beginning to turn pink as my heart begin to race. "Your house and Wendy—you wouldn't be scared to leave home?"

Celeste tightened her hand around mine.

"Maybe you can be my home," she said. "And I can be yours."

My eyes immediately flooded with tears and I threw myself

into her arms. I squeezed her as hard as I could, burying my face in her shoulder to try and stop myself from crying. I started to nod before I could speak, finally managing to get the words out, even though they were choked and teary.

"Yes," I said, pulling away and sliding my fingers into her hair. "Absolutely yes."

I pulled her into a kiss, the smell of her soap and shampoo enveloping me in an aura of flowers, like lying down in a meadow. Her skin was soft under my fingers, warm and sun-kissed from days under the desert sky. She kissed me back, wrapping her arms around me and pulling me against her.

After a moment, though, she leaned too far back and fell backward into the pillows with a yelp, pulling me with her.

I landed on her chest, laughing, while she sputtered, "Sorry, sorry! I-I haven't, um, done this very much—oh, god."

Her entire face was pink, and it was nice for once not to be the one who felt like I was about to catch on fire. I softly lifted myself off her, then readjusted, swinging my leg around so I straddled her hips. She had her hands over her face, so I leaned down and kissed her throat instead.

"It's okay," I promised her. "I've seen you do way more embarrassing stuff. Like, there was that time in middle school when you decided to chug an entire bottle of milk as fast as you could to try and prove you weren't lactose intolerant despite the fact you were *definitely* lactose intolerant—"

"I changed my mind, I'm staying in California."

I sputtered a laugh and reached out to move her hands from her face. She was flushed from her ears to her throat, blue eyes huge. Gently, I cupped her cheeks and leaned down to kiss her again.

Suddenly, the door to our room flew open, and Jasmine started to say, "Hey, good news, they decided to—"

She cut off as she noticed the position we were in, then scoffed. "Oh, my bad. Didn't realize you were being gay. I was gonna say that they reopened the Ferris wheel to try and give people something to do while the road's backed up, so Val and I are gonna go do that. I was gonna invite you, but it seems like you have other things to do."

My face reddened to match Celeste's as I straightened up, suddenly very aware of her between my legs. "Uh—"

"We're leaving in five if you change your mind about making out or whatever." She waved. "Anyway, have fun! Don't forget to use protection!"

She shut the door behind her.

If only to save face, Celeste and I decided to join Val and Jasmine at the Ferris wheel.

At that point, a lot of the festival had cleared out. The artists had packed up their stands and most of the food trucks had shuttered their windows. The final shows had been canceled, and with the mass exodus of people, Desert Bloom had lost much of the chaotic energy that made it what it was. It had been replaced by the sound was the desert breeze and the occasional burble of conversation.

In the hours since we left Facility B, Val had almost completely reverted to normal. Her teeth were still a little pointier than usual, and her fingernails looked a bit like claw acrylics, but it wasn't enough to warrant a second glance from most people. She definitely looked like she needed a nap, though, which I assumed she'd take in the car.

"Step on up!" the attendant said, gesturing to a candyshell turquoise gondola in front of him. The four of us climbed in, Jasmine and Val taking one bench, and Celeste and I on the other. The attendant latched our door, telling us to enjoy the ride.

We rose into the air, the view of the desert spreading out before us. The Joshua trees and sagebrush turned to nothing but little clumps this high up, with the red rock and pale brown roads in and out of the valley taking over the scene. The line of cars bottlenecked on one side, barely moving. It seemed no one was getting out of Desert Bloom that easily.

"You feeling any better, Val?" Celeste asked.

Val shrugged. "Oh, y'know. As good as I can feel after all that, I guess. I'm not sure I'll get the bile taste out of my mouth anytime soon. I think I brushed my teeth about forty times when we got back."

"I wonder what happened to the anthropophagi," I said, staring out at the desert and leaning gently into Celeste. "Or—the ones that got out, anyway. I guess they might still be around."

"People online were saying the FBI is gonna try to flush out the caves around the valley," Jasmine explained. "See if they're hiding there."

Val's eyes dropped to the ground. I was sure it struck a nerve to think about. She folded and unfolded her hands in her lap, closing her eyes.

"It was like all I could think about was hunger," she said. "Even when I knew you were there, I just forgot who you were. It was terrifying."

Jasmine wrapped an arm around her and Val accepted the hug.

Val continued, "I can't thank you enough for not giving up on me. I know I was kind of a bitch the last few days, but you all really came through."

"Of course we did. We'd be pretty shitty friends if we just abandoned you," I pointed out. "Plus, if we don't look out for each other, who will?"

"Exactly," Jasmine agreed. She rubbed Val's upper arm and added, "I mean, come on. We hid a literal body together. It doesn't get much more ride-or-die than that."

"Speaking of." Celeste lowered her voice to a whisper, so quiet I almost couldn't hear her over the sound of the music that was piped into each spoke of the Ferris wheel. "Now that everything's over…what do we want to do about Kaiden?"

"Honestly, I feel a little less bad about eating him now that I know he was in on No Flash Photography's little domestic terrorism plot," Jasmine muttered.

"His family still deserves to know what happened to him," Val whispered. She began picking at her cuticles, not looking at us. "Same with Eli and Raj. They did terrible things, but they were still somebody's sons. Even if they got what they deserved, I'd want closure for the people they were close to."

"I think the cops will take care of telling Eli and Raj's families if they find them at Facility B," I offered. I did my best not to think too hard about whether or not it was possible one or both of them could have made it out before the blaze consumed the place, but the pang in my chest still ached. "As for Kaiden… I wonder if we could leave an anonymous tip."

Jasmine and Val both raised their eyebrows while Celeste added, "Oh yeah—the cops opened an anonymous tip line for anyone who knows anything about missing persons from Desert Bloom. We could use that."

I gently lowered my voice. "What do you think, Val?"

She nodded, finally lifting her face. "Yeah. I think that'll help put this all to rest for me."

"Seriously." Jasmine kicked up one of her feet on the latch holding the door. "What a week, huh? Monsters, drugs, murder—not to mention Celeste and Zoey are together now."

Val straightened all the way up. "Wait, *what?*"

Celeste and I both blushed. I glanced up at her while she gently reached out and put a hand on my leg. My face got even redder.

"We haven't, um, exactly put a label on it," Celeste said, smiling sheepishly.

"I can't believe you didn't tell me!" Val's jaw dropped and she threw her hands up. "Am I the last to know? I am, aren't I? Ugh! This is what I get for turning into a monster and fleeing into the desert for a day!"

"It really only just happened," I muttered in an attempt to console her.

"It's true," Celeste agreed. She glanced at me, offering a small smile. "We haven't even agreed to be girlfriends yet."

I blinked, my mouth going dry. "Is that something you'd want?"

Softly, Celeste nodded. "Definitely."

"Oh my god, *shut up*," Val said. She bounced a little in her seat. "This is so cute! Wait, hold on, I need to capture this."

"Now look at what you've done," Jasmine groaned.

Val took out her phone and held it up so all four of us were visible on the screen. She flashed a cheek smile and held up a peace sign. "Everyone say *ghoulfriends*!"

"I'm not gonna—" I started to say.

But Celeste cut me off with a soft kiss to the cheek, which immediately made me turn beet red. Jasmine stuck out her tongue and winked while Val smiled as wide as she could. All at once, the three of them said, "Ghoulfriends!"

Val snapped the picture.

"Cute!" she cried. "I'm framing it."

"Oh my god," I muttered.

"Hey, come on." Celeste poked me between the ribs, then leaned in close and whispered, "It's a nice moment to remember, right?"

Her breath was warm on my cheek, and my heart did a little flip in my chest. While Jasmine and Val leaned in to get a better look at the picture, I turned my face to Celeste's.

"Sure. There is one thing I can think of to make it better, though."

So with the late afternoon summer sun on us, I leaned forward and kissed my best friend, feeling her heartbeat against mine. For once, after all this time, it felt like we had it all figured out.

And the future was ours.

my dearest darkest

one

While all towns have their ghosts, Rainwater's were special. They sank through its submerged sea caves and slithered up its cliffs. They bounced around its caverns and tunnels like electrical pulses in a brain, echoing memories of footsteps and laughter and screams through the ground and into the towering evergreen trees. The peninsula had a habit of keeping things long after they were gone.

And on May 16, when Finch Chamberlin crossed the town line into Rainwater, Maine, it decided to keep her.

"Terrible-looking campus, huh?" her father said, meeting her eyes in the rearview mirror. He nodded up at the soaring spires of Ulalume Academy as they came into view beyond the trees.

"Oh! I…I think it's pretty," Finch defended, looking down at her shoes.

"He's joking, sweetie." Finch's mother shot him a sharp look. "It's lovely."

Ulalume's towering, Gothic campus rose out of the fog-shrouded trees. The peninsula Rainwater rested on was just under forty square miles, vaguely crescent-shaped, with a rocky coastline and the occasional pebble beach. A single causeway led in and out.

The Chamberlins left their car in the guest parking lot. Finch's mother pulled her into a sideways hug, squeezing her upper arm while her father led the way, more interested in getting to the student services office on time for Finch's final audition for Ulalume's renowned music program than the fact that his daughter looked ready to crawl out of her skin.

"You okay?" her mother asked.

Finch chewed her lower lip. "Nervous."

"About?"

"Everything," Finch whispered, barely audible. She might as well tattoo it on her forehead. Or sew it on her jackets as a warning. DO NOT LOOK AT OR APPROACH OR THINK ABOUT, PLEASE. THANK YOU.

Her mom kissed the crown of her head. "You'll do fine, little bird. I'm here."

Finch closed her eyes, took a breath, and nodded. "You're here."

She was trying not to think about the fact that she wouldn't be for long, though. Assuming this audition scored her a spot in the music program, she'd be living here for the foreseeable future. Ulalume was a boarding school that housed three hundred of the most talented prodigies—and trust fund babies—that the administration had handpicked to join their illustrious institution. After two years of rejections, she was hoping this would finally be the year she got in—and procured the scholarship she so desperately needed.

Finch and her family stepped into the student services office a minute later. It was uncomfortably warm, and the persistent humidity from outside seemed to permeate the building's ivy-covered stone walls. Finch dabbed at her forehead with the back of her hand. She was glad she could play off her excessive sweating as weather-related.

"Oh—hey there! You must be Finch," the woman at the front desk said in a faint Maine accent, looking up from a glossy issue of *Cosmo*.

Finch's father confirmed, and an even bigger smile broke across the woman's face.

"Congratulations on the audition." She came around the desk and gestured for them to follow her. "I'll show you to the auditorium."

A twisted smile cut across Kyra Astor's face. "So, you gonna share some of that tequila or do you need the bottle for a couple hundred more selfies?"

Selena St. Clair, phone in hand, paused long enough to pull off a red Louis Vuitton pump and throw it at her. The shoe missed her by centimeters and hit the wall with a loud *thump*.

Kyra broke into hysterical laughter.

The two of them had snuck off to their favorite drinking spot on campus: the orchestra pit beneath the auditorium. The musty space was full of discarded music stands and broken instrument parts, but with most of the year's musical events wrapped up, it was quiet and private.

In fact, the school only had one major event left before summer: the Founder's Ball, Ulalume's end-of-semester celebration, and Selena had a head start on pregaming. In one hand was a bottle of expensive tequila, and in the other, her phone.

She took a swig from the bottle, then slid her phone back in her purse. "Did you invite the others yet?"

"Amber's still with her tutor working on some paper," Kyra said with an eye roll, "and Risa's pregaming elsewhere."

She held out a hand for the tequila. Selena passed it to her.

Their fingers touched for a beat, a flutter of warmth passing between them. Selena's cheeks flared pink while Kyra swung the bottle up and took a sip. Tequila dribbled down her chin and into the neckline of her silver dress.

Selena tore her eyes away, busying herself with examining her fingernails. She'd had them done yesterday, painted the same shade of ballet slipper–pink that most of the girls in her year would have on for the ball. It was prim, proper—expected. Which made it all the more jarring when Selena remembered how her preened fingers had looked woven through Kyra's red tresses the night before.

Her blush worsened. She was lucky the pit was covered and dark.

"So I'm stuck with you," Selena said, successfully faking an airy, disappointed tone. She steadied her breathing. The mask went back on. "Text them. Risa will cancel if she knows I want her here."

Kyra coughed out a small laugh to cover up her wince. Selena knew exactly where to press her fingers to hit bruises—to hit every girl at Ulalume's bruises.

"Selena, you don't—"

The doors to the auditorium flew open. A tangle of voices flooded the echoing space, instantly drowning out whatever Kyra had been meaning to say.

Selena's heart thundered. Ulalume had strict rules about alcohol—students could get in serious trouble just for having it in their rooms, much less actively drinking on school grounds.

Kyra's eyes bugged and she whispered, "What do we do?"

Selena threw out her hands and furiously mouthed back, "How should I know?"

"Is it okay if we stay and watch?" a woman asked, getting closer to the pit.

"Of course," a voice replied. Selena recognized it—Mr. Rizzio, the head of the music department. "Finch, if you want to head onto the stage, I'll set up the camera so I can record your audition for the admissions committee to review. Then we can get started."

Selena cursed, then reached for the bottle. "Give it to me!"

Kyra shoved the bottle into her hands.

Soft footsteps creaked above them as someone crossed to the grand piano at the edge of the stage. The house lights went down, and Selena lost sight of Kyra in the darkness.

"It's just an audition," Selena whispered. "We can hide until they're done."

"I'm ready when you are," a quiet voice said onstage.

Something about it made Selena pause. Even with the blood pounding in her ears and sweat slicking her hands. The voice was small, barely more than a chirp, but there was a sweetness to it she couldn't describe.

"She's a prodigy, you know," a man in the front row said. "You're going to be amazed at what she can do. All the other girls her age are out there chasing boys, but our Finch—she's got her keys and that's all she needs. Nothing can distract her."

Selena closed her eyes. *Finch.*

"Thank you, Mr. Chamberlin," Mr. Rizzio said. He called to the girl onstage, "We're all set down here. You can get started whenever you're ready, Finch."

Selena pressed her back against the wall of the pit, trying to keep her breathing even. Auditions didn't usually take more than fifteen minutes—they'd be out of there in no time.

Up above, Finch hit the first few notes. They were gentle, like wind chimes in quick succession. But as her fingers glided across the keys, the melody began to swell, growing louder and more intense. It wasn't the sort of song Selena would have expected from such a timid-voiced girl—the energy of it was huge, imposing, growing with a torrent of sound that echoed through the auditorium with a resounding punch that made Selena's heart quicken.

"She's really good," Selena whispered.

Selena could barely make out Kyra throwing her hands in the air. "*Literally* who cares?"

Selena rolled her eyes, then settled in, letting the sound of Finch's song wash over her.

It wasn't particularly long—maybe four minutes—before Finch slammed down on the final notes, a reverberating echo rippling across the auditorium.

"Wonderful," Mr. Rizzio said. "Next, we'll move onto the improvisational part of the aud—"

Without warning, a resonant *bang* burst through the silence as

Kyra nudged a music stand at the wrong angle, knocking it into the others and creating a disastrous domino effect. Kyra let out a choked yelp while Selena cursed colorfully under her breath.

The lights flickered on a few moments later and the entrance to the pit opened to reveal Mr. Rizzio standing with his arms crossed, eyebrows up. Selena, out of options, slid the tequila bottle into her dress sleeve and held it behind her back.

"You two," Mr. Rizzio said. "Come up here, please."

Kyra and Selena exchanged a look, Kyra's already pale skin now ghost-white. As they stood from the pile of collapsed music stands, Selena did her best to conceal the bottle-shaped bulge in her sleeve.

The upper part of the auditorium, with its art deco–style, gaudy light fixtures, carved wood accents, and cushy velvet seats, greeted them along with the horrified faces of two people Selena assumed were Finch's parents. Selena glanced over her shoulder—Finch sat at the piano a few feet away, mouth agape.

She was white, small, and waifish with the biggest set of luminous eyes Selena had ever seen, like two searchlights singling her out from across the room. Her hair was elbow-length and chestnut brown, an uncanny contrast to her pale skin.

For a brief second, Selena forgot how far up shit creek she was.

"Do you have a good reason as to why you're in the orchestra pit? During an *audition*?" Mr. Rizzio asked, sounding exhausted.

Selena and Kyra exchanged another look. Selena lied, "Um. We were looking for our friend's violin that she left down there. We didn't mean to interrupt."

"We're super sorry," Kyra agreed, nodding vigorously. "Like, *beyond* sorry, can't even put into words how sor—"

Selena elbowed her, cutting her off.

"Right." Mr. Rizzio pinched the skin between his eyebrows. "Okay. I'm going to give you the benefit of the doubt and assume this is a simple misunderstanding—"

As Mr. Rizzio spoke, Selena gently shifted the tequila bottle in her sleeve, trying to hide it behind her arm so the shape was less visible. As she did, however, it slipped into her hand. She was barely able to catch it before it slid onto the floor, and her breath hitched.

Mr. Rizzio didn't notice.

Selena withheld a sigh of relief. *Thank goodn—*

"Is that…" a voice muttered behind her. "*Alcohol?*"

The second she said it, Finch clapped a hand over her mouth.

She hadn't meant to say that out loud.

The blond girl tensed. She was tall, with a slim, athletic build and natural waves in her golden hair. She was white, but had a natural warm tan to her skin that spoke to days spent lounging in the sun.

As Finch's words met her ear, the girl whipped around and shot her the most poisonous glare she'd ever seen. Even in that moment, though, Finch couldn't help but notice the sharp angle of her cheekbones and the straight slope of her nose—and the way her pretty red lips curled into a scowl.

Finch turned vibrantly red from her throat to her ears.

She stammered, "I—um—sorry—"

Mr. Rizzio let out a pained, world-weary sigh. "All right. Selena, show me your hands please."

Selena winced. After a beat, her tensed shoulders fell and,

averting her gaze to the floor, she let the bottle of tequila slide into her hand. She held it out to Mr. Rizzio.

He took the bottle softly from her hand, reading the label over the rim of his glasses before nodding to himself and letting out a breath.

"Okay. Selena, Kyra, I'm going to have you head to the head-mistress's office. I'll meet you there once I finish up Finch's audition so we have a chance to discuss this and call your parents." He turned, meeting Finch and her parents' eyes. "Finch, Mr. and Mrs. Chamberlin—I cannot apologize enough for Miss St. Clair and Miss Astor's behavior. I promise you we don't tolerate this sort of thing at Ulalume."

Selena hung her head while the other girl—a white redhead with a long, sleek ponytail hanging down her back—looked to be on the verge of tears. She, too, turned and glared at Finch, only stopping when Selena waved her hand and summoned her to follow.

Just before they made it to the doors, Selena stopped and turned.

"I'm sorry for interrupting your audition," she told Finch, meeting her gaze with snake-green, kohl-rimmed eyes. "Good luck. Maybe I'll see you around next year."

She turned, heading out the door with her friend.

It swung closed behind her with a *bang*.

Finch tried to swallow, throat dry. *Why did that sound like a threat?*

"Well," Finch's mother said after a pregnant pause. "She seems...spirited."

"That's one word for it," her father said, narrowing his eyes.

But Finch didn't say anything. She was too caught up in the

sensation that radiated from her heart and into her limbs. It was like her skin had been stripped away, leaving her a ball of lightning and exposed nerves.

Selena St. Clair.

acknowledgments

*I*f you happened to read my last set of acknowledgments, you're probably aware that my first book took more than a decade to finish before it landed on shelves. Needless to say, that was not the case with this one. People aren't kidding when they say writing your second book is hard—in fact, it's really something of a Herculean task if we're being honest. I guess that's why I'm so lucky to have so many wonderful people who have supported me throughout this journey.

First, as always, thank you to my amazing agent, Erica Bauman. Whether it's meeting up for drinks in the city or answering my panicked emails, you've been there for me through a whole lot of ups and downs. I can confidently say I wouldn't be here without you.

Speaking of people who I wouldn't be here without, shout-out to my awesome editor, Annie Berger. Your ability to help me carve a decent story out of a marble block made of overcomplicated sub-plots is not only truly impressive but also very much appreciated.

To the rest of the Sourcebooks team: you've all been a joy to work with, and this book wouldn't be nearly as good (or aesthetically pleasing) without your insight.

And of course, to my sensational friends—when I first moved to Boston, I was a total stranger thousands of miles from home, and now I can't imagine my life without the community that I found here, even as many of us go our separate directions. I love you all so, so much. Special mention to my high school besties, Ally, Alex, and Simone, to whom this book is dedicated. Zoey, Celeste, Val, and Jasmine are who they are because of you.

And of course, to my family: you raised me to never give up, to always speak my mind, and to have the confidence to fail and be better for it. Also, hey, I didn't kill the parents in this one! See? I live up to my promises sometimes.

Finally, to all the readers, librarians, booksellers, bloggers, and influencers who have helped introduce people to my books: you are the beating heart of this industry, so never let anyone tell you otherwise. Your support is what makes books like this one possible.

And last: to my cat, Squid. You're a very, very good boy and I love you so much, even when you steal my socks and hide them in your cat tower. I'm so lucky you're mine. ♥

about the author

Kayla Cottingham is a YA author and librarian. Her first book, *My Dearest Darkest*, was a *New York Times* and *Publishers Weekly* bestseller. Originally from Salt Lake City, Utah, Kayla lives in Boston, where she loves to hike the woods, play RPGs, and snuggle with her ridiculously large black cat, Squid.